Charles Pero

THE Maze Murderer

Twisted Killer Series

SterlingHouse Publisher, Inc.   Pittsburgh, PA

Other titles in

The Twisted Killer Series

Tainted Blood

Torn Apart

Black Ribbon

The Riddler

Famous Organs

The Lunar Killings

THE Maze Murderer

Perothrillers

ISBN-10: 1-56315-391-2
ISBN-13: 978-1-56-315391-4

Hardback
© Copyright 2007 Charles Pero
All Rights Reserved
First Printing 2007
Library of Congress #2006940719

Requests for information should be addressed to:
SterlingHouse Publisher, Inc.
7436 Washington Avenue
Pittsburgh, Pennsylvania 15218
info@sterlinghousepublisher.com
www.sterlinghousepublisher.com

Pero Thrillers
is an imprint of SterlingHouse Publisher, Inc.

SterlingHouse Publisher, Inc. is a company
of the Cyntomedia Corporation

Cover Design: Brandon M. Bittner
Interior Design: Kathleen M. Gall
Images provided by iStockphoto.com

Printed in Canada

Dedication

For Rusty Fischer, who has always believed in my stories.
Thank you for helping me write a great book.

Acknowledgments

I want to thank all the real men and women who work each day to catch killers like the one I've described in this book. Without you, none of us would sleep at night or, for that matter, ever feel safe again. I would also like to add my grateful thanks to the following:

My sister, Angela, for your loving support.
Amanda C., for your keen insight—it meant a lot to me.
Jimmy, for listening and giving me great feedback.
Jackie Hartman—you've been a great inspiration to me.

Prologue

Special Director Frank Logan fusses in the back of the chauffeured limousine, his new jeans scratchy, his stiff shirt collar too tight. He looks at the looming high-rise poking out of downtown LA, like some daunting sky needle, and curses, unbuttoning his top shirt button at the last minute.

"There," he sighs, the ice in his thick rocks glass clinking with the motion. "*Much* better."

Inch by inch, the downtown traffic snarled even at 8 p.m. on a Saturday night, the gigantic building of mirrored glass and 6-foot high lettering creeps closer and closer. **DOUBLETREE PUBLISHING COMPANY** reads the glowing red sign atop the building's topmost floor, some 76 stories above street level.

Frank sighs, shaking his head, and returns his attention to the limousine's decked out interior. His literary agent, Bernie Segal, has spared no expense for this latest book launch, the most ambitious, according to Bernie, and most annoying, according to Frank, to date. Even Frank's favorite gin, Bombay Sapphire, has been placed in the chilled bucket usually reserved for champagne bottles.

On his lap is the advanced-release copy of his latest hardcover. He feels cheesy holding it this way, but Bernie keeps blathering on about things like "product placement" and "household name" and "go-to guy" and "face recognition," so he regretfully consented to tote it along, if only to shut the brusque, thirty-something Bernie up.

He looks at the cover, now runny and stained with the condensation from his gin and tonic. It's the usual true-crime stock art: fluttering crime scene tape, busted down door, bloody handprint on the wood frame, shadowy figure looming in the background, with only one new twist.

For Frank's latest book, his name is actually bigger than the title.

The author's photo on the back is bigger this time, too. He'd only glanced at it, once, and then quickly turned it over. It was that same glamour shot Bernie had been pushing ever since setting up the photo shoot some six months earlier: Frank in faded jeans and a fisherman's sweater, resting comfortably in an Adirondack chair on the dock of Bernie's summer home in the Hamptons.

It was supposed to make Frank look polished and dignified, cool and reserved; all he saw was a fussy, pampered old coot, posing for the camera when he should be off nabbing the bad guys.

Still, it was better than the alternative. If Bernie had gotten his way, Frank would have been pictured wearing his full FBI regalia, windbreaker, ID badge, shoulder holster and all, his gun in hand and his foot halfway through the process of kicking in a door.

Frank grimaces at the thought, raises the glass to his lips, and takes another drink.

In a move only slightly masked as passive aggression, he's been using the book as a coaster ever since the limo picked him up at his ritzy hotel six blocks away. "Bernie," he'd complained hours earlier when his smothering agent had called his room to finalize the details, "six blocks? In my days as a DC traffic cop, I used to walk that far just to grab a cup of coffee. I don't need a friggin' limo."

But Bernie had insisted, and now here Frank sits, pulling up to the glittering building and staring out at the madhouse just beyond his smoky, tinted windows. Reporters stand at attention on either side of two barriers, while various literary luminaries walk a red carpet—yes, Bernie had even finagled a red carpet from the publisher—in their tuxedos and ball gowns.

Frank fights the temptation to look behind him, wondering if perhaps Brad Pitt and Angelina Jolie are in the car behind him, perhaps slated for the release of their latest blockbuster and hence all the Hollywood-style hoopla.

Frank shakes his head instead, watching a liveried valet approach the back door. "Sure you're ready for this, Mr. Logan?" asks the bemused chauffeur, who's been listening to Frank grouse and gripe—and top off his high-ball—for five of the last six blocks.

"How about we change places, Louie?" Frank quips, holding up the author's photo emblazoned across the entire back of the hard-cover book. "A few more gray hairs, take off that tie, look a little tougher, and you could pass for me."

"Yeah," deadpans the much younger chauffeur, a cocky kid with ink black hair and a Brooklyn accent. "Maybe in a decade or two. Sorry, Mr. Logan, they're waiting for the legendary FBI man turned bestselling author, not some college dropout from NYU."

"Silly kid," Frank corrects him. "Don't you know most best-selling authors are college dropouts?"

Louie doesn't have time to respond. Before he can lose his nerve, Frank bounds from the back of the sleek, stretch limousine, beating the valet to the punch and smiling weakly to the photographers as he dodges the various local celebrities who have been invited to the launch.

At 56, cutting nimbly through the crowd of pampered patrons like a running back in his prime, Frank's body has the power and appeal of any man half his age. His face is masculine and strong, a bit weathered from his years on the planet, but overall no worse for the wear. Only his eyes betray him; eyes that reveal the fact that Frank has seen things most will never see—or perhaps *shouldn't* see.

Frank, the only one in a jacket and jeans, meets and greets those in his path to the best of his ability. Glancing at the watch on his wrist, he sees he's already five minutes late. Picking up the pace, he glides off the carpet through two automatic glass doors that whisk him into the interior of Doubletree Publishing Company.

He'd been here before, of course. Once to sign his very first contract, back before he'd made Deputy Director and was still a gun-shy rookie; to writing, that is. How his hand had trembled putting pen to paper on that auspicious day, and how Bernie had hovered, physically taking the signed contract from Frank's hands and handing it to his editor, as if signifying that he wasn't going to be let out of the tiniest little detail now that the deal was official.

Since then he'd been back a dozen times or more, for this marketing strategy meeting or that editorial knock-down, drag-out fuss with the legal department about naming names or insisting that no gory detail was too graphic if it made his readers think twice about jogging alone at 4 a.m. or not investing in a can of mace.

Now, as he makes his way through the crowd still lingering in the lobby, past the banners and posters all bearing Frank's image, past all the people holding his books, Frank instinctively spots the building's grand reception room just off the marbled hallway and makes a beeline for its darkened interior.

Through hordes of people still taking their seats, and all clamoring for a handshake or autograph, the limber Frank makes his way to the podium. He groans, hearing Bernie's well-rehearsed intro, as his agent of over half a dozen years—and just as many books—does the honors of emcee for this grand soiree.

Frank joins him onstage just as Bernie is wrapping up his spiel, "...and has already sold over 3 million copies of his latest book in 14 languages worldwide...," Bernie hesitates, spotting Frank, before continuing, "Ah, speak of the devil and the devil arrives....*Finally*!"

Frank, along with the crowd, can't help but chuckle. Say what you want about old Bernie Segal, but the man can work a crowd. "Ladies and gentlemen," Bernie concludes, looking Frank up and down and barely hiding a frown at his casual attire, "a man who—luckily for all of us—writes better than he dresses!

"Not only is he Deputy Director of the FBI's newest Special Circumstances crime unit, but arguably the best true crime writer Doubletree has published in decades. Please help me welcome the man of the hour. The one and only...Frank Logan!"

The crowd applauds wildly. As Frank walks up to the podium, he playfully pretends to box with Bernie. The slim, thirty-something Bernie plays along, although Frank can see the impatient expression on his face.

"Thank you, truly, no, please sit down. Thanks, thanks so much. And thanks to my agent, Bernie Segal, for that introduction. Bernie," Frank adds as he looks up from the podium. "You're fired!"

Once again, everyone chuckles. Everyone, that is, except Bernie, who concentrates, instead, on straightening his slick, Armani tie.

Frank, smiling at Bernie, continues more modestly, "No, but seriously...I thank you all...." An awkward pause greets the room as Frank pats the four corners of his casual jacket, at last retrieving his notes. "And I'd like to talk to you about what has been, not only the main subject of each of my books and the fascination of readers around the world, but what continues to be, the obsession of my life: Murder!

"Murder is my business; has been, I suppose, for nearly forty years. Starting from my early days beating the streets in Washington, DC, all the way to the body farm at Quantico during my FBI training, and later during my profiling work for the Bureau.

"Some say I've paid my dues solving murders. Others claim I'm making money off murder. Perhaps, in some small way, *both* are right. But I like to think that I'm not just solving the crimes I write about in these books, but in fact preventing them from happening again."

Somewhat cheesily, Frank holds up his latest book. The adoring crowd nods in recognition. For once, even Bernie nods approvingly. Frank continues. "Read these books closely enough, and you'll see what I've seen, learn what I've learned. Bernie can tell you, I'm not one to brag—although that certainly never stops *him* from doing it for me—but I can't tell you how many women have come up to me after reading my first few books to say that they never park in a dark lot anymore, or that they hold their keys like a weapon if they do, or that they lock their doors every night, and check their windows.

"Is that a bad thing? Hell no. Is it a good thing? Hell *yes*! Do I make a few pennies for helping you remember to bolt your doors and check your backseat before getting in the car? *Hell* yes! And as long as there is crime, as long as there are criminals, I'm going to keep writing.

"Thank you, folks. Thanks so much for taking time out of your busy schedules and coming here tonight. Now, if I understand his wild gesticulations to the right of me correctly, my agent here has a few last-minute things to tell you before I start signing books. Be patient, my hands aren't what they used to be! Bernie?"

At long last, Frank leaves the podium. A cheery assistant greets Frank in the wings of the reception room, checking off notes on a clipboard clutched in his hands and leading Frank by the arm to yet another room, where a long line of people are already waiting for his signature.

Looking over his shoulder, Frank spots Bernie addressing the crowd. As his handler pulls him away, Frank can't help but think how much more comfortable Bernie is in front of a crowd than he is.

"Huh," he chuckles to himself, all the while absently smiling for his adoring fans, "maybe he should write a book someday. I mean, why waste all his talent on talking me up?"

Who could have guessed Bernie was thinking the exact same thing?

1 The hall stretched out before him, a seemingly endless expanse of dark corners and closed doors. Seemingly endless, but not. There *was* an end, but would it prove to be his own? And there weren't an infinite number of doors, only three. But in this case, opening them, clearing them, seeing what was beyond them, could take a lifetime.

Vinny Smalldeano sighed, took out his standard-issue Beretta, and assumed the position as he began the long trek down the dangerous hallway. He avoided the stagnant puddles caused by the leaky pipes that stretched above him like a swarm of drooling snakes, and kept sweeping his eyes across the field in front of him, from corner to corner, all too aware that this "danger zone" could erupt into a kill zone at any moment.

His partner was searching the floor below him, two teams of snipers had their lasers trained on the fire escapes, and a recon team watched the front and back doors downstairs, should their subject miraculously elude Smalldeano and his team.

He shook the logistics from his head; part of his training was to rely on the team, not sweat them. He had to trust in their training as much as his own; each team member had a job to do. His was to lead; that's what he was doing.

He avoided another puddle, stepping instead on something soft and squishy. Smelling the foul odor of decay as it wafted up from his tightly-laced black boots, he realized it must have been a dead lizard or rat. He fought the gag reflex, moving forward instead, until he was just shy of the first door. A crooked apartment number hung from one rusty screw, the bottom of a 7 now the top, making the letter "L" instead.

There was no need to identify himself; this was an abandoned building and the perp was an immediate threat to the safety of himself, the rest of his team, and the ten-year-old girl he'd just snatched from across state lines in West Virginia.

Risking a glance around the moldy frame, he quickly judged the door's weakest point and aimed his foot. He sent the door flying from its rusty hinges, just like he'd been trained. It landed on its side, giving him cover if needed and saving him the trouble of walking across its unsteady surface should it have landed flat on its back.

The rank smell of weeks-old food and even older feces launched an aerial attack on his senses, causing his eyes to water and nostrils to flare. He resisted the impulse to flinch, training his eyes instead on the newest danger zone: the kitchen of the apartment.

His thick, wiry muscles were on high-alert, every cell in his body engulfed in the heady rush of adrenaline that coursed through his veins. Sweat dripped down the collar of his thick bulletproof vest; the gray FBI T-shirt beneath soaked to the core, his dominant abdominal muscles tensed at the ready.

His eyes flicked back and forth, his ears picked up the dripping sounds from the hallway, the settling of dust from his door-kicking, the sweat dripping off his nose onto the cracked linoleum of the claustrophobic foyer.

He was exhausted, emotionally and physically. This wasn't his first floor, but his fifth. Ten floors dotted the leaning tenement building. He and his partner had split them up and were now at the end of their rope. Witnesses had seen the perp dragging the girl in there earlier that morning; no one had seen them leave.

The first 8 floors had been cleared after endless hours of intense, heart-pounding effort. Every broken door, every dead rat, every rank puddle and stale sandwich had left him devoid of energy. His head pounded with a stress headache the size of the Washington monument, which he hoped to see one day from his office at FBI headquarters. As it was, that day seemed as far away as the end of this particular search and seizure.

He rubbed the thought away, pinching the bridge of his nose with his free hand to try and rid himself of a tiny measure of the pressure forcing a blinding white light across his vision. He blinked, once, twice, for focus and cleared the kitchen, moving quickly through the deserted living room to the first of two bedrooms.

He alternated his field of vision from the debris on the floor to the shadows in the corners. The day was rapidly dwindling; they were losing the light. If he didn't clear the next two rooms within the hour, night would fall and they'd have to resort to flashlights; he needed the clear light of day to peer into every nook and cranny.

He quickened his pace, crouching to enter the first bedroom and spying two potential causes for concern: a piss-stained mattress leaning against the wall—behind which the perp might be hiding— and a closed closet door.

"Fuck," he whispered softly, and then again and again and again: "fuck, fuck, *fuck*!" The ploy worked; his migraine momentarily subsided. With a clear head and sure purpose, he made quick work of overturning the mattress, behind which lay a family of dust mites and little else. Stealthily he approached the closet; there was no avoiding detection at this range.

Even he could hear his own heart beating; Vinny knew the subject would have heard the mattress clattering to the floor, dead springs falling clear from fabric long since rotted through. His boots could not avoid the broken glass of several dozen burnt pipes and heroin syringes, left behind by the crack heads and users who'd probably called this place home for years.

Vinny neared the closet, which faced a wall mottled with water stains, both natural and manmade. The smell was overpowering, but so too was the gut instinct that this was the magic doorway. The skin of Vinny's testicles was clenched in anticipation, and even his goose bumps had goose bumps. He tried to steady his own breathing, listening carefully, but all he saw was the door in front of him, all he heard was the dripping of water and the pounding of his own heart.

Still, his gut had gotten him this far, through years at the academy, a half dozen years on the street after that, through Quantico and, at last, to the final proving grounds. He navigated the minefield of drug-crazed shooters and federal politics, all with grace and cunning; he knew the perp was here, felt it as clean and cool as the sweat dripping down his thirty-two year old back.

He reached for the door, gun at the ready, eyes big as saucers, every tendon flexed, every pore open, mouth agape, ready to yell "Freeze!" There was no kicking in this door, not with the prospect of an unarmed minor in there with the perp. It opened out, and so he would open it out.

He reached for the knob, hand trembling, strong, big, sweaty, but sure. The handle was surprisingly cold to the touch, making him doubt himself, but only momentarily. He began to turn, slowly, slowly, only to....

The wall behind him evaporated in a cloud of dust as rough hands reached to grab his throat. They missed, finding his shoulders instead, but still with enough purchase to drag him back, back; the hands like vice grips, cold and remorseless, as in front of him the doorknob retreated slowly and his whole world fell away.

Back he went, until at last he found his footing and stopped his retreat, the dust of ancient drywall clogging his throat as he picked up his left foot and drove it backward through the wall, hearing a crunch and a curse.

"Shit, Smalldeano, what the hell?"

The voice, familiar.

The hands, released.

Instinctively Vinny turned, only to spy his special schools instructor, Cap Callahan, grimacing as he clutched his offended groin. "Since when the fuck did a prick like you stop knowing how to take a joke?" he asked, his face red, his balding hair plastered to his furrowed brow from endless minutes apparently spent waiting for the perfect moment.

In from the hallway spilled a half-dozen special agents, all wearing Hawaiian shirts and holding pitchers of beer aloft. The closet before him burst open, holding the rest of his team and a frozen, lifeless CPR dummy, representing the child he'd been ordered to rescue. Around her pale, rubber throat hung a handwritten sign that said, "What took you so long?"

"What the fuck?" he spat, adrenaline still surging through his throttled veins. "This was some kind of joke?"

Callahan limped from the wall, kicking drywall as he went. "You think I'd hide in a wall for five hours for a joke? This is your graduation party, asshole. You made it!"

"I made it?" Vinny asked. "But I thought I still had two weeks of training to go. I thought this field exercise was part of that."

Laughter filled the claustrophobic hallway as more and more agents filed into the room. "Your training was over last week!" Cap said, pouring himself a glass of beer. "Once you nabbed that child pornographer using the new APRHND software we've been tinkering with. This? This was just a lure to get you away from the books and into the bar. The paperwork's all done; your assignment's secure and just waiting for you to sign on the dotted line."

Pats of congratulation peppered his shoulders as his gun was whisked away and replaced with a glass of cold beer. Into his free hand, still trembling, Cap deposited a wilted envelope, stained by sweat and crumpled, no doubt from when Vinny kneed him in the balls.

"Where?" was all Vinny could think to ask.

Cap wasted no time in answering: "DC, my boy. You got your wish; you're going to headquarters."

The room fell away, the jokes, the camaraderie, the beer foam, even the anger of being lured into a fake rescue scenario and wasting five hours and twenty pounds in sweat. It was official: Vinny Smalldeano was the newest member of the FBI's elite Special Circumstances Killer squad, headquartered in none other than Washington, DC. Criminals be damned.

2 Frank Logan settled into his first-class seat as the redeye from LAX awaited take-off for the nonstop flight back to Dulles in DC. He certainly wasn't the first Fed to fly commercial, but he was surely one of the only few flying first class in these days of budget battles and belt-tightening. But that was okay, let them fuss about it back at headquarters. It was on his dime anyway; nothing they could do about it.

Besides, they were used to it. Ever since the publication of his first book half a dozen years back, Frank and the FBI had enjoyed an uneasy alliance. The Feds knew Frank was good for them, he knew they were good for him.

Frank's gritty look—graying hair, chiseled chin, sharp green eyes—made him the new poster boy for the FBI. It didn't hurt that his exploits always managed to come at a time when the FBI was reeling from one sort of miscue or another: another foiled hostage situation aired live on CNN, an interstate kidnapping with a grim ending announced immediately on the Grudge Report.

The handsome, weathered author, with his trademark blue jeans and comfortably worn T-shirt, made a nice counterpoint to the FBI's stiff suits and occasionally disappointing reputation. The more Frank hawked his books, the better the Feds looked. Then again, Frank's rise to the position of political poster boy had caused a few gray hairs back at headquarters, and he knew the rumor around 935 Pennsylvania Avenue was that he was nothing more than a glory chaser and a newshound, out for his own gain, the Bureau be damned. Though those who knew him best frowned at the suggestion, Frank knew that, in the end, results were all that mattered to the top brass. And when it came to results, Frank's track record was about as good as his books' sales figures. And these days, that was very, very good.

Frank scanned the half-empty cabin, noticing the wide-eyed flight attendants to his right as they bustled about, trying to appear as if they weren't star-struck. He sighed, wished he could sleep, knew he never would, and, instead, opened the daily package that had been Fed-Exed to his hotel room that morning.

The packet was thicker than it had been the past few days, but, looking at the date on his watch, Frank suddenly realized why: Today was Monday. There was always more murder and mayhem over the weekend, although, as the head of the FBI's Special Circumstances Killer unit, Frank knew it wasn't necessarily *his* brand of murder and mayhem. The title was new; the suspect was not. To qualify as a "special circumstances" killer, the murders had to be multiple, cross state boundaries, and display a recognizable modus operandi, or MO.

Frank should know; after 32 years in the Bureau, he'd been charged with assembling the task force, which necessarily meant dotting the i's and crossing the t's on its Congressional charter. Before approving his budget, Congress had made him pin down the difference between the typical serial killer and that of the special circumstances variety. After apprehending nearly a dozen of these types in his career, the task had been all too easy. Still, the budget they'd approved was a pittance compared to what he'd asked for, and Frank soon found himself behind the eight ball, instead of out in front of it, as he preferred.

Hence the packet on his lap. He looked at the return address in the upper left-hand corner: Central Clippings, Inc. Not the catchiest of small business names, but it certainly fit: the news clipping agency was quite literally located in the center of the country, and Frank had taken a personal tour of their Manhattan, Kansas headquarters—if one could call a single floor in a downtown bank building "headquarters"—before he'd subscribed to their hefty weekly fee. In return for his two grand a month, Frank got a daily—not weekly, but daily—packet of news clippings from around the country. The single keyword? Murder. Various filters cut down on the clippings he actually received. Solved murders, for instance, or murders in which a family member was involved, weren't included.

Even so, the number of unsolved murders that did pass through the various Central Clippings filters was often staggering and occasionally insurmountable. At headquarters he had a full-time staffer flag those items of interest that might signal a future—or current—special circumstances killer, but while on the road, he was on his own.

The packet opened with a tear, interrupting the giggling flight attendants, one of whom—the alpha female, with stiff hair and stiffer breasts—took it as her cue to come offer Frank a drink. He took a quick glance at his watch, wondered if the bar was still open, and with a quick wink at the leggy stewardess, effectively guaranteed that it was.

While he awaited his gin and tonic, he scoured through the garden variety news reports of murder the clipping service had flagged. A body found in Nebraska. A missing co-ed in San Diego, feared dead. A grisly discovery in a New Jersey storage shed. Frank took his drink from the stewardess without a word, ignoring her gasp as she eyed the assortment of pain and misery in his trembling hands, complete with grainy black and white photos straight from the AP wire.

He sighed, sipped, sipped again, feeling the cold, thin liquid lubricate his throat and ease his mind. Two grand a month. $500 a week. It was an expense the Bureau would have never approved, even if there'd been money in the budget for it, which, of course, there hadn't been. But he figured he owed it to the American people who, after all, were the ones who bought his books. If it cost him twenty grand a month to prevent special circumstances killers from preying on his fan base, he'd gladly pay. Two-hundred grand a month, if he had it.

It was a mentality the Bureau had never quite tolerated. Frank realized it was one they'd never understand, either.

3 Bernie Segal watched from the airport VIP lounge as Frank's flight finally took off, its taillights winking in the restless hours between midnight and dawn. The bar had long since closed, but with a signed copy of Frank's latest book, not to mention a well-placed twenty dollar bill for a bookmark, Bernie had convinced the bartender to pour him one last double—more like a triple—before he locked up for the night.

The miniatures in his carry-on bag didn't hurt, either. He nursed the dregs of his drink, wishing Frank a pleasant flight back to DC with a raised hand, as sure as it was steady. "Catch us some more bad guys, Frankie," he said with a scowl, using his private nickname for the famed Fed, one he'd never use to his face or, for that matter, in public. "Sell us some more books."

Bernie glanced around the deserted bar. A faulty beer light blinking in the corner provided the only illumination, save that of the departing planes outside the huge plate glass window he was facing. His flight was still several hours away, but he'd wanted to catch a ride to the airport with Frank, so he'd put himself out once again, readjusting his schedule to fit the breadwinner's. It was a small price to pay, he supposed. Several lonely hours in an empty VIP lounge in exchange for a golden opportunity to have some quiet time alone with Frank. Of course, it hadn't been very productive, not on the surface anyway, but Bernie knew his triumphs over Frank came in inches, not feet.

During the twenty-minute limo ride from the hotel to LAX, he'd been able to mix business with pleasure, planting the seed in Frank's head once again to let him pursue the weekly crime series Bernie had been pitching all over town.

Frank was staunchly against it, but the networks were all for it. Frank saw it as compromising a dozen open case files; Bernie just saw dollar signs. Frank saw it as risking the lives of future victims by exploiting the savagery of past special circumstances killers; Bernie saw it as "fuck you" money for his imminent retirement.

Frank had no idea of the vast difference between TV money and book money. It was like night and day; the networks were offering Frank's combined advances on all six of his books in exchange for a one-hour pilot. And that was just the pilot! God knows what they'd be offering for an entire series.

Bernie stared out the window, watching another plane take off. He toasted it, realizing just how far he—and Frank—had come. When the two had met in a grungy little SoHo bar some seven years earlier, Frank had yet to head up the Special Circumstances task force and Bernie had yet to crack the bestseller lists.

All that changed with Frank's first book, *Case File Confidential*. The book had been your typical tough-FBI-man-solves-tough-cases true crime book, complete with "8 pages of shocking crime scene photos," but to lure the best publishers with the biggest advances, a hungry Bernie had tracked down every single murderer profiled in the book.

With their exclusive interviews, not to mention a stiff cash deposit into their death row canteen accounts, Bernie had pulled off the historical: for the first time ever, readers were able to read the good guy's version of the case right next to the bad guy's. It was a startling contrast, and a bona fide media magnet.

In no time, Bernie had signed Frank to a six-book deal with Doubletree, a first for an active federal agent, and after the second book, Hollywood had come calling. When Bernie realized that he was spending more money on long distance phone calls than he was on cab fare to the New York publishers' offices, he knew that a move was in order.

It didn't hurt that Doubletree's corporate headquarters, they of the popular movie tie-ins, were located smack dab in downtown LA. He'd kited checks on his patchwork of half a dozen bank loans and splurged on a pricey suite of offices in Beverly Hills, then never looked back. Now all his hard work was paying off; the first adaptation of one of Frank's books was due to hit theaters sometime next fall, and if he could lock down the TV series to coincide with that season's sweeps week, they'd be on easy street for time immemorial.

Bernie toasted another plane and stared at the week's itinerary laid out before him on the wet, sticky bar. Scouting locations for the TV pilot wasn't easy, nor was it his job, but Bernie had long since secured for himself a reputation as a hands-on agent.

If the networks wouldn't commit to a pilot, sight unseen, he'd damn well shoot one himself.

4 It had been six weeks since tourist season officially ended, and long, grim months still remained before the snowbirds made their way south, bringing with them fat wallets and fatter bellies. Unlike her best friends, Monica and Amy, who worked for tips after school at the local pizzeria, Candace Myers made only six bucks an hour whether Gino's Ice Cream Emporium was standing room only on a hopping Saturday night or as barren as the desert on a rainy Tuesday afternoon.

At the moment she was all alone in the store, as usual. She didn't mind the solitude, though. Boring was bad, but standing elbow deep in a sticky tub of mint chocolate chip while a family of twelve waited for their free samples—never to spend a dime, mind you— was infinitely worse.

Six bucks was six bucks, no matter how you sliced it; better to make it doing her calculus homework and listening to her walkman than serving sunburned customers and making small talk about time-shares and Solarcaine.

The afternoon passed slowly, the activity up and down the boardwalk starting slow and getting even slower as her shift inched by as coolly as the ice crystals that inevitably formed on the crunchy cardboard tin of rainbow sherbet, October's lowest seller.

She'd hoped that her boyfriend of five months, Thad Coombs, would stop by after track practice, but, as usual, the big dope had gotten detention again for dropping cherry bombs down three of the boy's room toilets and would be spending an extra hour with the coach, running laps as penance for his childish prank.

So it was just Candace, Alicia Keyes playing through her head-phones, mint chocolate chip, and questions 12-68 on page 324 of her advanced calculus book for the next three hours. Odds *and* evens!

Ah, the joys of being a high school senior. She snuggled deeper into her FSU sweatshirt that she wore beneath her Gino's apron, a perk the owner allowed on account of the freezing temperatures that reigned supreme behind the four large, coffin-like coolers holding all 56 of Gino's "homemade" specialties.

The "homemade," of course, required quotation marks, even on the scoop shaped sign hanging above the door, owing to the fact that Gino ordered his ice cream, mint chocolate chip, rainbow sherbet, and the other 54 flavors, from a distributor in Boise, just like 2,367 other vendors touting "homemade" ice cream all across the country.

Her boss might have been a tad unethical, Candace thought, but aside from that time he tried to hit on her in the break room after his wife's funeral—and two bottles of Ouzo—he was a straight-up guy who always slipped a hundred dollar bonus in her Christmas card and made sure the shop closed early the night before an exam day.

One more semester, however, and she'd be rid of vanilla, mint chocolate chip, and even the crystallized rainbow sherbet. Hopefully forever. Off to Florida State University in Tallahassee, the state capital, where she planned to be a kindergarten teacher just like her mom.

In a world where most achingly beautiful high school seniors with part-time jobs in ice cream parlors and jock boyfriends have something to hide—teen pregnancy, AIDS, a nasty crack or heroin addiction, a rap sheet for shoplifting from the Gap, or perhaps even an eating disorder like one of their favorite models-slash-singers-slash-actresses—Candace was a deceptively simple girl with similarly simple goals. She was a virgin, technically anyway, and had over two thousand dollars in her individual bank account at Sunshine Lenders. She made her own car payment every month, though her dad still chipped in for half of her insurance, a secret they'd both managed to keep from her mother.

She volunteered at the local homeless shelter because she wanted to, not because it would look good on her college transcript. (Okay, maybe that's why she had *started* volunteering there, but after that first trip she really liked it.) She gave her friends a 50% discount on cones, even though she secretly made up the difference out of her own pocket once they left.

She had a quirky sense of humor that only those who knew her best ever had the distinction of enjoying. She was also a secret fan of *General Hospital*—thank God for TiVo—listened to Christmas albums until well into February, and wanted kids more than anything else in the world. (Just not with a doofus like Thad, the cute doofus.) The definitive "good girl," she lived for her family, friends, school, boyfriend, and job, in that order.

Unfortunately for Candace, she just didn't have that long to live.

5

He'd been watching her for hours, since she started her shift at precisely 1 p.m. That was the kind of girl Candace Myers was. He knew it from the moment he'd laid eyes on her some two days earlier, strolling down the boardwalk to her low-rent ice cream parlor in mauve bell-bottoms and a tank top that barely crossed her navel, innocently devoid of a flashy belly button ring, a fact that only served to thrill him even more.

At first, the tawdry outfit put him off; it didn't jibe with the research he'd done, combing through hours of school and medical files for weaknesses or petty teenage transgressions like cheating, skipping, or tardiness.

An honor student, loyal friend, dutiful daughter, faithful girlfriend, and punctual employee, the bare midriff, exposed shoulders, swaying hips, and budding breasts just didn't jibe with his own mental picture. But then he watched the other girls on the boardwalk, most too old, the rest not old enough.

He saw that the current whims of American fashion dictated a teenage girl dress in such a manner, at least until the bell curve slid down another slope and the current whim became something else. Most girls, he noted, wore less, and wore it worse.

He spotted her extra-thick belt, designed to hide the bottom half of her navel, and was proud that there were no piercings or tattoos anywhere on all that ripe, tan, exposed flesh.

She would do just fine, this one.

The first day, as October sprang to life clear and bright under the fading Florida sun, he'd watched her lug her bright pink backpack into the store, trade niceties with the older woman who worked the day shift, and then slip into her baggy college sweatshirt and sea-foam-colored Gino's apron.

For hours, he watched her do her homework, tidy up, eye the clock, serve a grand total of six customers, and then lock up before returning down the boardwalk to her modest economy car, most likely an early graduation present for Daddy's little honor student, soon to be a college co-ed.

He couldn't have asked for a better first victim. The papers would eat her alive, or dead, in this case, instantly memorializing her as an innocent in a world of crass, teenage pride. She would be the poster girl for rage, outcry, and revenge, and the spark that lit a fuse of a serial killer's, make that a special circumstance killer's, cross-country spree.

But still, every marathon starts with the first step.

On this day, he watched her show up right on time. His perch was a barstool across the boardwalk in some low-rent biker dive with cheap draft beer and stale pretzels and, best of all, a clear, unbroken view of Gino's.

He was in plain sight, this much he knew, but his ingenious disguise, not to mention his place of rest, would assure that any would-be, booze-soaked, white trash witnesses would remember only an undistinguishable tourist in a Hawaiian shirt, cheap Florida ball cap, cheaper sunglasses, baggy baggies, and generic blue flip-flops.

It was standard Daytona fare, entirely disposable, and had been purchased for under twenty bucks at the local tourist shop the minute he arrived in town. They'd be looking for John Candy in *Summer Rental* and he'd already be onto his next state, flying so far under their radar there wouldn't even be a blip as he settled in to spy on hapless Victim Number Two.

He'd established a pattern, long enough for even the dimwitted bartender to know his "regular" each afternoon was a single shot of well bourbon with a slow, smooth Amstel Light to follow. It was the perfect touch: just enough of a detail to let the cops know he wasn't afraid of them, yet nothing specific enough to tie him down.

Next time, it would be a shot of gin and a Bass Ale. After that, who knows? A margarita, extra limes. A virgin piña colada, no cherries. Cold sake at some sushi joint. For now all he needed was a clear head and an even clearer view, and from his barstool perch he had more than he could have hoped for.

Unlike other killers, those not worthy to lick his flip-flops, he had no sexual desire for the innocent girl working at the ice cream parlor to save money for gas, movies, and pizzas at the state university next fall. Though her body was flawless, her skin unimpeachable, her legs coltish and willing, he saw only tomorrow's headlines: **Local Teen Found Mutilated in Popular Ice Cream Parlor.**

It might as well have been written on the inside of his cheap sunglasses. As the night wound down, the bar crowd livened up, all except for the sole tourist sitting by his lonesome, nursing his beer and shot in his disposable get-up.

Soon it would be quitting time for Little Miss Perfect, and only now did the thrill of the hunt cause his blood pressure to rise ever so slightly, as it fought back the subtle buzz that followed his beer and shot. He watched his clock, saw 8 p.m. fast approaching, and knew from experience that, by 8:05, she'd already be emptying the trash behind the store. He paid his tab, neither tipping too much nor too little, and rushed to meet his fate.

Rush was the optimum word. Now the light buzz he'd been feeling for hours vanished in the wake of a crushing tidal wave of trembling adrenaline that almost made him walk out of his ridiculous blue flip-flops. He smirked, realizing you could plan for weeks, months, hell, years, and an unexpected jolt of adrenaline and a cheap pair of flip-flops could, quite literally, trip you up.

She was not expecting him. She hadn't heard the cowbell over Gino's door tinkle in her absence, nor the lock slide solidly into place and the "Closed" sign turn into view. Once inside, he turned out the lights, spilled her purse, slid on her backpack, and waited patiently for her in the cramped employee break room. It was little more than a broom closet with a picnic table and a microwave, but it was between Gino's locked front door and the soon-to-be-bolted back door. He heard her out there, rattling garbage can lids back into place, even the soft swish of her pink, pale hands rubbing together as his senses tightened with a killer's omniscience.

From his perch, he could even smell the tell-tale scent of her Bath and Body Works hand gel—raspberry, yeah, that was it, though they'd probably call it something snooty like "Country Raspberry" or "Blushing Berry"—as she rid her hands of pesky germs on her way back inside. Her back to the break room, she slid the bolt on the back door and turned off the light, realizing too late that an intruder was only inches from her soft, bare shoulders.

His approach was swift, silent, and effective. His perch afforded him quick access, his self-training gave him near perfection in the art of human submission: one arm up through her armpit and around the back of her neck, a classic half-nelson, and the other on her mouth to silence the scream that she was too shocked to voice.

As always, he had come prepared: Surgical gloves masked his prints, overbearing suntan lotion slathered across every inch of his shaved body clouded his DNA, and even the alcohol on his breath rendered his saliva untraceable. He was a silent killing machine, just gearing up for a long month of hell. She felt the pressure on her neck, sniffed the cloying scent of coconut oil, and, true to form, didn't resist the hand over her mouth.

The plastic cigar case that had been present in his garish shirt pocket for days yielded a syringe containing a mild but instant sedative that, a mere forty-six minutes after her death, would be completely untraceable. He sensed her vulnerability, applied more pressure to her tender neck, and quickly extracted the syringe with the hand that had, until just then, covered her mouth.

Even through the glove, he could sense the saliva on his palm, but it didn't slow the plunge of the needle into her soft, exposed throat. There was a whimper, a sudden gasp after the realization that this was not your normal, every day robbery, and then silence. Sweet silence. He knew from experience there were twenty-eight delectable seconds of surrender, and he used every last one of them to turn her toward him and gaze into her eyes.

Soft blue contact lenses stared back at him, wide with fear, ruining the moment. What honor student, what perfect victim, wore *colored* contacts? This tiny tidbit was not in his research, and served only to rob him of his picture-perfect image of this first, photogenic victim. Still, he would not be denied the satisfaction of guiding her to her death, or at least her last, few conscious moments. Death, after all, would take much longer.

When he was finished, he stared at the scene before him and thought it was appropriately "disorganized," as the FBI profiler would eventually determine. His weapon of opportunity would mesh with his predatory instincts, the locking of both doors would imply some-one familiar to the victim, and the missing backpack would further insinuate common robbery. It was a classic triumvirate and, though just as staged as the ice cream cashier's body would eventually be, enough of a hodgepodge of misread clues to keep the local cops chas-ing their tails. It was an inside-out triangle, three distinct clues each leading in three separate directions. Three potential suspect profiles, none of which would even be close to accurate. The evidence left behind would be negligible: A stray fiber from his mass-produced Hawaiian shirt, a generic flip flop print in melted ice cream, a body so cold it would be impossible to pinpoint time of death.

He hadn't covered all his bases, of course; that would imply yet another profile he wasn't yet willing to reveal. But he had covered just enough to shrink the balls of any lawman experienced enough to know better.

Finally, just before using Candace's key to let himself out, he pulled a pristine piece of paper from his back pocket, slipped it from its protective plastic casing, and laid it carefully on Candace's bare breasts.

Or, at least, what remained of them.

As he left through the back door, dodging Dempsey dumpsters and winos, his smile lit the bleak October night. He hadn't felt this good in ages. Well, not since the last one. But she, like all the others, had just been practice for the main event. This was the real thing, the first true test, and he smiled the smug grin of a man deeply satisfied with his work at the end of a long, hard day. If he'd had a boss, he'd have gotten an "attaboy" right there on the spot.

Perhaps even a pat on the ass.

As it was, he'd have to wait until the morning paper to enjoy the glory. Then again, the mint chocolate chip currently melting down the cone he'd "borrowed", and across his blood-soaked plastic gloves, wasn't too shabby, either.

6

Rocky Chicone had taken a lot of grief for his rather audacious nickname over the years—"Yo, Rock, where's Adrian?", "Go get 'em, Rock," "When's your next fight, Rocko?"—but those who knew him best recognized that the only time he put on the gloves was to fight crime.

His appearance was equally off-putting to the Sylvester Stallone comparisons. Straight blond hair, tortoise shell glasses, rail-thin frame draped over 6'2" of 35-year-old ex-basketball player, meant that the shouts of "Yo, Rock" that greeted him everywhere he went—inside and out of the Daytona PD—seemed more appropriate for just about anybody *other* than Lieutenant Rocky Chicone. He hadn't always had the nickname, of course, though most everyone in Daytona Beach, including his family of five, had forgotten that his given name was actually Charles Dade Chicone.

And, far from fighting, boxing gloves, or bloody noses, that nickname itself had decidedly more *academic* origins: His grandfather was a local fisherman famed for his likeness to Florida's most famous writer: Ernest Hemingway.

One day, a reporter showed up at Grampa Ernest's doorstep for the inevitable yearly Hemingway Days story, only to find little Charles sitting out front on the porch, rocking away, a copy of *The Old Man and the Sea* in his hands.

Seems Grampa Ernest was tired of being front page news each time those crazies down in Key West decided to celebrate their most famous resident with an annual look-alike contest, and so the round-faced, white bearded, sun-bleached recluse set his nine-year-old grandson out to greet the reporter in his stead.

With no one else to interview, the cameraman dutifully snapped a shot of little Charles rocking away on the sun porch, the bestseller on his lap. The next day a bold headline over the full-color picture read: **Hemingway's Missing In Action—"Rocky" Stands In!**

He'd been called "Rocky" ever since….

"Yo, Rock," cried out an officer new to the scene, not to mention the force, bearing the now lukewarm coffee Rocky had requested some thirty minutes earlier. "Sorry it took me so long, but the 7-11 up the street is jammed with the usual rubberneckers and…."

"Why the hell didn't you just go to the bar across the street and get some there?" Rocky asked, pointing to the deserted watering hole within spitting distance. "Christ, I thought you'd fallen off the pier or something. I was five seconds away from sending out a search party."

The rookie looked over his shoulder at the open bar across from the ice cream parlor, closed to the public by the yards and yards of yellow crime scene tape currently flapping in the wet, slick breeze of a late afternoon Daytona rainstorm.

A cadre of coffee sipping cops waved back.

"Shit," muttered the rookie.

"Shit is right," Rocky said with a grin, cracking the first bright spot in this long, depressing day.

It had started out inauspiciously enough. Rocky woke up as he did every morning, took a three-mile run in the hazy Florida dawn, and then showered for another long day on the state's glittering East Coast. Minutes later, the digital clock by his bed reading barely 5 a.m., his pager jolted on his belt, sending him dashing to the kitchen phone, where he wouldn't wake his bride of nearly a dozen years when he called into headquarters.

"Yo, Rock," said the voice of the morning dispatcher. "Captain wants you on the scene of Gino's Ice Cream Emporium, stat. You know the one? On the boardwalk? That's the one. Crime scene's already up and running. He wanted to give you enough shut-eye to be alert for the next 24. Hell, make that 48. Gonna be a long day and night, sounds like. Something about a body in a cooler? Guess that's the last new flavor old Gino'll ever create, huh, Lt.?"

"Nice," Rocky muttered wryly, shaking his still wet head and hanging up the phone as quietly as possible before creeping back into the bedroom to finish dressing. Within minutes, he was pulling up at the world famous Daytona Beach Pier, looking less like the set of *Beach Blanket Bingo* and more like the backdrop of some Hollywood director's latest true crime thriller.

And, yet again, Rocky was the reluctant star.

Patrol cars had blocked off the main parking lot, filled as it was with cars, both marked and unmarked, all of them beading up in the early morning drizzle of a grim October dawn. Personnel, both young and old, night shift and day, rooted around in trunks crammed with shotgun shells, evidence bags, and first-aid kits, searching for their long-forgotten rain gear.

Beat cops waved off lurking traffic in the early morning stillness with flashlights honed to a razor's point by bright orange cones affixed to the lenses. Rocky ignored the good-natured shouts of "Yo, Rock" as he expertly dipped below what seemed like miles and miles of familiar yellow crime scene tape and strode up the warped pier to Gino's.

Many, many hours later, he watched wearily as the pier slowly drained of law enforcement personnel. The scene had been bagged and tagged, the body, such as it was, carted away by the coroner, and, as night slowly fell and the gay pier lighting clashed with the long, grim hours ahead, Rocky held on to one key staff member engaging in his evening detection: The "coffee rookie."

"See ya, Rock," said the rookie unknowingly, as, one-by-one, plainclothes detectives, crime scene techs, and uniformed officers strolled down the pier and got into their cars, only to slip off into the slow, wet night to mull over the case in diners and fast-food joints throughout the city. A dozen different pockets of coffee-swilling, omelet-ordering, armchair quarterbacks, second-guessing every one of Rocky's moves.

"Not so fast…," Rocky grumbled, pausing to regard the rookie's nametag: "…Sanchez. I need a warm body for the night work. You up for it?"

"Night work?" Sanchez asked, peering inside the deserted ice cream parlor, walls, sinks, and fixtures plastered with black fingerprint powder until it looked like the bowels of some West Virginia coalmine. "Don't you want to check out the autopsy with the rest of the late-night ghouls?"

"What for?" asked Rocky, draining the last of his coffee with a flourish that said, *I've only just begun.* He held up a manila folder, thick with 8 x 10 glossies graphic enough to make even Charles Manson blanch. "I've got the crime scene photos right here, and the coroner's report will be on my desk when I get back in the morning. Everyone's gone, kid. Now's when the *real* work begins."

Rocky sent Sanchez off for two more cups of coffee—physically steering him by the shoulders in the direction of the bar across from Gino's, so as to avoid a repeat of the earlier caffeine infraction—and waited for him in the garishly-lit ice cream parlor, enjoying the temporary peace and quiet of the deserted crime scene.

Rocky liked to think of himself as "old school," not exactly a popular thing to be in this day of high-tech crime fiction and glitzy TV cop dramas. Much like the airwaves, movie theaters, and bookstores, the department itself was full of pseudo-profilers, boning up on John Douglas thrillers and holing up for weeks at a time in Quantico, Virginia, learning the difference between mass murderers and serial killers, and coming back with a certificate in one hand and a chip on their shoulders.

Rocky was no "mind hunter." There was nothing sexy about what he did. No techno-rock from this week's "it" band played in the background while he toiled over endless hours of blood samples and fingerprints. No sexy-slash-nerdy crime tech in a low-cut lab coat and daring bust line flirted with him coyly while they fought over who got the first look into the electron microscope to examine a spent bullet casing or torn fingernail.

"You first."

"No, you first."

"If you insist."

"Oh, but I *do*...."

He was many things in addition to being a good cop—a family man, a devout Catholic, a disciplined runner, an avid reader, a legendary napper, a closet Metallica fan, an easy crier, painfully ticklish—but there was no part of him that could relate to the kind of man, make that *animal*, who could stride into an ice cream parlor at eight in the evening and slaughter an innocent teen angel like Candace Myers.

He couldn't "walk in the murder's shoes," as some of his colleagues liked to brag. He couldn't "get into their heads." He couldn't see what they saw, go where they went, think what they thought, feel what they felt.

He didn't want to.

More importantly, he didn't *need* to.

He'd seen where they'd been. For Rocky, that was enough. He didn't need some flimsy FBI certificate to tell him which killers were organized and which were just plain bat-shit, just-killed-their-mother nuts. He could tell which suspects wore gloves, and which shaved their heads in an attempt to get rid of any follicle evidence.

Rocky was a stalker, and there was no one better to handle Daytona's latest vicious murder. That's why he was given free rein in a deserted ice cream parlor long after the so-called "dime store profilers" had all gone home, eaten dinner, and tucked their kids in tight.

The stalker and the rookie had a long night ahead of them.

7 The newspaper lay on the passenger seat, boldly announcing a "brutal" slaying in the land of "the perpetual spring break." The story itself was so predictable, he could have written it in his sleep, especially given his particular literary background; but nonetheless, he would carefully cut it out and stick it in his, up until now, empty scrapbook when, and if, he ever got back home.

For now, there was work to do, and as Florida's panhandle lay flat and thick in his rearview mirror, he silently crossed the border into the land of peaches and pecans, Bulldogs and *Gone with the Wind*.

There was nothing spectacular about his ride, nothing covert about his appearance. He wasn't covering his tracks so much as leaving them far, far behind, and as for the "thrill of the hunt," he was still satiated enough with the recent kill to be hours away from "stalking mode," as he liked to call it.

Still, next to the pristine Daytona Beach paper sat a fresh guidebook to Georgia colleges, a half-dozen of them within a fifty mile radius, ranging from technical schools to community colleges to beauty schools to full-fledged state universities. It was a veritable killer's buffet and, before long, he'd be hungry enough to partake.

For now?

For now there was just the memory....

"Candace."

A smirk crossed his narrow lips, tickled at his broad nose. Candace. He loved that name. *Candace*. Perfect. What a great, camera-ready, All-American, MTV, teenage name.

As predicted, the paper had made her out to be nothing short of a modern-day heroine. The virgin victim. The perfect student. The faithful girlfriend. The high school senior. Even an interview given by her grieving boyfriend had touted her "purity." Purity? He couldn't have wished for a better word.

Except, maybe, for immaculate.

Oh, and let's not forget unsullied.

And what about *chaste*?

And how he had defiled her.

As he cruised through the deep, dark night, he silently marveled at how quickly the dogged reporters on the story—it had taken three of them to do the slaughter justice—had been able to paint such an accurate picture of the slain teen queen.

True, a hungry bar patron with the munchies for pistachio praline had alerted the cops to an empty, open ice cream parlor just after 1:15 a.m., but the trio of reporters for the local rag must have worked double time to rouse her friends and family for interviews in the hours between then and just before dawn, the time the paper went to press.

It only proved his theory right: The papers wouldn't wait for politics, history, or science, but they'd sure as shit "hold the presses" for blood and guts, particularly when both had been splattered up and down the walls of a local ice cream parlor overseen by a teenage princess named *Candace*, saving up for college as she protected her precious, ripe virginity by only going to second—okay, third—base with her handsome, appropriately grief-stricken, captain-of-the-football team boyfriend.

It couldn't have been a more auspicious start to his eventual plan, but there were miles to go before Phase 2 could begin. He pulled into a rest stop, relieved himself, and threw the last of his bloody clothes into a generic trash bin whose contents would eventually end up in some local dump 60 miles away. He studied his college guide map over a cup of vending machine coffee and a bag of salt-free pretzels in the flickering light of a graffiti-covered picnic table with gum stuck to the bottom and boogers on the top.

He fingered the change in his pocket with one hand as the steady index finger of the other perused ground zero for his next crime scene. He settled on Peachtree Community College, a sprawling ode to academia covering some six city blocks just south of a retail and commercial district, mere minutes away from Interstate 95.

Quick in, quick out.

The best, the *only*, kind.

He could already picture it in his mind as he returned to his van, fired up the ignition, and left the rest stop, like the first murder scene, in the rearview mirror, never to be seen again.

The scene came so easily to him, like a memory, though it was still yet to happen: The comely co-ed in the local dive bar. Perfect. Dallying on a school night, avoiding her prissy roommate or, perhaps, just taking a quick study break from her light load at PCC.

He'd watch her from the shadows, nursing his second Amstel Light, fiddling idly with the stale beer nuts, hidden behind the local university color of choice, waiting until friend after friend straggled home, leaving her alone as she eyed the rowdy frat boys at the bar. Her simple study break evolved into something decidedly more erotic as she quickly checked her purse for the condom hidden safely behind her travel tissues and lip gloss in the corner pocket.

He would have already scoped out the fire exit, located, inevitably, between the men's and ladies' rooms, just past the ciga-rette machine and pay phone, quickly dismantling the alarm with a flick of his pocket tweezers and propping the exit door ajar with a matchbook from the very bar itself.

He'd let the frat boys flirt with her, one by one, watching as their youth and vitality oozed off their muscle shirts and cargo pants and ball caps in waves of cheap cologne, dirty underwear, and easy overconfidence. He'd let them buy her drink after drink, more money left in his pockets, after all, and graciously allow them to schmooze her in tag-team style, their Neanderthal brains painting porn-inspired pictures of threesomes and foursomes and orgies as her bladder slowly filled on cheap mixed drinks from the sports bar's pre-dictably alluring 2-for-1 special.

As she inevitably rose on long, wobbly legs to "powder her nose," the frat boys would lurk behind, too timid to follow, too eager to congratulate one another on their easy score with high-fives and head butts and celebratory toasts of watered down draft beer.

As they planned the night's festivities, he would split from the shadows in an instant of unrecognizable blur—"It could have been a guy, officer, it just happened so damn fast and, shit, I'd had ten beers by then"—and rush her through the open door, one gloved hand clasped firmly against her freshly painted, pertly parted lips and the other nestled in the small of her firm, athletic back.

Into the darkened alley they'd go, never to be seen again.

Well, *one* of them anyway.

After all, he'd have to leave a second maze somewhere.

Her ravaged corpse, tossed in a nearby dumpster, would work just fine.

8 Frank's quarterly budget meeting had run long, so he stopped for a few beers and a burger at his favorite greasy diner on the way back to the office. He casually deflected the usual curiosity from the middle-aged barmaid with the freckled face and masculine haircut, demurring with generic answers her subtle "any gory details to share this week?" probing.

She nodded, let him off with the warning that he "better have some good dirt for her next time," and so he spent the next forty-two minutes in glorious, peaceful silence. Okay, so a shiny jukebox in the corner blared bad 80s tunes and a few scattered co-eds from George-town endured even worse blind dates with their banal, casual chit-chat; but if it didn't have to do with blood, guts, or cutbacks, it was all white noise to him.

He carefully chewed his French fries, going easy on the ketchup, and avoiding the bun in favor of another light beer. For a dangerously old-fashioned guy—not a few of his ex-girlfriends had bordered on calling him a male chauvinist—he was surprisingly concerned with his physical appearance.

Aside from the bar and bookshelves, his scale was his most frequently used household appliance, and if the waistband of his size 36-jeans felt snug on Monday, he'd spend an extra hour at the gym every day until Friday. His old pals at the Bureau, most of whom only saw a gym the week before they were due to qualify for the current year's field test, wondered when he was going to switch from writing true crime books to diet books.

Frank didn't mind; it had more to do with staying sharp than it did slim. He'd long ago learned that his body had a certain equilibrium. Stray too far from it in either direction, and his mind suffered.

Clogging his system with too much fat and sugar only punished his mind in the end, and that was something he just couldn't afford. Even his drinking had a razor's edge to it. He knew just how much his system could carry, just how far he could take it.

He sipped at the dregs of his last beer of the night and sighed. He often grew tired of the endless self-control that ruled his life, but for now it was his only edge against the often younger, tireless, and let's not forget just plain buck-wild crazy, special circumstances killers who forced him to remain on his toes, day or night, dinner or breakfast, fat or thin.

Leaving the bar and stepping into the chilly October air of a typical DC night, he felt satisfied and invigorated, not full and sluggish. He walked the rest of the way to his office on light feet and trim legs, feeling spry and alert, until he topped the staircase to his office and found one of his daily newspaper clippings flagged and highlighted on the top of his desk.

"Shit," he spat as he sat down, suddenly feeling tired and old as he picked up the marked clipping. He knew what this meant. Typically, his assistant just slid a file of one to two dozen clippings on his desk, in between the usual desktop detritus that built up during the day. One clipping, highlighted and flagged, meant only one thing: a potential special circumstances killer.

He looked at the masthead on the clipping and groaned. "Daytona Beach?" he grumbled aloud, suddenly wishing he'd splurged on that third and final beer. "Do you have any idea how hot it is in Florida this time of year?"

No one answered him. No one cared. He glanced at his watch: 10:15 p.m. Shit, in the old days this place would have been bustling with eager beavers, all juiced up on free coffee and hot tips, ready to take names and kick asses. Now, he found himself staring out his office door at empty cubicles and humming computers, a maze of dead white space waiting until tomorrow to confront the endless leads and dead-end tips he knew piled up during a typical day.

He didn't blame his comrades. The dwindling budgets, the barriers they put up for overtime, the thankless tasks and futile cases—why would they want to stick around after normal hours? But what chapped his ass was that the stiffs who clocked out at 5 each night were the same ones who hounded him the loudest about publishing his books or spending his own money on an outside clipping service.

What the hell did they think he was doing it for?

He sighed, skimmed the article, and highlighted a few key concepts his assistant had missed. The body parts found in the ice cream cooler. Clever killer. The missing backpack. What did that mean? The spatter of melted ice cream leading out the back door. Carelessness? Or a cover-up?

He re-read the article for the last time, jotted down some notes, and bundled both into a special filing cabinet he kept locked beneath his dorm fridge filled with bottled water and the occasional yogurt cup. It could be something, it could be nothing. Just to be sure, he fired off a quick email to his contact at the clipping agency, putting in a request to add the keywords "Daytona" and "Florida" for the next seven days. He re-read the email before sending it, glad he did. "Georgia," he added to his list, reflecting on his own definition of a special circumstances killer.

"Cross that state line," he said aloud to his empty, well-lit office, "and your ass is mine."

He only wished his bravado could ease his suddenly sour stomach.

"You getting all this, rookie?" Lt. Rocky Chicone asked for the umpteenth time as the late night turned into the early morning and, one by one, the gaily lit shops and bars lining Daytona's world-famous pier went dark, leaving desolate Gino's the only bright spot on the boardwalk.

It was their second night on the case, and by now the two men fell into a clearly delineated pattern: Rocky, the patient mentor to Sanchez's uninitiated eagerness. Now the rookie dutifully referred to his rapidly filling notepad, repeating back what the patient Lieutenant had just told him mere moments before: "'Lack of fingerprints and the evidence of localized blood spatter clearly indicate signs of precognizant organization uncommon in your garden-variety psychopath.' Got it, Rock. What next? Another coffee break?"

Rocky peered out the window at the desolate strip. "Not unless you want to use the facilities here," he deadpanned, watching the rookie's face. Sanchez blanched as he looked at the nearest industrial strength coffeemaker, where the girl's spleen had been located some twelve hours earlier.

"No thanks," he whispered.

Rocky smiled. "Don't worry, kid, just a few more hours and we're done here. Now, ignore the gore, the obvious signs of blood and guts, the massive damage to the girl's anatomy, and look at the store itself. Scratch that: Don't just look at it, *see* it."

Rocky paused, making sure the rookie did as he was told. Dutifully, if wearily, Sanchez peered out from behind the ice cream cooler, upon which a dozen crime scene photos had been taped hours earlier, and surveyed the nearly pristine scene.

"Notice the lack of upturned tables and chairs?" Rocky asked patiently, not waiting for an answer before continuing. "They're all tucked in, nice and neat, just like Candace had left them when she tidied up, according to the log in the employee break room, at 3:45 p.m. What does that mean?"

"The killer moved with purpose, and killed quickly?" Sanchez responded dutifully, parroting his mentor's cadence, emphasizing the last to pose a question, even as he answered correctly. By now, he was familiar with Rocky's, aka the Stalker's, methods: Question, prod, and answer. Answer, prod, and question. Despite the late hour and two days without much sleep, Sanchez drank it up eagerly, convinced that a lesson in crime scene technique from Rocky was as valuable as anything he could learn from the Feds.

"Correct." Rocky nodded proudly, beaming at the unmistakable signs of life from his apparently apt pupil. "And the missing money from the register? The $45.78 missing in tens, fives, singles, and loose change? What would *that* imply?"

"Robbery *might* have been a motive," Sanchez said quickly, before adding, "but the obvious overkill says otherwise. It's common for killers to mask a kill with a botched robbery. The secondary blurring the primary."

Rocky nodded again, reaching past Sanchez to lift the heavily dusted cash drawer, revealing a pile of crisp twenties hiding beneath, each one bagged and tagged in red-topped evidence bags. "That, and the fact that any grade school robber knows the twenties are kept *beneath* the till. This is what we call 'lazy staging.' It's almost…playful. Whimsical. The killer is saying, 'I know it wasn't a robbery. *You* know it wasn't a robbery. But I'll go through the motions just to toss in that modicum of doubt anyway.'"

Rocky was on a roll now, his third, make that fourth, of the night. Sanchez, used to his superior's patterns by now, settled in against the still-chilly cooler and made himself as comfortable as possible.

This could take awhile.

"But there's a routine to it," Rocky continued, eyes glazed over, as Sanchez disappeared and all that remained was the dust and powder and blood and gore and chalk line of the day-old crime scene. "Like he was just going through the motions. Ticking off items he had on a list. Item Number One? Silence the victim. Easy enough. Number Two? Make it look gory, twisted, and sick, like some psycho who couldn't plan a clambake just wandered into town and decided to go off his rocker. Numbers Three through who knows how many? Those are a little harder to nail down.

"The killer isn't just organized, he's…what's the word I'm looking for…luxuriously indulgent. Almost…decadent…about his crime. It takes time to gut a person. Lots and lots of time. Oodles of it. Not the way a whacko would gut somebody, stabbing and slicing until the guts fly out and land in his lap; but it takes time and, more than that, attention to detail to do what *this* guy did.

"That spleen we found in your coffeemaker over there? Coroner said it had been sliced out with 'medical precision.' No errant nicks or stray cuts. No gashes or gaping holes. So, it's eight at night, middle of the Daytona Beach pier, maybe half a dozen other stores still operating on either side of Gino's here, and this guy's taking forty whacks—and then some—at poor Candace with nothing but an industrial-sized ice cream cooler and a flimsy deadbolt between himself and discovery. What's *that* say?"

Not waiting for a response, although the rookie was eagerly opening his mouth to give one, Rocky plunged on. "I'll tell you what it says, Sanchez. It says he waited, he watched, he prowled, he did his research. *That's* what it says. When the manger at the bank gets around to pulling Gino's sales records for the past five years, dollars to donuts we'll find that just before closing is his *slowest* sales period. It's gonna be a veritable flat-line through the business day.

"Peak hours for ice cream? I'm betting between one and two, just after lunch, and then five and six, just before dinner. But eight? At eight, all the tourists are back in their hotel rooms putting Solarcaine on their sunburns and cleaning up for dinner at the fish fry. All the locals are home in bed watching Must-See-TV. Further still, I guarantee we'll find that the first week of October here is Gino's slowest month. Fewer tourists, school's in session, weather's finally cooling off after the long, hot summer, not as much need for a frosty cone or thick shake. Our guy? He's not just any organized killer; he's the fucking *Dean* of Organized Killers. And for what? There was no sign of sexual deviance. No sign of 'forced entry,' if you will. The nipples were cut off, sure, great, big whoop. The vagina was parsed and snipped. Okay. So what? Those are both things I guarantee you he's *heard* that your garden variety psycho would do for kicks. Any Tom, Dick, or Scary with eight bucks and a Barnes & Noble discount card can read all about that kind of bullshit in Frank Logan's latest FBI tell-all. We found no semen, not a drop, so this nut's not even getting off on the violence.

"So what's the thrill for him? What's his endgame? More importantly, why *Candace*? Why Gino's? He walked away with less than fifty bucks from the register, left her class ring on that finger we found in the milkshake blender over there, and didn't even bust his nut in the process. Why?"

"The maze," Sanchez interrupted, staring at the bloodied sheet of paper currently encased in a thick evidence bag by the cash register. Candace's blood oozed through the cheap newsprint, blossoming past the lines and twists and turns like sea foam edging back toward the tide.

They'd found no significance to the maze—not geographic, not symbolic, not forensic—that would determine its presence on the body. For that reason, its presence was doubly chilling.

"The maze," Rocky said, nodding slowly. "The maze. What's with the fucking maze, Sanchez? What role does it play? What significance does it have? What the hell does the maze *mean*?"

Sanchez shrugged. "Mind games," he answered confidently. Rocky was nothing if not encouraging and, apart from the fraternal wisecrack about the belated convenience store coffee from the previous day, had yet to belittle him on his actual police work. "Maybe the girl, the blood, the spleen, all that bullshit, is just the icing. The maze? Maybe *that's* the cake."

Rocky smiled. Sanchez couldn't see it, but Rocky smiled nonetheless. His pupil had just graduated from the Stalker's School of Crime Scene Analysis. "Fuckin' A," he muttered, in place of a certificate or graduation ceremony. " 'The maze is the cake.' I like that, Sanchez. I like that a lot. When we get back to HQ, I'm gonna put that in the official report. Maybe you can copyright that when this is all over. Make yourself some dough. Who knows? But you're exactly right. This…whole…scene, that's all it is. A scene. A stage. A…a set.

No different from Hollywood. Candace? She's nothing more than a prop. A human prop in some twisted play this whacko's got running through his head 24 hours a day, 7 days a week, 365 days a year.

"I don't know who's watching with him. Manson? Bundy? Dahmer? His dead grandmother, mummifying in the attic? But it's playing, all day, all night. While he's at work, it's playing. While he's in rush hour traffic, it's playing. While he's screwing his wife, it's playing.

"Candace? She wasn't the star of this show. Not by a long shot. I'd say an extra, no doubt. A pretty prop. But nothing more than a device, handy for her spleen and ring finger and buckets and buckets of fresh, deep, crimson blood.

"This guy's a director, I can feel it. A bad director, but a powerful one. A smart one. And this movie's just begun. In fact, I wouldn't be surprised if this was just the opening credits. You know, the one with the eerie music in the background and the actors' names rolling to let you know, 'Hey, look out, this guy's a bad ass and he's just getting warmed up.' And you and me? Sorry to say it, Sanchez, but we're just bit players, too. We won't be the ones to solve this crime. No sir, no how. We won't be anything but a distant memory by the time the big boys get through dotting the i's and crossing the t's on this bad boy. This one's gonna go on and on, and we're gonna read about the grand finale in the papers, just like the rest of the world will."

Rocky wound down, the early mornings, brisk afternoons, and calculated evenings of the past days suddenly taking their toll as exhaustion set in like a natural sedative. After a minute or two of comfortable silence—Sanchez had long since moved past exhaustion and was in zombie land—the rookie asked the final question of the night: "So, what do you think is this guy's next move?"

Rocky shook his head rapidly, unaware that he was even doing it. "No idea," he admitted, a first for the night, causing Sanchez's young, dull eyes to instantly crack open wider. "But I can tell you this much for sure: Maybe not today, maybe not tomorrow, but in the very near future, we're gonna get a fax, a call, a page, or a tip about some other girl, some other carnage, some other crime scene, in some other jurisdiction, similar to this. But not *too* similar. The girl will be young and pretty, but she'll look just different enough from Candace that we won't be able to pin down an MO. Bundy liked brunettes with straight hair. Dahmer liked tall, thin black boys. But our boy won't be so predictable.

"She'll be just a tad older, a co-ed perhaps, or just a tad younger, a middle-schooler. Candace was fair complected. The next girl will be tan, a sun worshipper. Candace was an honor student; the next one'll be an average student. Straight C's, I predict. Oh, she'll be slaughtered, no doubt about it. The crime scenes will be 'eerily similar.' That's how the papers will put it, anyway. But the only real similarity, the only thing that will really matter, will be the maze.

"You said it best, Sanchez: This guts and gore, that's all the icing. The maze is the cake, rookie. The maze is the cake."

Rocky sighed, rubbed his eyes, then smeared his hand across his long, thin, gaunt face like a washcloth, trying in vain to cleanse himself of the night's thick, heavy detritus. "Speaking of cake," he sighed, slipping each crime scene photo back into its manila envelope and snatching up the maze, "how about some breakfast, huh?"

Sanchez nodded, just in time to hear his stomach growl. Both men laughed, a first for the evening. "You're on," the rookie said to the Stalker.

"Just one thing," said Rocky, taking on a mock serious tone as they prepared to exit Gino's. "Next time we're working a crime scene and I ask you for coffee, what's the first thing you're gonna do?"

"Look for a long line of cops," Sanchez said, grinning.

Rocky grinned back. It had been another long night, and once again, the grins had been in short supply. Chances were, they wouldn't be any more plentiful in the hours, or days, or weeks ahead. Best to smile when you could.

"Right, Sanchez," Rocky said, as the two men stumbled down the pier toward the parking lot. "Wherever you see a long line of cops, that's where you'll find hot coffee, too."

"Or a titty bar," Sanchez joked.

"Or a hot dog vendor in a thong," Rocky quipped.

"Or a movie set."

"Or a free buffet."

The two men ran out of jokes just before Rocky opened his passenger door for Sanchez, who'd long since lost a ride home with his daytime partner. "Thanks," the rookie said, meaning much more than the open door.

"No problem, kid," Rocky said, knowing what he really meant. "No problem at all. Thus endeth the lesson."

"I dunno, Rock," Sanchez said, settling into the leather seat of Rocky's standard issue Chevy Caprice. "Seems like it's only just beginning."

"You got me there, rookie," Rocky said with a sigh as he shut Sanchez's door and ambled over to his own. "You got me there."

10

Detective Will Morgenstern had been using his deceptively southern drawl for years now, in an attempt—most often a successful one—to outwit robbers, pimps, rapists, addicts, hopheads, creeps, convicts, slugs, bangers, thugs, and murderers.

Today's "performance" was no different.

"Howdy there, pardner," he said unassumingly to the rumpled mass of human scar tissue sitting across from him in the 12' x 12' interrogation room known popularly as "the pit" throughout the East Fulton County Sheriff's Department.

Though it could have been so named because the room was reminiscent of many squalid foxholes or other such "pits," or because it was so eerily similar to Edgar Allen Poe's claustrophobic and threatening short story *The Pit and the Pendulum*, the *real* reason behind Interrogation Room #3's colloquial nickname was more of a smell than a sight reference: It literally smelled like a pit. That being an *armpit*, of course.

The rancid perpetrator taking up space in the plastic, orange chair across the glorified picnic table that separated the two men wasn't doing much to play down the particular aroma, either.

"Care for a smoke?" Will asked the suspect, a local cable repairman known throughout the county for his alleged—this was the first time he'd ever actually been charged for the crime—predilection for sneaking back into the houses he'd just serviced and raping the single female homeowners. The suspect, known in local circles as "Spock," a nickname earned by his pointy ears and perpetually crooked fingers, nodded greedily at the blue and yellow pack of generic cigarettes, a carton of which Will always kept in the bottom of his desk drawer for just such occasions. As far as he was concerned, it was $18.79 well spent....

Though he rarely smoked and often competed in the annual tri-county marathon for law enforcement personnel, Will nonetheless lit two cigarettes at once and passed the second to Spock. He watched carefully as the deft young man managed to crane his neck down just far enough to reach his hand, which was, after all, handcuffed to a bolt screwed into the top of the table.

"Thanks," muttered Spock noncommittally. The suspect smiled self-deprecatingly around the lit cigarette at the detective. Somehow he managed to avoid Will's penetrating stare; his greasy face remained a mask of false charm and a willingness to please.

"No problem," Will nodded, expertly exhaling without inhaling as he tapped a matchbook from a local topless bar—another prop the happily-married detective and father of two kept safely hidden in his desk drawer for effect—again and again on the heavy wooden table.

It was an age-old tactic. Psychology 101, in fact, but nonetheless well-proven over time. Will had perfected his expertly-honed interrogation techniques as he rose through the ranks from duty cop to homicide detective to his present rank of lieutenant. A dry version of Chinese water torture, it had the similarly aggravating effect meant to put a perp off center. Just where Will Morgenstern wanted him to be.

"Look, man," Spock blurted, if only to get Will to stop the matchbook tap-dance momentarily. "I don't mean to sound ungrateful and all, but I'm a little hung-over, if you don't mind?"

Spock glared ominously at the matchbook, and Will smiled self-deprecatingly. "Sorry, pardner." He grimaced apologetically, not stopping the tapping for a second. Indeed, his pace increased ever so slightly in order to increase the pressure. "Bad habit. My old lady hates it. Girlfriend does, too. Helps me think, though. You don't mind, do you?"

Spock blinked. Round one went to the burly lieutenant. "Guess not," he said resignedly, sucking his cigarette down to the nub in three tight, cloying bursts of burning paper, sticky lips, and searing lungs. In between tapping, Will dutifully lit another and passed it over. Spock nodded, winced through the halo of smoke that already surrounded him, and sat back in his chair, his nicotine fix sufficiently "fixed."

Will never stopped tapping.

Spock never stopped watching him.

Some hypnotists used gold watches. Will used a matchbook from The Bump & Grind. The effect was eerily similar.

"Do they ever resist?" Will asked suddenly, apropos to nothing. Risking everything.

Spock blinked. Once. Twice. Then the chains that bound him all but sang as he clenched his fists. "Don't know what you're talking about, *sir*," Spock spat, mixing deference with disrespect as his tongue flicked beneath his crooked, yellow teeth.

"No, I…I…I just mean," Will stammered, as if he'd sprung the trap too soon and was quickly backpedaling. "These women come home from work, find a note from the friendly cable guy saying everything's okey-dokey, they watch a few hours of HBO on their big screen TV for the first time all week, have a glass or two of wine to celebrate, go to bed, and then you come in at 4 a.m. and rape them.

"I guess I'm just wondering if they're ever awake enough to fight back. Or would that be too much work for a little guy like you? Crawl into the wrong bed with the wrong girl, say some chick who outweighs you by twenty pounds and does her Tae-Bo video faithfully every day; things could go south for a scrawny bastard like you real quick-like. Care to enlighten me?"

"Wouldn't know where to begin," Spock nodded, his pointy ears glowing red as Will probed deeper and deeper into his fractured psyche. "Sounds like you should be talking to one of them perverts out there on the streets. Not me, man. I'm as straight as an arrow. Go in for women, young women, okay, sure, but not raping them in their bedrooms, dude. Have to take to the Internet to catch those whack jobs. You know how to use the Internet, don't you, pardner?"

"Funny you should say that, *pardner*," Will drawled purposefully, extinguishing his cigarette with a dramatic flourish and enjoying himself as he drew things out. Spock was done with his as well, but Will purposefully pocketed the pack, watching the suspect's tongue dart left and right across his thin, anemic lips like a lizard checking the air. "'Cause while you were out on a call this afternoon, techs from our crime lab took a little tour of your laptop. Wanna guess what they found?"

Spock finally smiled. "Nothing, *pardner*," he spat confidently, the last word like a sour egg on his tongue. "Don't got no laptop, never have."

Will looked nervous, on purpose.

Stammered, on purpose.

And stabbed at the air with a finger, on purpose.

"You mean you d...d...don't have a *laptop*?" he mock-sputtered, fake-flailing again. "Not even the one you bought at a pawn shop on...let's see what my records say here. That's right, down on South Peachtree Street? Cash? Say, October 12th of last year? 3:48 p.m., to be exact?"

The control had magically returned to his voice.

Spock's tongue was once again darting.

Will's fingers never stopped tapping out the metronome beats with his matchbook.

"Not even the one you use at the Cyber Café on Folsom Drive? Cash, again? Not even the one you keep in the P.O. Box at Mail City in the Cumberland Mall? Not even...this little lady right here?"

With that, Will pulled a battered laptop from his messenger bag placed casually atop his wooden chair and just out of sight behind his large frame and squared shoulders. Spock was on overdrive now, his thin, pale lips darting in concert with his dim, beady eyes, which were now blinking in concert with Will's matchbook.

On the screen of the laptop was a picture of a very frightened young woman in a very compromising position with a very well-endowed—Will had to give him that much, at least—local cable repairman. The geeks in IT had already positively identified the grinning face that matched the throbbing member as none other than James Masterson Wilson, aka "Spock."

In the corner of each photo, there on the bedside, carefully posed next to a slimy Spock, was a bedside clock reading the hour: 4 a.m. Will didn't need a criminal profiler from Quantico to tell him the clock was as attractive to Spock as the woman's helpless pleading or her warm, unyielding flesh.

"That's my old girlfriend," Spock sang out. "It was fully consensual, totally down with the chick, dude. She's into all kinds of kinky shit. She wanted me to take that picture, for real. And she'd never press charges, that much I know. Plus, I was drunk. You'll never pin that one on me."

Will shrugged. The slime was probably right. His first victim, a local woman who did, in fact, know Spock on a social level, had made one initial complaint and then promptly disappeared. Will knew she hadn't done so on her own volition, and that months from now some hapless jogger would find her body, bludgeoned, strangled, or worse, skeletonized and scattered in some humid Georgia clearing.

"You got me there, pardner," Will drawled again, using the rectangular mouse pad in the center of the console to click three times. One. Pause. Two. Pause. Three. Pause. More pop psychology. More dramatic effect. More sweat dripping off Spock's already greasy forehead. Magically, three vivid jpegs blinked to life on the laptop's fingerprint-powder smudged screen.

Three more women, each face down in their own soft, frilly pillows, filled the screen. Behind each one smiled a grinning Spock, hamming for the camera, most likely on a high-tech tripod borrowed from his own cable truck. In the corner of each photo was the telltale bedside clock reading the hour: 4 a.m. Will left his suspect babbling, scratching at the table for forgiveness.

Or, at the very least, a free cigarette.

As he left "the pit" to head straight for the men's room and a quick rinse with Listerine, not to mention a thorough hand-washing, his partner of two years, Sarah Dukes, stopped him in the hall.

"No rest for the weary, Lieutenant," she said purposefully, handing him his jacket and car keys. "A jogger found the body of that missing co-ed in the dumpster behind one of the bars on fraternity row. Lucky us: You and I got the case."

"Great," Will sighed, settling for a thin stick of Dentyne as he turned tail and followed his partner to the garage three levels down. "From one slimeball to the next."

Sarah, who'd been watching the interrogation carefully—a smile of pride growing across her pretty face—from behind the frosted mirror in the middle of the squad room, noticed how easily Will switched from Southern good ol' boy to Yankee snob in the blink of an eye. It was one of the things she loved about him.

11

Vinny Smalldeano followed the pert secretary from the elevator to his new office at FBI Headquarters in the nation's capital. Make that his new…cubicle. In a single, crushing moment, all his childhood dreams were dashed; no dart board on his office door, featuring the black and white wanted poster of the latest creep he was chasing. No coat rack in the corner, featuring his standard issue gray jacket and matching fedora. No file cabinets overflowing with solved cases and attaboy letters from the top brass congratulating him on his latest triumph. And certainly no window overlooking the Washington Monument.

"Is this actually the basement?" he asked the secretary. Raven was her name, at least according to the official ID badge clipped to her revealing décolletage. To Vinny, it seemed like they'd gone down more floors than actually existed.

"The basement?" She heehawed, as if he'd been joking. "You wish. This is the basement's basement, the lowest of the low. But get used to it, you'll be spending a lot of time here. Contrary to what the press might have you think, these special circumstances guys don't see much field work. It's basically just cataloging clues and racking up the profiles. Usually they're chained to their desks, picking apart crime scene photos and passing gas. You should smell this place come Miller time; it's worse than the tox lab upstairs!"

Raven passed her marble-pale hand back and forth below her pert little nose for emphasis. They stood awkwardly next to each other for a moment, eye to eye in the deserted, airless space.

Vinny was humble, but he wasn't brain dead when it came to the opposite sex. Typically, the younger women he encountered enjoyed checking him out, they called him "eye candy," and weren't shy about letting him know it. So far, Raven had been more interested in her black painted fingernails than his athletic physique, causing him to wonder if perhaps she batted for the other team.

"So where is everybody?" he asked pointedly, nodding a clean-shaven, square-jawed chin toward the rows and rows of empty cubicles standing sentinel beneath the whitewashed, windowless walls.

She snorted knowingly. "They're at Crawford's retirement party, which reminds me, I'm late!"

She hesitated, perhaps sensing he had more questions. He did: "Who's Crawford?" he asked.

She smirked. "The guy you're replacing, you big lug. What'd you think, you were such a big shot back in NYC they were gonna shift some veteran around to make room for you? You got lucky, pal. Crawford's out, you're in. Welcome to the party. Speaking of, if I don't get there soon, I'll miss the girl popping out of the cake."

Thought so. He nodded to himself, his suspicions about her sexual proclivities now confirmed.

Oblivious to his old-fashioned values, she walked a few steps away before turning back with an apologetic glance. "Hey, man," she said conspiratorially, "I'd ask you along, you know, but it might be kinda awkward, me dragging the new guy along even as I'm saying goodbye to the old guy. Better you're here sitting in Crawford's desk when everybody gets back. You know what I mean? Might be better for morale that way."

"Oh yeah," he mused aloud, "much better. Why don't you show me where he keeps his coffee cup and I can be taking a swig out of that when everybody walks in. I can't think of a worse way to be introduced to 'the team' than to have me report the day of the guy's retirement party. Couldn't I have reported for duty tomorrow? Whose idea was this?"

She looked around, as if someone might hear. "You're joking, right?" she asked, half-whispering. "I mean, you do know who your new boss is gonna be, right?"

Damn! He knew he should have read that dossier the FBI had sent him on the train, but he'd been so preoccupied with living the dream, he forgot to stick his toe in the shallow end of reality. His shrug was all the answer she was going to get.

"Dude, they have bookstores in NYC, right? I mean, get a clue. You're working for the one, the only, Frank Logan. Media darling. All around hottie. Bestselling author. And oh yeah, head of the Special Circumstances Killer Unit; i.e., your *boss*! You better not come to the party; seems like the new guy might have to spend some quality time boning up on the boss man."

"What can I say?" Vinny asked, trying to ignore the blush creeping up from his tight white collar. "I guess I'm not much of a reader."

When her stare of disbelief was all that filled the uncomfortable silence between them, Vinny cracked a joke by mock-whispering, "He can't hear us, can he?"

She brayed laughter. "Boy, you *are* new. His office is about as high up as you go. The only time he graces us with his presence is if we've screwed up royally—or he's published a new book."

She smirked and then—Vinny could almost see the light bulb going off over her jet-black hair—Raven dashed off to her desk and returned quickly with a battered, dog-eared, no doubt drooled-all-over copy of one Frank Logan's popular paperbacks. "Keep it," she said, tossing it onto the flat white surface of his desk, such as it was, before inching back down the hall and toward Crawford's much bally-hooed retirement party. "Consider it a cubicle-warming gift. I'm saving up to buy his latest in hardcover, anyway."

"What?" he asked to her retreating backside. "Bossman doesn't buy the whole team a copy?"

She was too far away from him to hear or, if she did, too busy reaching for her car keys to respond. It was just as well. He stared at his dossier, a three-inch thick binder running down everything from the history of the Special Circumstances unit to where to find the staples and rubber bands. He sighed, wondering which piece of literature the great and noble Frank Logan would want him to read first. He grabbed the well-used paperback, already suspecting the answer.

12

"Can someone tell me why this dumpster wasn't checked three days ago when the BOLO came out on this poor girl?" Lt. Will Morgenstern asked of no one in particular as he and his partner, Sarah Dukes, strode under the crime scene tape and straight to the offending trash receptacle.

"Apparently the manager gave the detectives on scene the wrong trash day," said some faceless uniform when it was apparent that nobody else at the scene was going to speak up. "Everyone assumed the cargo had been picked up, and nobody ever bothered to actually look inside."

Will shook his head. Sarah braced herself. Uniformed cops scattered, particularly the one who'd just delivered the unpopular message. "You mean no one took the time to peek under the lid? Who got the initial call? Wait, don't tell me: Picarillo and Southie, right? Those two couldn't find tits at a whorehouse. Sorry, Sarah."

"No you're not." Sarah smiled as Will went straight to bended knee to scout under the oozing dumpster. "But that's what I love about you."

"Bring me up to speed, will you?" her senior partner asked as his penlight probed the murky layer of ooze and slime at his feet.

"Lisa Field was a sophomore at Peachtree Community College," Sarah began ominously, reading straight from her ever-present little black book. "Majoring in...drum roll please...political science."

"Don't they all?" Will sighed. "Go on."

"Right." Sarah smiled woefully, watching Will the master at work. "She and her roommate needed a break from their mid-terms so they strolled down fraternity row until they landed at Wet Willie's here. Lisa's roommate, a freshman named Trish, called it quits at midnight, but Lisa wasn't quite ready to go just then. Trish made Lisa promise to call her at 1 a.m., in her words, 'just to be safe.' Lisa promised, waved goodbye, and never made the call."

Will stood up, dusted off his pants, and traded in his first pair of latex gloves for a second. Sarah began keeping a mental count. He would go through no less than a dozen pairs of gloves at a typical crime scene. Three-day old murders? That usually meant two dozen, minimum. She tried not to smile as he took over.

"Lemme guess," he said, peering into the dim space between the dumpster itself and the brick wall facing the back door to Wet Willie's Sports Bar and Emporium. "Half a dozen frat boys 'vaguely remember' chatting her up at the bar and, while they were fighting over which one could carry her books home, she decided to take a break from the testosterone and call Trish for their 1 a.m. check-in. Right?"

Sarah regarded her notes. "Estimates of the last time any of the boys saw her *was* around 1 a.m.," she said, frowning. She hated it when he was right. He was bad enough to live with when he was wrong, which wasn't too often.

"Anything dirty on any of these boys?" Will asked knowingly, rolling a wad of weeks-old gum he'd just peeled off the back of the dumpster between his thumb and ring finger. "Warrants? Imposters? Failing grades? High school sex scandals? Steroids? Slave girl web cams under their names? Dropouts? Anything?"

"Clean-cut jocks." She sighed wistfully. "The stuff of my locker room dreams. Nothing but parking tickets, bad grades, and worse credit between them. Bartender says they're all regulars for the Thursday Night Bladder Bursts; knows 'em all by name. They're all still in town, all gave truthful witness statements, and none of them have missed a class or football practice since."

Will shook his head. "It won't be them," he said with grave certainty, unconsciously eyeing a burly uniform who was keeping onlookers from the gym next door on the other side of the flapping yellow line. "Jocks are too stupid to stick around. One of them would have split by now, be hiding out in some cheap hotel room—or SUV trunk—somewhere two states over."

"Who we'd find because he was dumb enough to put the hotel

room on his credit card," Sarah chirped. She'd heard this speech once or twice before.

Will smirked, aware he was being pompous. Not that it stopped him, of course. She watched as he approached the body, cloaked beneath a dingy white sheet from the coroner's van, which was parked nearby.

Will waved to Fern Smith, the county's first female coroner. She waved back, winked at Sarah, and then tapped her watch as if to say, "Hurry it up." Will ignored her, taking his time as he walked around the prostate figure beneath the depressingly ominous blanket.

"She been examined yet?" he shouted to Fern. When she nodded back, he unceremoniously whisked off the sheet to reveal a naked woman in perfect physical condition, her lime green thong panties still entangled around one bruised, grimy ankle now stiff with rigor mortis.

Various stains blotted her skin—a ketchup smear in particular covered her left nipple—while various gum wrappers and beer labels were matted in her hair, both "upstairs and downstairs" as Will most sensitively noted.

Other than that, the body was pristine. No mutilation, no asphyxiation, no entrance wound, no exit wound. Aside from the coffee grounds clogging her nostrils, her face looked almost...beatific. Peaceful.

"What do you want to bet she was alive when he shoved her in there?" Will nodded, a ballpoint pen carefully probing her left nostril to displace an avalanche of still pungent coffee grounds coated with dry mucus.

She'd clearly breathed them in as she died.

"How?" Sarah asked. "There's not a mark on her, save for some ketchup and mustard. How do you force a girl into a dumpster to just...lie there and die?"

"Dollars to donuts when Fern gets her back to the lab and cleans her up, she'll find a pinprick between one of her fingers or behind her hairline or, hell, who knows, up the old whazzoo, for that matter. Either way, our guy waits in the dark for her to take a piss break or, in this case, phone a friend at precisely 1 a.m. and, the minute she does, he bum rushes her out the back door and straight into the alley.

"Once out here, it's dark, one in the morning, the busboys and bar backs have already gone home, the gym next door has been closed for hours. He's got all the time in the world. Sticks a needle where the sun don't shine. God knows what the stuff will turn out to be, but I bet it isn't gonna show up on any tox screen unless we look for it. By now any Tom, Dick, or Scary who watches the Forensics Channel knows the names of a dozen lethal drugs that mask everything from a heart attack to SIDS.

"He snatches her, sticks her, dumps her, and she lies face down in coffee grounds and beer suds and a day-old hot dog until whatever drugs are pumping through her veins take effect, and that's it. Lights out for Lisa."

Sarah shook her head. "At least she was unconscious," she murmured reverently to herself, saying a silent prayer for the innocent, if not slightly reckless, young co-ed.

"What's that?" Will asked, probing the nooks and crannies for himself as Fern waited impatiently by the coroner's van.

"Unconscious," Sarah repeated. "You ever get a strong whiff of fresh coffee grounds when you're taking out the trash? It's like Tabasco sauce. Or ammonia. No way she'd lie there and snort that stuff if she was conscious."

Will nodded, quietly impressed. He looked at her for a beat, about as big a compliment as she was likely to get in this lifetime, until his probing ballpoint hit pay dirt. There, wedged between marble pale buttocks so firm you could bounce a quarter off them, Will pried loose a plastic cigar case.

It pulled away with an odious sucking sound, not to mention a noxious whiff of pent up body gasses, but Will barely noticed as he quickly unscrewed the top to find inside a piece of paper, quickly bagged and tagged with, by Sarah's count, his eighth pair of latex gloves of the afternoon.

"What's up?" she asked as he carefully examined the newsprint found inside.

"Oh shit," he said, his regularly pallid complexion quickly growing a whiter shade of pale. "Oh no shit, oh no please, oh no!" He flipped open his cell phone and hit the speed dial for the main line at the precinct.

When someone answered, he spoke rapidly, calmly, and with precision: "Whoever this is, get Captain Deltano right away. Don't ask why, you'll only piss me off. And, trust me, you *don't* want to piss me off. Not today, anyway. So listen carefully: My name's Lieutenant Will Morgenstern. Out in the field with that missing coed? Right, the hot one on the news. Listen: Tell Deltano to be ready at the typewriter and to fire up the fax machine. We got a signature left behind at the crime scene, and my guess is he's gonna want to communicate with other jurisdictions about it."

As Will waited for Deltano to get to the phone, Sarah shrugged her shoulders at her partner, as if to say, "What's up?" Without taking his attention off his sleek, metallic cell phone, he silently held the plastic wrapped piece of paper out to her.

"Oh shit," she parroted him, taking in the garden-variety maze sheathed in the rapidly crinkling evidence bag.

The maze was simple to solve.

Getting the bright red blood from a pristine corpse with which to solve it?

That was far from simple.

13 He drove through the night after Lisa and the dumpster trash, barreling up the Georgia coast and zeroing in on a cut-and-paste corporate circle just outside of Duke University in Durham, North Carolina.

He was eager to capitalize on the time lag between the co-ed's death and her delayed discovery, and, while he had far from hidden her, the lucky break of bumbling detectives in the Fulton County Sheriff's Department gave him a window of opportunity he hadn't quite expected but now relished.

He was eager to toss a casual civilian into the mix. He'd done the prom queen, nixed the co-ed, now it was time for some tight-assed secretary with her Liz Claiborne blazer and Nike running shoes, dented laptop and fading "Mom's Taxi" bumper sticker. A mother, preferably. A wife, absolutely.

The MO was mandatory. Absolutely critical. He could see it now, filling the front pages of a hundred different newspapers in a hundred sleepy little towns: "We don't know who the next victim will be. They've been single. They've been married. They've been young. They've been old. High school. College. Professional."

The gas station coffee cups were piling up, the stolen road maps and guidebooks—never buy evidence when you can steal it; that was his motto—rode shotgun, the best co-pilot he could ever have.

The words of none other than Tony Robbins oozed through the stereo, motivating him in ways as yet unknown but immediately apparent. He'd actually met the man himself once, at a seminar or charity event, and even in speaking with him in the green room for less than five minutes, he'd been captivated by the sound of his voice. He didn't listen to the words, though, as potent as they might have been to entrepreneurs since time immemorial. No, it was the inflections of the eloquent motivational speaker's voice that so relaxed him. The up and down severity of the master motivator's on-tape pitch. Lull them, wow them, lull them, wow them. It was a soothing pattern.

And in between kills, *he* needed to be soothed....

He had a feeling that this was the calm before the storm. If he knew his cops, and boy, did he know cops, they'd have already hit on the maze clues. Two states. Two girls. Two murders. Two different crime scenes. Two different colors of hair. Two different ages.

It was enough to keep them at bay for only so long.

The maze was what would clue them in. He had forty-eight hours, tops, before the cops from two jurisdictions would finally hook up, compare notes, and alert the FBI. It was garden-variety serial killer antics, he knew, but it wasn't the mystery that got him off.

It was the chase.

Letting them know who he was was every bit as thrilling as watching a little-known drug subdue a healthy, beautiful co-ed into submission. Watching her slump down the side of a grease-smeared dumpster, filling his hands like so much putty, gave him the ultimate thrill. That was the exact moment he knew he could do anything—absolutely anything—he wanted to with her.

And, better yet, for as long as he liked.

Knowing he could do anything—*anything*—that he wanted to her was more of a rush than actually doing it. So was the chase. He was impatient for them to find him, now, and yet desperate that they didn't.

It drove him, competing with the lulling effect of the motivational CD playing in the background. Now he would have all the time in the world to take his third victim. And that, he relished. Like a stripper waiting for her customers to notice her new boob job, he craved the attention that would surround his fourth.

And his fifth.

And his sixth.

Lull them, wow them. Lull them, wow them.

It wasn't just a speaker's pattern. For him, it was a way of life.

For the girls, it was a way of death.

14

Six hours later, Sarah, Will, and Captain Deltano were seated in the precinct's most luxurious conference room—the one with carpet and wallpaper, reserved for the occasional press conference and the annual Mayor's visit—waiting to be patched in for a conference call with the Daytona PD.

"What's the scoop, Cap?" Sarah asked, pouring herself another cup of coffee from the machine next to the water cooler. It wasn't that she was thirsty, or even particularly tired. She was just taking advantage of the perks while she could. And coffee that didn't taste like week-old roach piss? That was a perk worth staining her teeth for.

Five years ago, the smell of coffee so close to viewing the dead co-ed's last whiff of life would have turned her stomach. Now it was just a means to an end for the hardened veteran: More coffee meant more man-hours spent catching the twisted fuck who killed the co-ed, then shoved a plastic cigar case up her ass.

"Anyone?" she asked as she rested a long, elegant hand atop the pristine stack of white Styrofoam cups awaiting the next press conference or Mayor's visit.

"We're not supposed to be using those, Sarah." The Captain frowned, clearly nervous about the upcoming phone call and fussing unnecessarily. It had been years since a serial killer passed through Atlanta. Now he was having flashbacks. And not happy ones, at that.

"Oh Cap," she pooh-poohed, pouring him a tall cup of the black stuff. "Live a little." He smiled, despite himself, as she handed him the cup. She sat next to Will, not even offering him a cup. A devout tea drinker, he stuck his nose up at Sarah's ever-present coffee mug any time he could. In this case, she didn't mind. Had he been a coffee drinker, she would have never been able to stump him back at the crime scene with her intimate knowledge of the smell of coffee grounds. Ah, the joys of petty miracles.

"To answer your question, Sarah," the Captain said, a jowly man of indiscriminate years, who'd been a fixture at headquarters since either of the detectives in the room with him had even thought about going to the Police Academy. "We're coordinating with a jurisdiction in Florida who may have found similar evidence to ours on a recent murder victim. Seems a teenage girl was slaughtered there last week while working after school at an ice cream parlor. They seem to think there's a...similarity."

Will scowled. "Our girl wasn't slaughtered, Cap," he said petulantly, overstating the obvious to a man who needed neither reminding *nor* attitude. "Wasn't even a scratch on her, come to think of it. This is just a waste of time. Not to mention, their victim sounds like some high school teen queen. Ice cream parlor? That's not a co-ed job. Unless Hooters is branching out into the lucrative world of Rocky Road and Peppermint Twist."

Cap frowned at the off-color joke. "Yeah, well, seems you're not the only one finding mazes at murder scenes these days, Will. Sarah."

Will's face blanched. "You mean?" he asked, no need to finish.

"I mean," Cap grunted after a loud slug of fresh coffee, "that we've got two murders, in two states, involving two girls, different MOs, and the same exact fucking signature: two mazes, solved with the victim's blood."

Will smiled triumphantly. "That's just it, Cap," he bragged. "Our girl? Nothing. Aside from the pin prick Fern found at the tip of her pubis, there wasn't a scratch on her. How do you fill out a maze without any blood?"

Cap frowned, setting his coffee aside. "Gimme some credit, huh, Will?" he spat. "I had the lab fax over her DNA profile, *and* the one taken from the maze. Turns out, the teenager in Florida has the same profile as the blood on the maze. As the blood on OUR maze, Will. Waddya say to that, Mr. Smarty Pants?"

"Oh shit," Will said, frowning. "Oh...holy...shit."

Finally, just as the phone rang, Cap smiled. "That's what I

thought you'd say, you know-it-all, smug S.O.B. Now pick up the goddamned phone and quit acting so superior. If this *is* a serial killer, we could be working with these guys from Florida for quite some time. Let's try to make a good first impression, shall we?"

15

Bernie Segal, literary agent extraordinaire, fumed in the long line during rush hour at Taco Bell. "This would never happen to me in LA," he kept telling himself in a mental mantra. He tried not to blow his lid as the dimwitted teenage cashier kept handing bag after bag of bean burritos and Choco-Tacos to the overloaded car full of overweight secretaries in front of him. Of course, back in LA he'd have his assistant, Guy, run such trivial errands for him, but while he was still on the road, he was forced to do things the old-fashioned, make that prehistoric, way.

So far, the scouting sessions had gone as planned. Lots of local flavor, lots of great exterior shots, lots of local—not to mention unemployed—film school grads to avail himself of should any of the six cable networks he was courting give him the proverbial green light.

He smiled contently, momentarily forgetting that he was third in a line of eight cars waiting for his stupid value grande meal, when he suddenly noticed the driver of the front car handing back one of the white bags with a very distressed look on her face.

Through the blaring horns and talk radio he distinctly heard the word "void" called out by the very frustrated cashier. "Shit!" he spat, jerking the rental car into park and instinctively reaching for the stack of newspapers lining the passenger seat.

His job was to stay on top of pop culture. A family falls down a well, Bernie was on it. Kid shoots up a school, Bernie could magically get the stepmother's number and ink a deal before Geraldo found out about it. Some might go so far as to call him an ambulance chaser. While not exactly wincing at the term—he recognized it as all too apt—he nonetheless preferred to be called "media savvy."

Back in LA, he would be feasting on the industry trades and, in between a flurry of phone calls, enjoying the highlightings and clippings Guy would have already had waiting for him from that morning's stack of tabloid-esque stories from around the country. But now he was forced to resort to a handful of local Southern rags and, of course, that old McStandby, *USA Today*. Still, his eyes were ever alert for the sensational, the exploitative, the bloody, and so when a days-old Florida rag and a more recent Georgia paper both had similar headlines featuring "brutal" (Florida's word) and "savage" (Georgia's term) killings that both papers called "unsolved," his phone was already dialing before it had reached his ear.

Naturally, Frank was out of the office—or simply using his Caller ID to screen one of Bernie's typically nag-filled calls—but it didn't stop Bernie from leaving the following message: "Frank. Bernie. On the road here doing a little talent scouting and just ran across a couple fresh murders that might be headed your way. Looks like, yeah, first Florida, now Georgia. The papers are scant on details, aren't they always, but they're doing everything *but* saying the two crimes are related.

"Here's the scoop: Hoping you can fill me in when you get a second. I know we're flush off the new book sales, but we really need another hardback to push once the new one goes into paperback, and that's a few short months away. Sorry to sound so crass, pardner, but that's me. Give me a buzz on my cell when you get a break from being a superhero. You'll be my top priority. Ciao."

Bernie mulled over the message for countless minutes as the first car finally straightened out their order—nothing a free bag of cinnamon taco chips won't cure—and drove away satisfied, forcing Bernie to shift back into drive and drift forward into second place. He wondered if perhaps he hadn't come on too strong. It wasn't rare for Bernie to poke Frank for news on a current case. Hell, half the books wouldn't get written if Bernie wasn't prodding Frank along at some point during the case, but this case wasn't even official yet.

Bernie flushed, realizing he'd perhaps overstepped. It was this damn TV pilot. It had him edgy, off his game. He was so eager for Frank to be working on a new case to profile, something the public hadn't already read about ad nauseam in his books, that he was linking two cases—in two separate states, no less—that might not even be related.

"Fuck Frank," Bernie finally spat as the lifeless cashier screwed up yet another order and he slid the car back into park. "He'll forgive me for being a soulless rat bastard when he's cashing that million dollar paycheck the networks give him."

Bernie smiled, no longer angry at the tongue-tied Taco Bell worker.

Hell, he wasn't even hungry anymore.

16

You would think that the head of the Special Circumstances Crime Unit, or SCCU, would warrant an office as prestigious as his title, but as Senior Agent Frank Logan settled into the well-worn leather chair behind the glorified picnic table that constituted his so-called desk, he looked decidedly out of place in the somewhat humble surroundings.

Those who would complain about his temporary file cabinets and outdated phone, his obsolete PC and the dusty picture of Bill Clinton that constituted the entirety of his wall coverings, would get the standard Logan line: "Why the hell would I decorate *this* dump? I'm never here."

Those who knew him best, however, including his efficient and long-suffering assistant, Margie Holcomb, knew enough not to argue. Most years, Frank clocked a whopping 270 days on the road. (Or, to be more precise, in the air.) He had more frequent flyer miles than most rock stars and more power than most presidents, and his cluttered office was the least of his many worries.

What worried him most were killers. Men. Women. Blacks. Whites. Kids. Teens. Adults. Seniors. Teachers. Lawyers. Doctors. Nurses. Wives. Husbands. Sons. Daughters. Didn't matter who it was, where they lived, or what they did for a living; if they killed more than one person under what the FBI termed "special circumstances," Frank Logan would soon grow to know them on an intimate and quite costly—to them, anyway—level.

Yet Logan was quick to caution those would-be agents and local cops who immediately assumed he was some Jack Crawford or Clarice Starling wannabe that he was no profiler.

Not by a long shot.

Amazingly, Frank had never taken a single class since leaving the academy over thirty years earlier. There were no certificates lining his wall, no citations, commendations, or awards. He was what the agency referred to as a "lifer."

There was no wife, no kids, no dog, no cat. Not even a house-plant sullied the ledges of his modest bachelor pad in Georgetown—or his beach house in Malibu—and his closet, living room, bedroom, and any other room, were as austere and outdated as his office.

No one knew what drove him, for few knew him at all except, perhaps, his literary agent Bernie Segal. (And what a sad commentary *that* was.) He was jovial when need be, charming to members of the opposite sex, popular with the fellas, in like Flynn with the top brass, and had the ear of anyone and everyone who could help him on both coasts, especially in the District of Columbia.

He was as wise as he was kind, as spry as the physical situation demanded, though this happened less and less as his legend grew, and on this day he wanted nothing more than to be left alone.

Like most things Frank Logan wanted, it was not meant to be.

"Morning, Frank," said his assistant Margie, precisely six minutes after he'd arrived, straight from a red-eye flight after scouring a South Carolina tobacco farm for the remains of a special circumstance killer's eighth victim.

She'd wanted to confer with him right away, but experience, and time, had taught her to give her boss at least five minutes of what he called down time. Adding an extra minute only helped to soften the blow. "To what do we owe the honor on this fine day?"

"Morning, Margie," he grunted, ungraciously accepting the cup of coffee she handed him perfunctorily. She was as familiar with his habits, routines, and desires as any spouse. "Please tell me coffee is all you're bringing into this office today. I just spent four days up to my knees in pig shit, only to find half of a jaw bone. I'm not in the mood for another special circumstances killer today."

"Sorry, Frank." Margie pouted unsympathetically, knowing Frank was *never* not in the mood for another case. "But this one just came in from the South. Imagine that, you must be real popular down there."

She handed him a pathetically thin file marked with a bright red case number splashed across the manila folder. Before he could open it, she summarized it for him: "Two girls. Two states. Two MO's. Two crime scenes. Two reporting agencies. Special circumstance? You tell me. A maze found at each scene, filled out in the victim's blood. You'll find the victim's files in there, not much to go on, yet, and the contact info for the original reporting agencies. Welcome back, Frank. Let me know if there's anything I can do to help."

Frank restrained himself from telling her where to put her precious folder, and instead held up a hand to delay her exit. "Tell me, Margie, since I know you're the head gossip around these parts; I've been hearing rumblings about a new partner the brass is assigning me. You wouldn't know anything about that, would you?" He grinned knowingly.

"Of course I would," Margie said with a twinkle in her sea-green eyes, shining mysteriously under her helmet of bright red hair. "That's why you've kept me around so long. I know *all* the secrets."

Frank couldn't argue with that. The two had been paired together during his very first year as a supervisor and now, some three decades later, she was still there. Her short frame had rounded out nicely over the years, her eyes had settled into a cobweb of laugh lines, no doubt enhanced by the lively banter she exchanged with both agents and staff nine hours a day, five days a week, 50 weeks a year—and perhaps even on her two weeks of vacation time—come rain or shine.

If Frank Logan was one of the five most powerful senior agents in the FBI, Margie was one of the five most powerful *people* in the FBI. Perhaps the whole darn town. Her knowledge of procedure, history, decorum, and routine made her the go-to gal for everyone from the Senior Director all the way down to the newest greenhorn in the mailroom. Despite their decades-long friendship, however, Frank knew the only reason she was still assigned to him was because he only saw her two or three times a month, leaving her free to answer questions near and far for the entire agency. Far from being her boss, Frank often felt as if he was at Margie's mercy.

It was a fact she never let him forget.

"Well," Frank said impatiently. "I'm waiting...."

Margie sighed, her eyes sliding to the back of her head as she recalled, nearly verbatim, a conversation she'd overheard in the cafeteria some weeks earlier. "Logan's a loose cannon," she began, her short, chubby fingers making quotation marks in the air before and after each sentence to let her boss know the words she was speaking were not her opinion, but those of the muckety-mucks who, no matter what their combined power and prestige may have been, still signed their checks. "He's been going solo too long. Ever since the death of his last partner. He thinks he works better as a lone ranger. But that's not the agency way. We'll find him the best of the best; we just won't let Frank know it until it's too late."

Margie finished with a flourish, her fingers tired from all that quoting. Frank sighed, shaking his head as he admitted, "I'm surprised it took them so long. Waddya think? One week? Two?"

"Three," Margie reassured him with her trademark irony. "Three days, that is. Jawbone or no, the Cigarette Slayer was your last solo case, Frank. Whenever you get up to speed on this new one, these Maze Murders I've just handed you, you'll be dragging along a new partner on the red-eye to the latest crime scene. Sorry, Frank. But you know what they say, don't shoot the messenger."

Frank nodded, marveling that Margie had done it yet again. "Cigarette Slayer," he frowned, now using a few quotation marks of his own as he recited the nicknames of his latest, and newest, case. "Maze Murders. How do you do it, Margie? How do you take one look at a murder book and come up with a nickname for the killings? Do you have a deal with the *Washington Post*? Huh? Waddya get? Fifty bucks, a hundred, for every serial killer you name?"

Margie grinned coyly. Hell, the old gal was actually blushing. "I have no idea *what* you're talking about, Frank."

"The hell you don't," Frank said with a grin. "How long have you and I been together now? Thirty years or thereabouts?"

"Thirty-three and counting, this June," she corrected him.

"Thirty-*three* years," Frank marveled, letting out a whistle. "And, what? Let's say I get about fifteen of these murder books a year, give or take. How many of them do you think you've named so far, Margie? Ten a year? Twelve? Fourteen? Fifteen?"

There was no need for an answer. From the Capricorn Killer to the Axe Handler to the Wood Chipper to the Son of Satan to the Seattle Strangler to the Kiss-Me Killer, Margie had named them all. If only the readers knew the diminutive secretary was the mastermind behind the buzz words that filled their tabloid TV and true crime books for the past three decades, they'd promptly lynch all those big-name journalists who had been taking the credit for coining the terms.

"And now…you've already named this one, Margie?" Frank asked, looking at the file folder on his otherwise bare desk.

"Not *named*, Frank," Margie insisted, collecting her trademark cool. "Just…kind of…suggested. It's easier that way. Professionally speaking. Now instead of asking me, 'What's the deal with those murders involving the mazes stuffed up the victim's wazoos?' you can simply say, 'Hand me the Maze Murder file.' It's not a matter of ownership, just one of convenience. I really don't see what the big deal is."

Frank looked at the words, *Maze Murder*, scrawled in Margie's easily recognizable hand across the file folder, and had to grin. "It's no big deal at all, Margie," Frank said, scrolling his long, thick finger down to the pertinent info scribbled at the bottom of the file. "I see you've nicknamed the killer as well."

"Hardly," Margie scoffed, surreptitiously edging toward the office door.

"Oh really?" he asked, his finger resting next to the pre-printed box labeled, "Killer ID." "Says here in this box you've decided to call our killer 'Maze.' Or is that just an abbreviation?"

Margie sighed. "Just trying to make your life easier, Frank," she said. "Now instead of asking me for 'the Maze Murder file in which the killer leaves behind mazes,' you can just say, 'What's up with Maze today?' Or, 'What's the latest with this Maze character?' If you'd prefer I stay out of your business, *sir*, I'd be glad to do so."

Frank shook his head. Now he'd touched a nerve. "Why start now?" he quipped, knowing the only way out of a three-day funk around the office was a quick joke at his own expense. "I lack your, shall we say, *imagination*, for these kinds of creative touches. I suppose instead of complaining, I should be thanking you."

"Yes," she agreed over her shoulder as she fled the office, his apology apparently accepted. "You *should*."

Frank sighed, sipped his coffee, and began leafing through the skimpy folder. "Maze," he mumbled aloud, already losing himself in the gory crime scene photos, technical measurements, and minutia of his next assignment. "What will she think of next?"

17 Maze would have liked to have lingered at the third crime scene, but duty called. This time the victim was found so fast, he didn't have enough time to stick around and grab the local paper, fresh off the presses. Instead, he had had to appease himself by stopping at the first Internet café he'd found on the road, paying his $5.00 per ten minutes in cash, and logging into the *Raleigh-Durham Reporter* with a fake username and generic password to read the story from afar, something he was loathe to do, except in those rare situations he deemed as emergencies.

He read the story three times, quickly, and then a fourth and fifth, more carefully. He'd longed to print it out, complete with titillating crime scene tape flapping in the stiff North Caroline breeze; so tempted, in fact, that his mouse arrow lingered over the ever-present printer icon at the top of his Web browser for two full minutes of his precious time allotment. In the end, his self-control had won out and he'd merely committed the article to memory.

There'd be plenty of time to print it out later.

The article, like the two previous ones, had been specific about the gory details and skittish about the important ones. Despite the close proximity of the three states—so perfectly aligned that even a fourth grader could have followed his stubby finger up a map of the Southeast coast—North Carolina was desperately behind the learning curve and had yet to link the dead secretary to either the co-ed in Georgia or the cone pusher in Daytona Beach.

At least, not in print anyway.

He marveled at the way they handled the "unnamed piece of evidence," burying its mention toward the end of the two-column, front page story, where the survivors of the victims and names of the first rescue unit on the scene were listed in those monotonous details so few readers ever bothered to digest.

"Unnamed piece of evidence," Maze chuckled. "What will they think of next?"

18

Detective Holly Madison of the Durham PD didn't resent picking up the FBI agent at the Raleigh-Durham airport just seven hours after discovering the body of the missing secretary.

In fact, she was honored after she heard who it was she'd be chauffeuring back to the station house for a 6 p.m. conference with the rest of the Homicide Division. After all, who *hadn't* heard of the legendary Frank Logan?

The man who'd single-handedly worked more special circumstances cases than any other agent in the FBI, even back when they were called mass murderers, then spree murderers, then serial killers. The man was an icon in the field of death. So much so that, as she sat in the Delta Sky Miles Lounge awaiting his arrival at Gate #14, she wondered if he was actually on speaking terms with the Grim Reaper himself.

She chuckled over her club soda and lime, itching to be off duty so she could add a belt of Absolut, maybe even a shot of cranberry, to the tepid mixture that had been sitting in front of her for nearly an hour now. She consoled herself with the fact that she'd been given babysitting duty of Special Director Logan, which meant she'd get the midnight to six a.m. shift at his hotel, one of the new Hiltons or Marriotts dotting that Industrial Park the college was so proud of. Either one would be sure to have a lobby bar and, once the living legend was making nice with the Sandman, she could wrap her hands around the biggest Absolut and club soda a woman had ever seen.

She wasn't normally a big drinker, but the memory of that poor woman's body—nearly decapitated, it was, the hands and feet missing, as if the killer didn't want them to identify the body—had disturbed her. Big FBI guys like Special Director Frank Logan? They probably enjoyed glazed crullers and Starbucks as they swapped cemetery humor atop the victim's bodies, barely even registering the bite marks, bullet holes, missing nipples, and severed heads lying strewn at their feet like so much litter. But three-year detectives like Holly? She'd be having nightmares for years. Decades, even. "Sorry honey," she'd be saying to her future husband, a well-meaning, understanding, long-suffering bloke who'd just have to get used to her night sweats and nightmares.

Already she was having trouble sleeping, though she'd never admit it to the officials at the precinct. Even now, sitting in the light of day at the airport bar, surrounded by well-heeled travelers and the sultry bartender who'd been flirting with her over the smoked almonds for the last half-hour, she could still see flashes of the secretary's exposed shin bones and the jagged tears and poking gristle at the joints of her missing wrists.

She'd been at the movies when she got the call. That was the ironic thing, the reason none of the guys down at the squad would ever believe a dead body—a real, live, oozing dead body—would ever give her the willies. The name of the movie she'd been taking in that day: *Zombie Killers 3*. So how could a bona fide slasher flick junkie, an aficionado of all things gory, gooey, gurgling, and gut-spilling, ever admit to the department shrink, let alone the guys in the bullpen, that she hadn't slept more than four hours in the days since she'd arrived at the scene?

A medium popcorn had been situated in the empty chair next to her. (There were always plenty of them at the 3 p.m. matinee.) Large Diet Coke in the cup holder. Half-empty bag of Twizzlers in her lap, covering the dull green light glowing from the ever-present cell phone clipped to her belt. The only two teenagers who were still remaining, out of the eight pathetically predictable characters who'd appeared at the beginning of the movie had just discovered the secret remedy to lure all the zombies into the abandoned mineshaft to blow them all up. She still had thirty minutes of lukewarm special effects and fake blood left to see when the familiar vibration jolted her into a straight upright position. "Shit!" she'd spat, immediately apologizing to the elderly couple three rows behind her who were fast asleep and drooling into their Kiddy packs.

Out into the lobby, she'd flipped open her department-issued cell phone—three sizes bigger than those on the civilian market, or roughly half the size of most high-top sneakers—and was met with the breathless voice of their normally unexcitable dispatcher. "Holly, a jogger just found that missing secretary, the one that's been in all the papers. Uniforms are securing the scene as we speak. You were next on rotation, and Captain says get your ass over there pronto. His words, Holly. It's a bad one, so bad the jogger who found her thought she'd been mauled by a bear. Good luck, girl."

And that was that. Goodbye popcorn, Twizzlers, soda, brain-munching zombies, and two remaining teenagers. She'd leapt into her seven-year-old Honda Civic and high-tailed it down to the crime scene: a simple storage shed just behind the research lab where the ill-fated secretary had worked.

Her name had been Rhonda. Holly had read it in the papers, but it had never stuck until she'd been standing over the woman's dead, battered, mutilated body in that tiny storage shed and the uniforms kept calling her "Jane Doe."

"They should call her 'Chain Doe' with wounds like that," one loudmouth uniform had quipped. "It must have taken a chainsaw to separate her extremities from her limbs."

"Shit," goofed another, joining in on the fun. "I was calling her John Doe until the moment I found her tits in that shoebox over there."

"It's Rhonda Fucking Holcomb," Holly had spat, pulling rank and the woman's name out of her ass, a holdover from seeing her face splashed on the front page for the last 48-hours. "Now clear out and let us ladies get to know each other a little better."

With the uniforms gone, along with their bad jokes and mouths full of chewing tobacco, and the crime scene techs still half an hour away, Holly got up close and personal with the mutilated corpse of Rhonda Fucking Holcomb. Wife of David Reginald Holcomb. Mother of two, Lucinda Chelsea Holcomb and Brad Williams Holcomb.

She was naked, her "well-nourished"—that's what the coroner called any woman who wasn't a crack whore or Mama Cass—body as pale as Italian marble and slathered with dried blood, most notably from her missing extremities.

In those quiet, intimate moments, Holly had studied every inch of Rhonda Holcomb. Her pale, cold eyes. The blood still caked in her left ear. The duct tape still clinging to her limp, lifeless, red hair. The chipped tooth. The bite mark in her fleshy abdomen, just south of her cesarean scar. Holly didn't realize she was crying for her, mourning her loss, until the coroner had shown up and shooed her out with a brisk but familiar, "Don't let the boys see you crying. Here, take this tissue."

Holly had thanked Dr. Catherine Mead profusely before walking out of the storage shed, past the uniforms still craning their heads around the shed entrance for a better look, past her Honda Civic and straight to the curb where, in front of roughly fourteen cub reporters, she promptly threw up half a bag of Twizzlers, twelve ounces of Diet Coke, and two-thirds of a medium popcorn.

So much for being one of the boys.

19 Senior Director Frank Logan sat in yet another conference room, surrounded by yet another cadre of earnest, hard-working, well-meaning cops, and sighed. *How many more of these can I take?* he thought, as some greenhorn in uniform was given the onerous duty of wrangling the forty-year-old slide projector back to life.

He watched as his new pal, Holly something or other—*Sounds like a snack cake. Holly Debbie? Holly Twinkie? Holly Hostess?*—fidgeted nervously in her seat against the back wall while a dozen older, fatter, and dumber detectives filled the front row of the cramped room. He'd been impressed with Holly, her bright smile, shapely breasts, mid-priced perfume, bright eyes, and efficient manner, a welcome change from the inevitably rumpled, nicotine-stained, coffee-laced male escorts usually sent to fetch him from the local airport upon his arrival in a new town. With their gruff "hello's" and quick pace, he'd rarely felt as welcome and honestly embraced as Holly had made him feel. Despite his steadfast rule of never smiling at the locals until their first week together was ancient history, he'd found a grin playing at the corners of his mouth long before they'd claimed his bags and climbed into her tiny Honda.

"Tell me what you saw," he'd ordered as soon as she'd left the traffic loop, merged onto the highway and he saw her short, but sensitive hands relax upon the wheel. "Down to the nitty gritty. Don't hold anything back. I need to know from the first reporting detective so I can be prepared when your politically-connected supervisors give me the old song and dance back at the station."

He'd seen her smirk, watched the wheels go round and round in her head as she weighed who to trust more, the legendary FBI man with the impressive Forensics Channel resume and bestselling book series, or the good ol' boys back at the station. It didn't take her long to take sides.

"Feet and hands were removed," she began, easing into the right lane and cruising at just over the speed limit, none too eager for the ride to be over. "Not precisely, either. No scalpel or MD here, sir."

"Please," he'd said soothingly from the passenger seat. "Call me Frank."

"Yeah, right," she'd chuckled. "As if. Anyway, *sir*, there were lacerations about the face and head, especially at her neck, which was practically severed. Again, a rough cut, something jagged and dull, used with much force. But not overkill. I kind of, well, far be it from me to make any kind of assumptions with you riding shotgun, sir, but…I kinda got the feeling the violence was forced. Like, maybe, he was showboating, doing it for the cameras, you know?"

"Why?" he asked, intrigued but trying not to let on that he agreed with her. "Why do you say that, Holly?"

He watched a faint blush creep up her fine, delicate throat to her drawn cheeks—he recognized that telltale look of sleep deprivation right away—as she registered the fact that not only had he remembered her name, but had used it in the familiar. Then it was right back to business.

"Dunno," she grunted, though he knew instinctively that she was lying. "Just a gut feeling, you know? Like, the feet and hands being missing? What's up with that? Everyone and their brother knew who she was the minute we found her. She wasn't 200 feet from her place of employment, and her frickin' head was still attached. Her cesarean scar was laid bare. So why bother?"

"Perhaps the killer was interrupted in his work," Frank theorized.

"Then why take the hands and feet?" she pointed out, growing excited despite her days-old lethargy. Frank wondered if he was the first to raise such questions with her, if her supervisors had even asked her opinion yet. Dollars to doughnuts they hadn't. "I mean, if he's interrupted, how'd he get them past whoever was doing the interrupting? And hands and feet? They're no picnic to get past prying eyes. Throw 'em in a backpack, sure, but why bother if you're leaving the head behind? And the bite marks? There was no pattern, no rhyme or reason."

"Not unusual for a crime of passion to lack all logic," Frank cautioned but, just like *himself*, Holly had her instincts and was clinging to them viciously.

"But it *wasn't* passionate, sir," she insisted. "None of the bites went too deep, and there seemed to be nothing sexual about the crime. I know what you're going to say, sir: 'Sex and passion don't always go together, Holly.' But why was she naked, then? Why bother with taking off her clothes? What I think is, I think this guy had time, I think he enjoyed it, but not for the usual reasons. I think he's got a bigger plan, and I think he's gonna do it again. Soon. Real soon."

"Where did you find the maze?" Frank asked, realizing that at some point during Holly's diatribe he'd actually taken out his black notebook and begun scribbling down random passages, quoting her verbatim as if she might actually be a colleague.

"Halfway down her severed esophagus," she answered matter-of-factly, an obvious bluff as her trembling hands once again gripped the steering wheel as she took the exit toward downtown Durham. "Stuffed in one of those test tube thingies? But not the kind you'd find in a hospital or doctor's office. Crime tech says it was plastic, the novelty type you see in roadside souvenir stores with one cigarette inside, or a chocolate bar or something. You know, 'Emergency Nicotine Break' or 'Emergency Chocolate Stash,' that kind of thing."

"Anything…particular…about the maze?" he asked knowingly.

"You mean besides it being filled out in blood?" she asked with a snort. "Not much. Except for the fact that it wasn't *her* blood."

He nodded, as if she was telling him something he didn't know. "Whose blood do you think it is?" he asked.

"Well, sir," she hemmed before taking the plunge. "Chances are, it's some unnamed victim we haven't found yet. Some poor girl whose body is rotting in another storage shed, or garage, or dumpster clear across town somewhere."

"Try Georgia," he said quietly.

He was impressed that, despite the white knuckles that clearly sprang up on her clenched hands, she never took her eyes off the road, despite the explosive implications of the bombshell he'd just dropped.

"Is that why you're here, sir?" she asked casually, easing into the parking lot of the precinct. "Because there's another victim? Crossing state lines? Back in Georgia? And that's her blood on that maze?"

"Try *two* victims," he remarked as she turned off the engine and they both sat idle in the car. "Georgia. Florida. Blood from the first victim was used to solve her maze, *and* the second maze. Blood from the second maze was, apparently, used to fill out yours. That makes three victims. Three states. Three mazes. That's why I'm here, Holly. I'm here to catch this guy. I'm here to figure out his 'special circumstance.' I'm here to prove he's not so special, after all. And then it's my job to take him down."

Now there they sat, Holly, perhaps the sharpest mind in the room, relegated to the "back of the bus" in the strict caste system of Southern law enforcement.

That's okay, Frank thought. Before he was done, everyone in the room would know that Holly had been dead right about a lot. Down to the motive, the crime, the time, the quick profile she'd managed to construct based on everything she knew.

Holly Madison, if he had anything to do with it, would get her props this day.

He turned around as the uniform finally got the ancient slide machine back in working order. As the blood-spattered storage shed floor filled the screen in the front of the room, Special Director Frank Logan turned to look at Holly.

She didn't see him, didn't catch the look of grudging respect and professional admiration so present in his penetrating gaze, cast almost admiringly in her direction. Holly was too busy looking at the business card Frank had given her just before they got out of her car at the station. The card of the best darn shrink in all of North Carolina.

20

"Two isn't enough? Two? Two dead bodies in two different states? Peter, you're killing me here!" Bernie Segal didn't just talk into the phone, he barked into it. By some standards, he could be considered handsome; fit body, stylishly close-cropped haircut, priceless clothes, and a face that, when in repose, looked smooth and serene.

Watch him on the phone, however, and the face knotted into something canine, something predatory, the brunt of his features contorting into something unrecognizable and, frankly, just a tad obscene.

He was in the parking lot of yet another Southern truck stop, a megalopolis of sorts, where one could take a shower, weigh himself, get a spritz of cologne out of a rusty machine for 75 cents, buy a book on tape or pair of overalls, order fried chicken or potato logs, and buy gas, all under the same 70s-inspired, multi-colored roof.

Bernie's rental car was gassed up and parked in a sea of similar-looking compacts, distinguishable from one another only by the personal taste of the junk food wrappers scattered on the dashboard.

He had a bottled Starbucks mocha something in his left hand, the closest he could get to a real cup of coffee in this town, and his cell phone in the right. Pacing and barking, barking and pacing, he was midway through yet another long distance dog and pony sales pitch to one of Hollywood's hottest execs.

On the other end was Peter Heifitz, *the* Peter Heifitz, of the upstart Forensic Network's two most popular shows, *Cops on Camera* and its highly successful spin-off series, *Cops on Camera: Fresno*. Rumor had it there was a third show in production, though the network execs weren't quite sure if they favored Boise over Bergen County. They'd even taken to calling the Forensic Network "Heifitz TV," and it was rumored that Peter had taken points *and* stock in both series to get them off the ground, making him double trouble in the world of cable TV.

Other rumors abounded: Heifitz was being groomed for bigger and better things, meaning bigger and better shows, at the more legitimate networks. That Peter was gay. That Heifitz was not only not gay but, in fact, engaged to *Cops on Camera*'s leggy Brazilian-American hostess, Ciarra Sinclair. That Peter himself had served time before being born again, thus accounting for his willingness to put cops on a pedestal. (And make a mint doing it!)

One thing that was based in fact was his age: Peter Heifitz was all of 22 years old.

He was also, without a doubt, the new go-to guy for the genre he almost single-handedly introduced to the American public: law enforcement reality TV.

And he had Bernie Segal right where he wanted him.

"Listen, Bernie," Heifitz replied in his irritatingly sing-song fashion, one oft-imitated as much by his detractors as by his fans, "two dead bodies isn't enough for me to get the networks to buy me a cup of coffee, let alone the budget to shoot a 60-minute pilot. Get me three, get me four, and we can talk turkey."

Even Bernie, he of questionable moral values and a string of civil lawsuits in his closet, was struck by the heartless tone of Peter's reply. "These are *women*, Pete. And somebody's killing them. Logan will catch them, you have my word. His clearance rate is 100%. That's unheard of in the FBI."

"But not in the Special Crimes division," Peter corrected him. "How old is that unit? Five, six years old? So he's been lucky. He's due for a fall; no one can stay gold that long. Don't get me wrong, I love the guy. Peter Heifitz building a show around Frank Logan? It's a no-brainer, but I gotta have enough for a series. Two women don't cut it, Bern. I don't want to do half-hour shows anymore. An hour's where it's at. And two women doesn't get me a series full of one-hour shows."

Bernie sighed, listening to the endless growling of truck engines as they circled in a yawning loop around the gargantuan parking lot before merging with the highway beyond. The sun beat down on his head, making his twelve-dollar hair gel stiff and greasy, all at the same time.

"Listen, Pete, I'm not trying to tell you how to do your job, but look at it this way: You've got the first show, say the pilot, to profile the first victim. Some nice crime scene shots, a dramatic recreation or two...I'm scouting the local sites as we speak. Second show? Profile your host, Frank Logan.

"You get some great shots of Frank in action, some back scene crapola down at headquarters, a stack of his paperbacks, maybe even him at a book-signing or two. Next show? Second victim. More reen-actments, more local flavor, some interviews with the first cops on the crime scene, give them their props. Fourth show? You can talk about how similar this case is to, say, one of Frank's earlier cases.

"Idea," Bernie added, interrupting himself. "You might even be able to get a jailhouse interview with one of the sick fucks he put behind bars forever. It could even be a weekly feature, you know, pig-gyback on the whole Hannibal Lecter thing, right? There's gonna be more victims, Pete, trust me. I've been with Frank long enough to know there are *always* more victims."

Bernie waited, feeling cheesy for goosing the spiel, but not cheesy enough to apologize. He waited. Then he waited some more. All the while the sun beat down, and he had to pee.

The little prick, Bernie thought to himself, *he's making me wait. On purpose. Probably read about it in some book on high-stakes Holly-wood negotiation, some self-help guru BS he's bought into. Meanwhile my feet hurt, my prostate's shrinking, and I think my hair's on fire!*

The silence on the other end meant that Peter was contemplat-ing Bernie's idea. Or answering another call. Or filing his nails. Or checking his email. Or getting a blow job, who knew. And then, at last, Peter spoke: "There's promise there, Bern, I'll give you that. Maybe, and I'm just brainstorming here, but maybe the first half hour of each show could be a current case, and the second half a tie-in to an old case. Kind of a two-for-one deal, right?

"I mean, think about it: everybody's read Frank's books," Pete made his case, his sing-song voice going higher as his enthusiasm spread, "but nobody's ever seen any of them profiled on television. And I'd do it, Bernie. I'd do it up right. You think Frank's a star now? Wait'll I get a hold of him, pal. He'll be his very own galaxy. It might work. Let me noodle it around, Bernie, run it by the bigwigs. I know what they'll say, though, 'Two bodies aren't enough.' This thing goes special circumstances, Bern, you've got yourself a green light. If it stops at two, you might as well take it to the History Channel."

Bernie smiled, hearing the click of Peter's phone on the other end of the line. *History Channel my ass*, he thought serenely, downing the last of his bottled coffee as he headed back inside to take a piss and maybe even splurge on some vending machine cologne.

This thing's going primetime if it's the last thing I do.

"Greetings, gentleman," Frank began, casting a nodding glance and a wink in Holly's direction as he continued, "and...*ladies*. My name is Frank Logan, Senior Director of the Special Circumstances Crime Unit, better known as the SCCU, headquartered in Washington."

He paused for the inevitable "what an asshole" eye rolls and "big name dropper" elbow nudges between the locals, then proceeded almost as if by rote. "I am speaking to you today with the understanding that what I am about to say does not leave this room, does not end up in tomorrow's newspaper, does not end up in a quick email to your wives, lovers, boyfriends, or hunting buddies.

"If it does—and if you're wondering if I have the seniority to back up what I'm threatening, believe me, I do—if one word of this discussion leaks, if one crime scene photo makes it onto your own personal Website, or is even printed without the proper authorization code from the FBI, you won't just be directing traffic by this time tomorrow, you'll be directing *school* traffic. Make that *middle* school traffic.

"I'm going to tell you privileged information. It's going to matter. Maybe not today, maybe not tomorrow. Maybe not for this victim, maybe not even for the next victim, or the next, or the next after that. But, trust me, it's *going* to matter. The clues we uncover, the plot we unravel, the words we use, will come back to haunt us if they are leaked to the press, or anyone else, for that matter. That is why I threaten, scratch that, that is why I *promise* you, a severe and instant demotion should what is said in this room today, right now, ever leave this room except in your brain pans."

One more pause, a few more eye rolls, much less elbowing, and finally it was time for Frank to officially begin. "Now that we understand each other, what we have here in the unfortunate Mrs. Rhonda Holcomb is not an isolated incident. Not a single murder, but one in a series of murders."

Ignoring the ripple of emotion sweeping through the room, Frank continued. "The maze so cleverly uncovered by Detective Holly Madison here,"—quick nod, wink, and props to one very surprised Holly—"has been thoroughly tested by the labs back at Quantico to reveal that not only is the paper identical to that found in two previous murders, one in Georgia, one in Florida, but that the blood used to solve the maze in your case was identical to the blood from the victim in Georgia.

"The victim in Georgia? The maze found on, or should I say *in*, her body was filled in with the blood of what we believe is our first victim, in Florida. In case you're still trying to connect the dots, I'll save you the trouble: We are dealing with a special circumstances killer. Worse yet, a special circumstances killer who's now crossing borders. State borders, that is.

"So I'm not here to step on your toes, drink up all your Scotch, or steal any of your women." Quick wink to Holly, just the same. "I'm here to get a feel for the locale, soak up the crime scene, get straight with all the evidence, connect a few dots of my own, and I'll be out of your hair in, say, 48 hours. That said, I'm all ears."

Frank remained standing, pegging each officer in the room to the back of his chair with a steely glance born of hard-won experience. It was a little game he played with himself, from break room to board room to conference room across the country: Which local, good-old-boy, tobacco-plug-spitting, homophobic, redneck prick would show his fat, hairy ass first?

After all, there was always one and, until he'd nailed him good, Frank's work there couldn't really begin. The countdown continued in his head, 14, 15, 16.... This group was good. Most times, some beefy, nicotine-stained hand had shot up long before now. He was impressed.

19, 20, 21...We have a winner.

"Yes, officer," Frank said to the inevitably beefy hand stretching up the inevitably hairy arm through the tight sports coat tugged snug beneath the double chin that rounded out the flattop above the face of the man currently scowling at him. "What do you have for me?"

"Shouldn't that be 'What do you have for *us*?'" asked the thick, nasally voice. "And it's *Detective*. Detective Smathers."

"Ah, Detective Smathers, yes." Frank smiled, not meaning an inch of it. "What I have for you are questions. And plenty of them. Unless you have something to add, I suggest...."

"That's just it," Smathers interjected, feeding off the grumbling of his fellow locals and feeling his oats. "How are we supposed to help you if you don't give us any of the particulars of the two previous crimes? I mean, how can we figure out which clues are relevant, which information to leave out...."

"Smathers, is it?" Frank suddenly asked.

"*Detective* Smathers, yes," the beefy cop responded proudly.

"Right," Frank said smiling. "Listen, I know you're only doing what you think is right: standing up for the locals. It's admirable, really. I know you've probably read a few of my books, or seen me on *America's Most Wanted* or the Forensics Channel. That's great. More power to you. But I left all that bullshit outside this conference room door, Smathers, and I'll suggest you do the same. Your loyalty to the troops here in Durham is a liability to this case, not an asset. It clouds your judgment, makes you feel like hiding things, keeping them to yourself. 'Aha,' you want to say, 'look what escaped the eagle eye of famous FBI Director Frank Logan.' I feel for you. It's only natural. But know this: There's only one person in this room that I care about right now, and she's lying, spread-eagled and bloody, in those crime scene photos scattered across that table in front of you.

"*She's* why I'm here. Not to win one for my team, or steal one from yours. As far as I'm concerned, and I'll put this into language you can better understand: We're both on the same team. Got it, *Detective* Smathers? Now, you know me a little better, and I don't have time to know you. What I *do* have time for, roughly 47 hours and 26 minutes of it, to be exact, is to learn all you know about this poor woman and what happened to her four days ago in your town.

"So, where do *we* begin?"

Frank Logan smiled as the hands around the table, all but those belonging to Smathers, that is, began to rise, tentatively at first, and then with purpose. Soon, the clues came spilling out. By the time his low-tech, spiral-bound notebook was nearly full, four precious hours had passed and none other than Detective Holly Madison had been named as his personal liaison for the duration of the case.

It was the least he could do.

22

Pokey Gero was a teacher's worst nightmare, a truant officer's wet dream, and three suspensions away from Tuscawilla State Farms, the local juvenile detention center slash work farm slash boot camp-slash-thug mill. And he was only in the seventh grade, technically speaking anyway. Age wise, he actually belonged in the *tenth* grade, but a few failed grades, two arrest warrants, and three consecutive expulsions from John F. Kennedy Middle School had cost him some much-needed educational momentum.

On this frosty October morning, he was busy spending his lunch money at the convenience store across from his bus stop. Through the blinking neon beer signs and credit card stickers, Pokey watched as the rest of his classmates, sniveling little goody-goodies that they were, boarded the long yellow school bus in a decidedly ordinary fashion.

"Queer baits," he muttered gleefully to himself as he grabbed two Budweiser tallboys from the beer cooler and ambled confidently up to the sales counter. There, a convicted pornographer and well-known pedophile by the name of Teddy Rambeiux joyfully rang up the sale and handed Pokey three quarters and two pennies as change.

Though it was illegal in the state of South Carolina, or any other state in the union, for that matter, to sell alcohol to minors—and, despite his advanced age, rap sheet, and peach fuzz moustache, Pokey Gero was still considered a minor—Teddy Rambeiux was nothing if not a slick businessman. Ever since the advent of digital cameras and a quick weekend "how-to" course together, Pokey had been providing Teddy with pictures of naked JV cheerleaders showering after practice.

As such, Teddy's Website, www.afterschoolsmut.com, was the most popular—and expensive—on the Web, charging its 420,789 subscribers a whopping $14.95 per year for "guaranteed weekly updates."

The process was simple: Each Friday, Pokey went to school with Teddy's digital camera. After school, he hung around cheerleader practice, chain smoking Marlboro Reds and pulling the wings off flies until the frisky pre-teens hit the showers. There, peering through a hole the size of a silver dollar, Pokey snapped his weekly updates. By that night, Teddy's site was dutifully updated and the perversion could begin.

Without Pokey, there would be no Website. No updates. No subscribers. No six figure, tax-free income for one enterprising ex-con. Selling the zit-faced, knobby-kneed, oversexed fifteen-year-old two beers every morning was the least of Teddy's worries.

Shit, he would have sold the kid a hand grenade if he'd asked for it.

Without a word, Pokey took his beers, his change, and a quick strip of beef jerky. "On the house," Teddy mumbled gratefully before Pokey limped across the convenience store parking lot, past the trailer park to the right, and into the deserted field where he spent most mornings when he didn't go to school, which were *most* mornings.

Wiping beer foam onto his dirty jeans, Pokey took a seat on his favorite log and proceeded to nurse his "breakfast of champions." The air was still crisp and, peering around in all directions to make sure no one was looking, he hugged his muscular arms around his cut-off T-shirt. The dew had gone frosty in the early morning chill, and Pokey reveled in crunching his feet on the near-frozen grass as he swilled cold beer, finishing off his first can of the day.

He took longer with the second, finally breaking out his crum-pled pack of cigarettes and lighting one with the sterling silver lighter he'd stolen off some teacher or another during one of his many deten-tions after school. The initials inscribed on the front of the lighter meant nothing to him: "D. J." Nor did the touching inscription on the back: "Through the best of times, through the worst of times, you were my endless love."

He snorted every time he read it. *How gay*, he thought for the millionth time as he exhaled a cloud of cigarette smoke admirably large for someone so young. Then again, he'd been smoking and drinking for years.

After two beers, a mouthful of beef jerky, and no less than six cigarettes, Pokey finally felt the inevitable tug at his bladder and ambled over to his favorite spot to relieve himself. Throughout South and North Carolina, there were many vacant lots such as the one Pokey favored during his weekly bouts of truancy. A weedy field. Rusted car parts scattered across a lawn long since grown wild. Broken glass, the odd unrecognizable doorknob, and the crumbled frame of a house long since abandoned. Be it hurricanes, frigid winters, or sheer neglect, all that remained of this particular house was the fireplace, now showing signs of age and standing half as high as it might have in the house's family-sheltering heyday.

Amateur photographers saw picturesque ruins. Pokey saw only a restroom.

As he tried to finish spelling his name with the last of his considerable bladder contents, Pokey spotted an odd sight out of the corner of his eye: A mannequin waving to him from the other side of the crumbling fireplace. It wasn't waving, exactly, but that was definitely—yes, yes, it *had* to be—a pale plastic hand sticking up just below the red brick foundation. Pokey zipped up his pants, wiped his hands on a tuft of frost-crunchy grass, and walked around the fireplace to inspect his cryptic find.

It was no mannequin.

It was a lady.

A naked lady.

The fact that she was dead made little difference to Pokey. He'd been watching *CSI* since the series began. Likewise, the Forensics Channel, along with his before-and-after school snacks of alcohol and nicotine, was a staple of his daily diet.

She might have been dead—her skin a pale, waxy yellow, frost covering her eyelashes, long, blonde hair, and thick pubic patch—but she sure was hot. And naked. Naked. And hot.

He took out Teddy's digital camera and started flashing pictures. Something about the eerily quiet scene—not to mention the beautiful dead woman in his camera's viewfinder—told him what he was doing was wrong. But then, most things he did were wrong, so he was quite used to the feeling.

He snapped and snapped and snapped. Walking here, closing in, pulling back. With an amateur photographer's uncanny instinct, he unconsciously snapped her most poignant moments: a frozen tear caught halfway between nose and lips. A broken fingernail. A strange bruise across her feminine bicep.

It was only when he lowered the camera to take a shot of her hands that he started feeling queasy. Like the time his father had caught him smoking out behind his bedroom window and made him smoke the whole pack. There was a word his teachers would use: Nauseous. Yeah, that's it. He was feeling decidedly nauseous.

And for good reason: Three of her fingers were missing.

Pokey stepped back, grass crunching under his unlaced hi-top sneakers, only to hear a different kind of crunch. He looked beneath his feet to find a fingernail. Sadly, the finger was still attached.

Pokey whirled, as green as grass, and heaved until his side ached. Until he was sure his ribs were broken. Until his very shoes felt empty. When he was done, two cans of beer, chunky beef jerky, and that morning's Pop Tart were spread across a wide swath of grass. Out of the corner of this putrid mixture stuck a piece of paper.

After Pokey had been discovered lying face-down next to his favorite drinking log by Sergeant Vern Bronstein, the local truant officer, cops would locate the piece of paper under his putrid pile of breakfast treats. When the officers had separated it from the bits of cherry filling and cured beef that clung to it like glue, they could barely make out its contents.

A maze.

23

Newly-crowned Special Agent Vinny Smalldeano felt about as comfortable in a bookstore as a pedophile in an old folk's home. What's worse, he knew it showed. The co-ed cashier behind the sales counter had smirked knowingly at him as he'd fumblingly asked for the "police procedural books" after twenty minutes of searching the shelves by himself had earned him squat.

"You mean the true crime trash?" she'd asked knowingly, with a quick ponytail flip and a lazy eye roll. "Try aisle thirteen, right next to gay studies."

"That's kind of bad planning, isn't it?" he'd joked, sweat forming at his brow and eager for a little human contact after having spent so much time wandering the store alone.

"Not really," she responded, punching numbers into a calculator without looking back up at him. "We find the same kind of guy reads one as reads the other: White male, thirty-ish bordering on forty, thinning hair, reasonably physically fit, not overly so, college educated, middle income, marginal IQ, obsessed with cops."

Vinny caught his breath: Save for the thinning hair—he prided himself on his feathery brown mop—she'd just described him. All that was missing was for her to gaze up, wink, and say, "Sound familiar?"

She didn't.

Vinny felt robbed. So he headed over to aisle thirteen. In his hand was a half-finished Irish Mocha Java that had cost him most of six bucks at the bookstore's poser café. He felt stupid buying it, but when in Rome. It was either that or a $4 diet soda. He figured for two dollars more he'd at least try to look like he belonged here.

He wished he'd never come in the first place but his old part-ner—a damn good agent and new mother of a two-week-old baby girl, the reason for her mommy's long planned six-month maternity leave—had suggested, "If Frank Logan's gonna be your new partner, you might want to brush up on him. And what's the best way to brush up on a world famous, critically-renowned, bestselling author who just happens to have a famous criminalist's background? The bookstore, Vinny. You've got to get over your fear of bookstores on this one."

Truth be told, it wasn't a fear, exactly. More like an insecurity. Vinny had always been street smart, instead of book smart. Despite his *Sopranos* sounding name, however, he was no knuckle-scraping knee-breaker from the old neighborhood. True, he'd grown up in the shadow of the Big Apple, the third son in a family of six Italian-Americans, but his home had been a sleepy little burg in upstate New York, not the mean streets of Brooklyn.

He'd played baseball, football, and helped his old man out at the corner grocery store he ran for the better part of his seventy-eight years. His favorite shows growing up had always been *Adam-12*, *The Mod Squad*, and, though he'd rarely admit it these days, *CHIPS*.

His dad liked those shows, too. So much so that he'd set up a 13" black and white TV in the break room of his shop, a rare splurge for a man who wore his shoes till the toes showed and sold damaged bags of Oreos as "gourmet cake toppings" so as not to lose a cent on remainder items.

Together, the two would take turns keeping up with their latest episodes of the hit cops and robbers show of the day. Throughout the 70s and 80s, Vinny toiled away next to his father, proud to stand shoulder to shoulder with a real man. But come high school gradua-tion, as Vinny prepared to take his rightful place next to the old man behind the butcher counter, the elder Smalldeano had given him his walking papers.

"You go off to college, Vinny," he'd said. "Be a cop, like your heroes. I know you got it in ya. Here's some money I've been saving. Should be enough to get you squared away until that, whadda they call it? financial aid kicks in."

And so, with an envelope containing three thousand hard-earned dollars and a passion for cops and robbers, Vinny Smalldeano had headed off to the nearest state college, becoming the first in his family to get more than a high school diploma.

Even then, though, books scared him. In high school, he'd skipped by on his smooth Italian looks and even smoother reputation as a born athlete. Coaches, who doubled as nearly half of his teachers, passed him easily so he'd be available for play in whatever sport they were coaching. The rest of the teachers passed him just because he was so darn cute.

Four years of college had found him ready to apply for a position with the local PD back home when his roommate, a skinny Hispanic kid and "career student" with more degrees than he had pairs of shoes, squashed that idea: "Screw the locals. None of them have degrees, or they got 'em at night school. What you're looking for is the FBI. They're the ultimate cops and catch the ultimate robbers."

And so, here he was, thirteen years later, a respected veteran who'd nailed his share of bad guys while toiling at the Syracuse field office and, after six months of training under the elite umbrella of the SCCU, was at last headquartered in DC.

But even Vinny knew he was no Frank Logan, though his gorgeous wife of seven years, Tina, and even their two boys, Dirk and Vinny Jr., told him otherwise. Tina, a statuesque blonde he'd met at the Academy—she was in admissions, the cool, confident co-ed clerk to his inept, bumbling raw recruit—reminded him endlessly of his true mission in life. "You're the best there is at catching the bad guys, Vinny. I don't know if it was all that TV as a kid or what, but you don't learn what you do every day in a book. You learn it on the streets. And that's where you belong. Now go catch some bad guys!"

Still, even Tina had been star-struck when the brass had called him earlier that morning to tell Vinny who his new partner would be. "Frank Logan?" she'd squealed into the cell phone as Vinny drove to the nearest bookstore. "*The* Frank Logan. Oh my god, do you think it's bad form to ask for his autograph on the first day? You didn't, did you? But you will, right? For me and the boys, Vinny? Oh, and Shirley down the block. She loves it when they interview him on the Forensics Channel."

"I haven't met him yet," Vinny had explained. "He's on a case in North Carolina right now. I'm supposed to take the red-eye out tonight and meet him in South Carolina. No word why, or where, or when. No one told me why the newest recruit for the SCCU is being paired with its ranking member. All I know is that someone's supposed to meet me at the airport and bring me up to speed."

"So you're not coming home tonight?" she'd asked, heartbroken. It was Vinny Jr.'s sixth birthday, and ever since uprooting from all his old friends in Syracuse earlier that month, he'd been down in the dumps. "Sorry, forget I asked. He'll understand. We *always* understand." Even Tina's hopeful tone couldn't mask the biting sarcasm that lay underneath. "So where are you now?" she asked.

"I'm at the bookstore," he'd said, pulling into a space in the mammoth parking lot that fronted the mammoth, three story bookstore. "Getting some light reading for tonight's flight."

She'd laughed until he'd hung up.

And now he stood in front of the true crime section, deciding which of Frank Logan's latest bestsellers to purchase—***Fear of the Mind***: *How to Outwit the Criminal Thinker* or **In the Mind's Eye**: *Confessions of a Criminal Thinker*. He stared at the glossy author's photo on the back of each paperback and made his decision that way. One looked like a much younger Frank Logan, his trademark sunglasses poking out of the pocket of his tailored sports coat. The second looked like an older, wiser Frank Logan, sunglasses now firmly in place to hide the crow's feet and laugh lines he'd gained since his last author's photo shoot.

He bought them both.

He still couldn't tell which Frank Logan he liked best.

24

Detective Holly Madison listened as Frank Logan shouted orders into his sleek, futuristic-looking cell phone: "Ship those files to the new crime scene, stat." It was no easy task over the screaming of her detachable siren, currently piercing through traffic on the way to a small local airport on the other side of town, where a chartered helicopter awaited her VIP: Very Important Passenger.

"I was just *in* South Carolina," she heard Frank screech into the metallic flip-phone. "Why couldn't this happen a week ago?"

The awkward silence in the car—even the sirens seemed to quiet down for a moment or two—told both occupants the comment was in bad taste, even among cops, for whom gallows humor was not just a survival skill but a job requirement. "Sorry, Margie," Frank said, as he eyed Holly with a silent apology, the first time he'd glanced her way since they'd left the station house some ten minutes earlier. "That was awful of me. You know I didn't mean that."

There was some more ordering, some more apologizing, until Frank clicked the phone shut without so much as a "goodbye," or "thank you." "Christ," he sighed audibly as she let him vent. The radio in her Crown Victoria was tuned perpetually to the local classics station, muted on volume level three, where it trod the thin line between background music and soundtrack, depending on the situation. "What a *bitch*!"

Holly thought a moment, then risked actually speaking. "Who? Your assistant?"

It was the first time she ever saw Frank Logan laugh. "Yeah, well, her, too," he sighed after an outburst of uncharacteristic guffawing that softened his features and lightened his eyes. "But, no, I was actually referring to this case. Apparently, another body has just been found in South Carolina. Unfortunately, the witness who found the victim was some kid who threw up all over the maze.

"Do you have any idea how strong stomach acid is? We're lucky we found the maze at all, but the blood evidence, which we've been relying on so heavily up to this point, was completely eradicated. The kid's DNA markers are all over the thing. So now we've no idea if the maze was filled out with the victim's blood, the kid's blood, or *your* victim's blood. That, and the fact that she's a true Jane Doe, in every sense of the word.

"The first victim, in Florida, was found hours after her murder and easily identified. The next two were local news until they were found, and then family members rushed to identify them. But in this case, no one's gone missing in weeks and nobody's looking.

"So now, as if all we've had to contend with so far hasn't been bad enough, there's no way to establish the order of these victims. Is this guy killing by state, moving up the Eastern Coast? Or did he backtrack just to throw us off the trail?"

"Can't the Medical Examiner pinpoint time of death?" Holly ventured, proving once again that Frank Logan had not put his confidence in her in vain. "I mean, that way you'd know if she was killed before our victim or after. Right?"

"Generally speaking," Frank sighed, "yes. But as luck would have it, South Carolina experienced a sudden cold snap just after I left and the body was partially frozen when discovered. At first, the locals thought it was just rigor mortis, but when they cut into her they found ice crystals in her chest cavity. That means the M.E. can't pinpoint it within six hours, let alone six days. We've no way of knowing when she was killed. Was she Maze's third victim? Or his fourth? Shit, with this many victims in this tight of a time frame, she could have been his first for all we know."

Holly hadn't chauffeured too many high-profile FBI Directors around lately, but she was pretty sure this kind of stuff happened all the time. "Frank?" she asked tentatively as the airport finally appeared in the near distance. "Is there something…else…bothering you about this case? I mean, I know the order of the victims is important; I'm certainly not discounting that. I'm just wondering if maybe you're upset about something *other* than the order of the victims."

As Holly was waved through a clearance gate and directed toward an idle hangar, Frank Logan looked deeply into her eyes. For a moment, she was suspended, frozen in time, driving the narrow straightaway to the hangar on auto-pilot. She imagined for that split-second, that blinding instant, what the serial killers who sat across from Special Director Frank Logan felt as he interrogated them years after their crime, after they'd had enough time to grow bored spooking out the guards or other inmates and wanted something a little more...challenging...to fill their hours as they counted down their slow, dwindling days until lethal injection or the electric chair.

She was pinned to the driver's seat like a bug to a biologist's tray.

"You're right," he finally sighed as she regained her composure and pulled into the hangar, where a cordon of officers, both uniformed and plainclothes, state, local, and federal, awaited her very special cargo.

As they eagerly rushed the car, however, Frank Logan pressed his door lock and explained, "It's just that, the traveling, the case files, the jurisdictions, the days, the nights, the helicopters. It always seems the minute I'm getting to like someone, someone...special, some psychopath drags me away."

As fists groped for the passenger side door handle and gently tapped the window with tarnished police academy class rings to interrupt the brief interlude, Logan eyed Holly with the precision and passion that made him so focused. "I'm only sorry I didn't get to know you better," he whispered before unlocking the door, only to be whisked out by strong arms who were already handing him case files, faxes, and a metallic travel coffee mug full of liquid caffeine.

Frank Logan, who had cut his trip to Durham short by just shy of 36 hours, left his pretty detective liaison sitting in the driver's seat, staring after him, watching the long, purposeful strides he took toward the whirling blades of the all-black helicopter sitting across the hanger. He never looked back.

25

Gina stumbled into the all-night diner and waved at Basil, the chef with the golden spatula, and Gracie, the geriatric waitress with the golden touch. Both knew her by sight, by name, street name, anyway, by reputation, and greeted her warmly.

She was right on time.

"Regular, Sugar?" asked Gracie, pouring her a cup of black coffee in a mug so big you could practically swim laps in it.

"Please, Hon," Gina responded, pouring in five packs of sugar and spooning it softly without clinking the sides, an old habit she'd picked up ever since she ran away from home just three years earlier.

Her stepfather had stirred his coffee loudly. Morning, noon, night. Didn't matter. Only the sound remained. It clanged through the house, letting everyone know who was boss. "I'm stirring my coffee," he seemed to be saying with every loud clang against the side of the glass. "Hear that? And there's not a damn thing any of you can do about it. *Clink. Clink. Clink.* What's it mean? It means I'm up, I'm about, and you better watch out."

She did. Skulking through the house, avoiding him, clanging or no clanging. She got real quiet, real quick, the first day her mama brought him home. The leer in his eyes, the beer on his breath, the dirt under his fingernails, the bulge in his dirty coveralls. Gina knew he was trouble the minute she'd laid eyes on him.

But her mama? She was in love, and there was nothing to do but watch and wait for the other shoe to drop. When it did, right into her ribs that time she wasn't quite quick enough with the coffee pot—a costly "mistake" that left her pissing blood for three days—she knew it was time to go. It was only a matter of time before the kicking would lead to beating, then pounding, then midnight visits into her bedroom, the door locked, the pants down, the horror come home to roost at last. She might have been a straight C-student back then, but she was no dope. She'd read enough true crime books in her day to know what happened to the pretty, skinny, leggy stepdaughters when their mamas were working double-shifts down at the warehouse, plugging widgets into whatcha-ma-call-its to make gaily colored plastic toys for this Happy Meal or that prize bag.

She wasn't waiting around to become another child molestation statistic, that was for sure. Come midnight on Halloween, she broke open her piggy bank, socked away her candy, laid her Cat Woman costume out on the bed, and took off with little more than a backpack full of bite size Baby Ruths and a few thong panties, just in case.

She hadn't let her spoon clang against her coffee cup since.

Now, three years and seven hundred miles later, she worked the stroll by the refinery six nights a week. The hours were mean, the men were rough, but the money was good, and her profits were her own. The fact was, she had over three grand in the bank. More than enough for a bus ticket somewhere safe, clean, and quiet. More than enough for first and last month's rent and a few weeks off while she looked for a safe, dull, routine waitress job somewhere close by. More than enough for long, baggy jeans and clean cotton underwear and long-sleeve shirts and a quiet life of nun-like chastity and three showers a day, sans thongs.

"How many days and counting, Hon?" Gracie asked as she gently placed two pancakes and one fried egg on the scarred diner counter in front of the hungry hooker with the silent spoon.

"Just twelve more," Gina sighed, taking in the fresh smell of sweet batter and the sticky blueberry syrup that Gracie always kept warm just for her. "Found an apartment complex a couple hours away that takes cash. Looked it up on the Internet at the library. Went ahead and reserved myself a two-bedroom for six hundred bucks a month. Two bathrooms. I can switch if I get bored. You know, have a sunflower or watermelon theme in one. Maybe that palm tree and pineapple theme that's all the rage these days in the other. When I get tired of staring at sunflowers while I piss, I just get up and move over to palm trees and pineapples."

"Just make sure you're through doing your business before you get up," Gracie cackled with a nicotine chuckle, and watched as the skinny hooker devoured her meal in six quick bites. Even at that, she managed to wolf it down daintily. Gracie sighed and moved back behind the counter to watch as Gina sipped the rest of her coffee in sweet, albeit fleeting, abandon.

Of all the hookers who came in each night, and there were a dozen or so of them, Gina was the only one who seemed to want something more out of life than a fast buck, a spent condom, and her next score. Gracie had been on shift the first night Gina had come in, dazed and shaken after turning her very first trick. That night, the old gal had consoled the young one, even offering her a quick nip from the bottle of brandy she kept in her locker in the moldy break room. Gina had stirred it quietly into her coffee, the spoon never touching her mug once, even with her hands shaking to beat the band.

Gracie had been tempted to call the cops right then and there. Why, the girl didn't look a day over sixteen and, at that, not fit for these mean streets. Most of these other girls, well, you could tell they weren't fit for anything else. But Gina? She was special. She was one you couldn't forget. Still, there was nothing the old gal could do but sit and watch as Gina's greasy Italian pimp slammed in through the front door and dragged her back out onto the streets.

When Gracie went by to clear off her table that night, she nearly fainted when she found a tip. And not just any tip, but the whopper of the night: five whole bucks, folded into a neat square beneath the coffee cup. Gina had been in six nights a week ever since. Sometimes battered, sometimes high, sometimes bruised, sometimes shaken, but mostly just...numb.

Then, when her pimp was murdered in a drug deal gone bad a couple months back, it was as if all the shackles had been taken off. All the girls were free agents and seemed to blossom in the wake of his death, Gina in particular.

She'd even made Gracie a pledge: Three months, she'd said. Three months and as much money as I can save, and then I'm out of here. She was the first hooker Gracie had ever met who stuck by her word. And now it was twelve days and counting. Gracie watched as Gina hustled out into the mid-October cold, a brisk wave thrown over her shoulder as a shiny silver Rent-a-Car slid up to the curb.

The old gal sidled over to the table, no longer surprised to see a crisp five folded over beneath her coffee cup, her plates clean, stacked, and waiting. *Twelve days and counting*, she thought. *I'm sure gonna miss her. She's not going to be easily forgotten, that one.*

26

Maze knew it was time. Time for another one. More specifically, time for a useless one. The others had been strategic, calculated, careful, logical, and progressive. Connecting the dots, he'd gone according to plan. His plan. The only one that truly mattered.

He'd seen the plan in his head for years now, but only just recently—thanks to certain events in his professional life—had he been fortunate enough to put it into action. And even so, he'd never been sure the plan would work.

Killing? That he'd done before.

Serial killing? Or as the politically correct language du jour referred to it, Special Circumstance Murders? Yeah, he'd done those, too. Only no one had ever found out about those.

Now he was ready, willing to risk it all for the sake of his grand design, his murderous masterpiece, and so far so good. Sure, there were a few glitches. The kid with the queasy constitution and extra-strength stomach acid in South Carolina. The wily detective in North Carolina who'd found that body just a tad too early.

But all in all, it was just like he'd pictured it in his head. Even the name they'd given him was fitting: The Maze Murderer. Or, shortened for higher readability scores and more papers sold: just plain "Maze." Even in this day and age of celebrity killers and inmate interviews, it was still kinda hard to forget *that* one.

But now it was time to turn up the heat and make it harder on the Feds, the locals, the reporters, the talking heads on CNN. He'd been given credit for the other murders. Even with all the variables thrown in, he'd been satisfied that, within weeks, his mazes had been discovered but his pattern hadn't.

Now it was time to disrupt the flow.

Get dirty.

Get difficult.

So he took to the streets. There'd been no time to case this one. No research done, no tidbits of information gleaned from tailing her around town or digging into the local high school yearbooks or scouring the Internet. Too busy with traveling back and forth to work, with the necessary hunt, with the kills. But some things never changed and, besides, it wasn't the first hooker he'd killed.

It certainly wouldn't be the last.

He stopped at a local Pump and Pay first. Low-rent. Dirty parking lot. No slots for your ATM card at the pumps. Not the kind of place to have surveillance cameras behind the register and, even if they did, not the kind of place to save them indefinitely in the squalid break room with the fading pin-up pictures and giveaway hardware calendars.

By this time tomorrow, even if he was surreptitiously taped, his image, in the gray hooded sweatshirt, baggy jeans, and running shoes he'd paid cash for at a K-Mart three interstate exits back, would be long since taped over. He smiled, paying cash again as he bought a double-sized Styrofoam cup worth of soda and two tall boy Coors Lights. The pert teenager behind the cash register rang up his sale with gusto, or as much gusto as one could at 1:55 a.m. on a grim October morning. "Kinda cutting it close, aren't you, mister?" she asked through lips overdone with blue raspberry lipstick, slurring her words as her dull eyes bored into him, expecting a reply to her cashier chatter.

"It's all in the timing, young lady," he said hoarsely.

"Enjoy 'em," she said as he prepared to walk out into the empty parking lot, holding her life in his hands as he wavered at the front door.

"Oh, I will," he replied over his shoulder, sparing her.

She went back to her *Jet* magazine, none the wiser.

Around the corner he dumped the soda and replaced it with the containers of both beer cans. Sucking greedily at his straw, the pressures of the day—the phone calls, the faxes, the last-minute economy flight—evaporated as he headed straight to the local strip. The beer was gone by the time he found the red light district, a seedy little runway just south of a grimy industrial park brightly lit by the security lamps of an all-night refinery that belched God knows what from its smoke stacks out over the local citizens as they slept, none the wiser, in their single futons.

He found an 80s rock station and turned it up, crumpling the beer cans in the rental car and folding them between the seats where they would be sure to brush up beside his thigh later and remind him to throw them away.

The maze was safely locked in the glove box, along with the vial of blood from his last victim. An old-fashioned feather pen, bought for pennies at a flea market but nonetheless effective at solving dime store mazes with sticky gore, completed the triumvirate awaiting his latest victim. He found her by sheer physical selection: Her height made her a stand-out amongst the shorter, thicker tramps trolling the street in fishnet stockings and day-glow thongs barely hidden beneath too-short leather skirts.

He rolled down the passenger side window and breathed in a rush of cheap perfume before her perky breasts pushed playfully against her tight tube top in the space just above the door handle. He gave her a quick but astute once over: greasy hair, bad skin, ribs show-ing, lipstick on her teeth, still-healing needle marks on the arms, poorly hidden with cover-up Clearasil, and the greedy scent of des-peration.

A blue daub of pancake syrup tugged at her thick, young lips. A cheap gold necklace spelled out the name "Gina." This was no hooker with a heart of gold working to feed six kids back at the battered spouse shelter. This was a skank no one would miss.

Perhaps, if he was lucky, for months.

27

Frank Logan looked at the familiar Beverly Hills area code flashing in his cell phone window and grimaced. "What now?" he mumbled to himself, causing the corpulent teenager behind the Taco Bell counter to point back at herself in a concerned, *Who me?* gesture. He shook her off with a hand gesture, tapping a button to mute the ringing phone.

"Sorry," he said, paying for the grande burrito especiale combo with cash. "Don't you hate people who bring their cell phones into restaurants?" He was hoping for a quick resolution to his phone faux pas but instead only dug himself a deeper hole.

She frowned, nodding out at the sea of lunch-rush customers and commenting, "If'n I did, I'd be plumb out of business, sir."

He nodded, red-faced, and brought his plastic tray full of empty calories out to a postage-stamp-sized courtyard featuring four plastic picnic tables, each sporting a bell-shaped umbrella.

He was famished and realized he hadn't eaten all day. Even the famously amiable media darling got irritable when his blood sugar dropped, and his was currently in the basement. Not a good time to call your agent back.

He watched pick-up trucks, trucks with pick-up, and more pick-up trucks lumber by on the small town's main drag as the lunch rush, such as it was, slowly wound down. He sipped slowly at his soda, ate his meal even slower, and when it was over, longed for a cigarette. He had a stick of gum instead.

"Bernie," he said when the super agent picked up on the second ring. "What's going on?"

"What's going on?" Bernie practically shrieked, and Frank could picture him in his office, a stress ball in one hand and a trade paper in the other, one of those high-tech earpieces stuck fast to his head. "What's going on? You tell me. I'm flying all over the country, traveling hither and yon, leaving messages for you in three states, and this is the first time you've called back in 16 hours? 16 hours, Frank. That's a lifetime in this business. I don't have to tell you that, right?"

Frank rolled his eyes, saying, "It's an active investigation, Bernie. I know what you want when you call. And I can't give it to you. Not yet. You know that. Never have I commented on an active investigation, not for the next book proposal, not to excerpt in the new hardcover, not ever. Know why? Because while you may *think* it's life or death if we sell the next book, *I know* it's life or death to these women. How many times do we have to have this conversation, Bern?"

"As many times as it takes, brother. As many times as it takes. I'm not asking for the specifics, Frank. Just the broad strokes. The basics. I can't pitch the series if I don't...."

"What are you pitching the series for anyway, Bernie? I thought I put the kibosh on that in LA. We've got the film coming out next year; you won that fight. The new paperback comes out just in time for Christmas gift-giving, and what a lovely stocking stuffer that will make. The book that's in hardback now will come out in soft cover just in time for summer reading next year, followed by the movie tie-in with the new cover. Aren't you afraid of getting overexposed?"

"Overexposed? Overexposed? Who are you all of a sudden, Paris Hilton? This is what we've worked for, to become overexposed. You know what overexposure becomes, Frank?"

"I dunno, Bernie. Annoying. Repetitive. Redundant. Meaningless."

"It becomes permanent, Frank. It lasts forever. The books, the movies, the TV, the print, it sticks around. Sticks like glue. And suddenly the guy who wrote a few true crime books becomes a legend, and legends don't die, Frank. Nor do their bank accounts, if you get my drift. Don't you want permanence, Frank? Don't you want immortality?"

"Not at the cost of an innocent victim, Bernie. I just can't give you details. Read the papers. I know you got 'em there. Don't just scan them, read them. We can't give the reporters everything, but we give them enough. Should be enough for you too, my buddy, my pal. If it's not enough for these TV people, then...."

"They're not just *any* TV people anymore, Frank. They're the Forensics Network. I just got off the phone with the execs, and they're hot for you, man. Salivating. Drooling. Leaving DNA evidence all over the fucking place! You know why? Because of this case, Frank. Because it's current. They want you for a mid-season replacement in the spring. And they're offering half a million. Still think what the local rags are printing is enough? I need more than enough. I need what the guys down at the network can't read for themselves in the paper. I've got to go there knowing I'm the inside source. I've got to prove it to them, Frank, and if I can't, I'm afraid we...."

"Half a million dollars?" Frank asked. Even he, a man of few words, had to hand it to the kid from Beverly Hills. "For one series? Or am I missing something? Is that for, like, three or four years?"

For the first time in a long time, Bernie Segal laughed. Long. Hard. Loud. Genuine. It trilled through the cell phone, traveling the miles on a mellifluous note that made Frank smile, despite the fact that the laughter was no doubt at him, not with him. "For one series, Frank? Who do you think you're dealing with here? That's per episode, my man. Per episode. Now, what can you give me?"

An awkward pause followed while Frank did the numbers.

Then he sang; sang like a canary.

28

At long last, Vinny Smalldeano was face to face with the legend himself. And not just on the back cover of one of his book jackets, either. In fact, they were in the lobby bar of a mid-priced Holiday Inn in a tiny town called Carrington, South Carolina.

It was an awkward meeting, to say the least, but Vinny had braced himself with one of the small bottles of rum in his hotel room before slipping into a casual sport coat, crisp khaki slacks, and an even crisper white Oxford shirt, no tie, before heading downstairs for their inevitable rendezvous.

It hadn't been planned, of course. He had no idea if the one, the only, Frank Logan was even expecting him. He'd just been told to "find Frank" via a brusque recording on his hotel phone three minutes after he'd checked into his room.

"Find Frank," he'd muttered over and over during a ten-minute shower.

"Find Frank," he'd muttered into the mirror as he blew-dry his ink black hair, curling the graying edges back behind his ears. He could get them colored once he arrived back home.

"Find Frank," he'd muttered into the mini-bar as he went back and forth between a Scotch and soda and a rum and Coke. The flight from DC, where he'd been fully briefed and credentialed for his new assignment, no doubt to the chagrin of a dozen senior agents he'd leap-frogged over to get this assignment, had left him fagged out, so he opted for a quick Cuba Libra, sans lime.

Caffeine and booze, the perfect mix for the frequent flyer.

"Find Frank," he'd chewed over his ice as he downed the drink in three quick slurps, gesturing to the empty room with his empty glass, as if perfecting a soliloquy for this particular dress rehearsal.

"Find Frank," he'd whispered in the elevator on the way downstairs, breathing into his hand to see if the alcohol was too overpowering. Just to be sure, he snapped off two chalky white breath mints from a roll he'd found sequestered in his rarely-worn sports coat. They were so old that, when he bit into them, they barely made a crunching sound. He'd swallowed them both by the time the elevator stopped in the lobby.

And now, voila, he'd found him. (Or was it *Him*? If Vinny were to believe the various credentials, accomplishments, and hype woven throughout his "about the author" blurbs, it would most certainly be the latter.)

Seated at a table for two, examining what appeared to be glossy black and white crime scene photos in a darkened corner, perhaps the most famous living, current FBI director sat nursing a gin and tonic, a pile of lemon twists telling Vinny he was no teetotaler. Frank was talking on a sleek-looking cell phone, barking orders at someone on the other end. Vinny tried not to eavesdrop, but the bar wasn't that big. It was only when he heard the names "John Walsh" and "Bill O'Reilly" that his ears perked up.

"I'll be here for another day or two, Bernie," Frank Logan said into the cell. "It just can't be helped. You of all people should know that by now. Unless they can interview me on location, there's not much I can do about it. I'll be back at the bureau in 72 hours, unless this schmuck strikes again.

"What do you want me to do? Tell 'em if they can accommodate me, I'll send 'em a few sample chapters from the new book. Exclusive, of course? Right. Exclusive to both of them. Call me later if you're still on the road scouting sights for the next TV special, I'm supposed to meet my new partner in a few. Ciao."

The cell phone flipped closed. Frank took a drink, immediately switching from bestselling author mode to FBI Director.

"Frank Logan?" Vinny asked after a quick swipe of his sweaty palm on his crisp, new khakis.

"Yes?" The Director didn't look up.

"Vinny Smalldeano, sir." Vinny hemmed and hawed, eyeing the bartender as if he could somehow deliver him from the uncomfortable silence greeting his introduction. "I'm, uh, well...."

"My new partner," Frank said calmly, finally standing up and revealing that the pictures on the table weren't crime scene photos, after all, but head shots from Vinny's own confidential FBI file. "Yes, I've been expecting you. Sorry if you overheard any of that name-dropping on the phone. I know I sound like a schmuck, but my agent's the only civilian with my cell phone number and travel itinerary, and it's with good reason."

The two men shook hands. Not overly firm, not limp, but just firm enough. The perfect FBI handshake. Testing each other. Feeling each other out. Putting all of that profiling to good use.

They released hands almost simultaneously, a good sign, Vinny thought, and Frank caught the attention of the bartender with a practiced nod of his head. "Another for myself, Pete, and, wait, lemme guess, a Cuba Libra for my friend here?"

Vinny couldn't help but laugh, spotting the open laptop on the unoccupied seat across from Frank. "What'd you do, download my room charges already?"

Frank returned the grin. "Hardly," he said. "There's a splash of cola on your collar and the faint aroma of rum on your breath."

"Oh geez," Vinny groaned, trying to eye his own collar like a dog chasing his tail. He finally gave up. "Is this how it's going to be? Me the bumbling Watson to you the genius Sherlock Holmes?"

Frank removed the laptop so Vinny could sit down. "Hardly," Frank said, surreptitiously closing Vinny's file as well. "But I should say the same of you. From your files here, I'm quite impressed. Few agents rise so high so fast."

Vinny's BS meter went off at full-tilt. "Sure you have the right file there, Frank? I've been a senior agent precisely 2.7 years longer than most of my peers. I blame it on my family ties, not wanting to travel to all those hot spots the footloose and fancy-free younger agents don't mind packing off to, but I guess I just prefer the *Washington Post*."

Frank nodded at the old joke.

The bartender came, delivering their drinks and a fresh bowl of smoked almonds as he expertly removed the pile of curled lemon shavings from the middle of the table. Vinny absently wondered how many times he'd done that so far tonight. Vinny grabbed his drink and took a bigger swallow than he intended. It was all he could do not to cough it up like a dazzled freshman during Hell Week.

Seated across from Frank Logan, Vinny couldn't help but feel like the student at his teacher's knee. Still, he was surprised by Frank's pleasant demeanor and willingness to share.

All the way to South Carolina, Vinny had expected Frank's gruff exterior to match his gruff tone. He'd been thrust on partners before, always the bridesmaid, never the bride, only to find resentment, turf wars, and vague insecurities that surfaced quicker than a submarine in a Tom Clancy movie.

But Frank was open, warm, and immediately off-putting.

Vinny questioned it immediately. To himself, anyway.

By his third drink, he was brave enough to begin voicing his questions aloud. "Why the warm reception, Frank?" he asked after a particularly satisfying handful of smoked almonds. "I mean, aren't you the slightest bit apprehensive about taking on a new partner?"

Frank gave his best "pshaw" look, a well-practiced and wizened grin framed by arched eyebrows and plenty of hard-won laugh lines. "I look at this way, Vinny…. Is that your real name, Vinny? I mean, is that what I'm supposed to call you?"

"Vinny." He nodded. "Right. That's it."

"It's not Vincent?" Frank asked, chewing his ice calculatedly. "Vincenzo?"

"Just Vinny."

"From birth?"

"What? My birth certificate isn't in my jacket, Frank. It's Vinny. Straight-up. Always has been, always will be. You can call me Vin, if you like. My last partner did. When she was mad at me, that is."

"Well, Vinny," Frank sighed, pushing his last drink of the night away only half-finished. "I'm not mad at you. Fact is, I need you. I'm not as young as I once was. Not as spry, not as quick. Plus I've grown a little too fond of my evening nightcap, if you know what I mean. And between the traveling, the book-signings for my latest release, wrangling with the media, I barely get four hours of sleep a night as it is.

"Cases like this one, Vinny, they take it out of you. I'm not speaking down to you, get that straight right up front. That's not what I do. If I get carried away, sound like I'm pontificating, so be it. Fact is, we don't have much time for that whole 'getting to know you' grace period other partners get."

"Instead you read my file?" Vinny asked, welcoming Frank's hard edges and relieved to finally be past the way-too-pleasant BS stage of the meeting.

Frank smirked. "What? You didn't check out one of my books on the plane, huh?"

Vinny laughed out loud and shrugged by way of answer. "Try two," he finally admitted.

"Right," Frank said. "So you know me, I know you. Good. Point is, this is your first *real* Special Circumstances case. I'm not saying you haven't handled multiple kills yet, I know you have. But those weren't so special. A double murder here, a murder-suicide there, a spree kill or two, I'm not discounting those cases of yours at all. But they're not called 'special' circumstances for nothing.

"There are lots of agents in DC. Why'd I pick you for this assignment? Why'd you rise to the top over all the other guys I hand-selected for my team? Dunno. Can't explain it. Call it instinct, call it beginner's luck. Then again, maybe I just didn't want someone jaded by one too many SCCU cases. Point is: You're here. I'm here. We're together. No sour grapes here. At least not on my part.

"You're smart enough to come off wary, looking sharp, bright-eyed. I'm smart enough to take advantage of a younger agent who's survived this long in one of the backstabbingest, most political agencies in the country. So that tells me a few things. You're quiet, don't make waves, do your job, know how to fly under the radar. Good things all.

"You also partnered with a woman, tells me a few other things. You can put up with a temper; you're a good listener, not moody, good-natured. More good things. You're here. On time. I've got your flight schedule here. Got in exactly 42 minutes ago. That's just enough time for a shuttle ride over, check your messages, take a shower, make yourself a drink, and boogie down here. Didn't go to dinner first. Call your wife. Rent a movie. Take a nap. Whatever. You show up, stand straight, shake hands, and get down to business. It's what I need. It's what *you* need. Trust me, you work one of these cases all the way through to the end, whether you catch this mug or not, you're set for life, Vinny. Talk about a trial by fire.

"And you're with me now. *We're* working this case. By the time I'm through with you, you'll be doing this in your sleep. Trust me. And it's not an idle threat. Or a compliment. To me *or* you.

"Get a good night's sleep tonight, Vinny. It'll be your last. You think you've seen crime scene photos before? Think again. Think you've been up against hard-asses? Think again. Think your last partner could be a bitch? Think again. I'm telling you now, a few drinks in, to save us both some ego moments tomorrow when we're both bright and bushy-tailed and dealing with the locals: I'm in charge here. It's not blustering, posturing, whatever. I'll give you the same speech I give the locals: There's no time for training. You keep up or ship out.

"I say jump, you say how high. I say duck, you duck without looking for stray bullets. You listen, you watch, you learn, you take notes, you fetch coffee. We're both men here. We both drink coffee. I don't have time to get it. You will. It's that simple. I'm not on a power trip, I'm not pulling rank, I just know more than you do and it's gonna take both of us at top speed to take this sucker down.

"The order of priorities is simple on this one: My first allegiance is to the victims, past, present, and most of all future. My second allegiance is to the FBI, in general, and the SCCU, in particular. My third is to you."

Frank paused, reconsidered his half-finished drink, and finished it off in one swig.

"Anything else?" Vinny asked with a slight edge to his voice.

"Good," Frank said. "You're more than slightly annoyed, less than actually pissed. Any other reaction, I'd worry about your integrity, your commitment, hell, even your manhood. It's good to be pissed, but don't be pissed at me." Frank sighed as he handed Vinny a thick file. "Be pissed at *him*."

With that, Frank stood up, leaving Vinny with half a bowl of smoked almonds and the Maze Murderer file. He wondered if Vinny knew it was the first time the file had left his hands since it had landed on his desk.

He had a feeling that he did.

29 Frank smiled to see Vinny's head still buried in the case file at breakfast the next morning. It was six a.m., and it looked like Vinny was already on his second cup of coffee. Only the edges of his thick, dark hair were still wet, and a menu and overturned coffee cup on a plain white saucer sat across from him.

"Waiting for the old man to get up, huh, Vinny?" Frank asked, hair as damp as his suit was crisp.

"Naw," Vinny said with a smile, glad to take a break from the grim measurements and deadly statistics he'd been devouring for the last two hours. "I saw you in the gym when I came through the lobby this morning."

"On your way in from a morning jog, no doubt." Frank smirked, then signaled the waitress for a cup of coffee as the two partners engaged in a little one-upmanship. "Two miles or three, my boy?"

"Make that four, old man," Vinny cracked, covering his cup so the waitress wouldn't top him off. The two shared a good laugh before ordering eggs and bacon, no toast.

"I'm an evening runner myself," Frank said after his first sip. "But I have to admit," he added after his second, "I only run to drink."

"How's that?" Vinny asked.

"Well," the senior agent confessed, looking around as if a future biographer might be lurking next to the Belgian waffle stand. "After my second wife walked out on me, I realized I might have a slight drinking problem. So I made a pact with myself: I could only drink on those days I ran, and I could only drink one drink per mile."

Vinny was busy adding up the curled lemon twists from their meeting the previous night. "Wow, Frank, you must have run a marathon yesterday!" he quipped good-naturedly.

"Fuck you, pal," Frank spat, nearly choking on his third sip of coffee. "But, yes, first thing I do in a new town is run until I can barely get back. Best cure for jet lag known to man. Plus it gives you a feel for the town, you know? How many churches? How many titty bars? That kind of thing. Then, when the locals get holier-than-thou on you at your first meet and greet, you know who's full of shit and who's not."

Vinny nodded, sensing that the bonding period was now officially over. A short lull, another cup of coffee for Frank, and breakfast arrived. The two men ate quickly, in short bursts and contemplative silence. When Vinny looked up from his empty plate, he could tell Frank was finally ready to get down to business.

He couldn't, however, tell whether he was relieved or disappointed.

"Tell me about the file," Frank said, stacking their plates for the waitress so they could have more room.

Vinny nodded. He'd been expecting this. "Gut reaction is he's far from through," he began, tapping the unopened file folder with which he'd become so familiar of late. "It's like he's restless, moving around. No, not just moving around, moving *toward* something. Something…specific. It's like he's got a game book, and we're only seeing a few pages."

"Is it a big playbook?" Frank prodded, swirling cream and sugar into a fresh cup of coffee he'd never finish.

"Huge," Vinny nodded. "Could be as big as all 50 states."

Frank nodded. "What about the mazes? Why wasn't that your first gut reaction?"

"They're important," Vinny said, getting a faraway look in his eye. "But I have a feeling they're more for us than for him. Like this guy's watched too much TV and figures he's supposed to have a signature, you know. Like he'd be letting us down if he didn't do what the most famous killers did. Like a celebrity who writes a book because he thinks he should."

Vinny snapped back to reality. "Oh, sorry Frank."

Frank laughed. "Don't be. My literary agent isn't. And my accountant's not, either. Go on."

Vinny stopped blushing and continued. "You're right, this *is* my first multiple, but I've sat in rooms with killers before. Real killers. And I knew this wasn't their first. That they'd hidden 'em, those first ones, and hidden 'em good. They all had a hunger that was insatiable. They all got off on it. This guy? I get the feeling the endgame is more important than the blood and guts. Like he's just doing this to get our attention, and only so he guarantees himself a private meeting with the one and only Frank Logan."

Frank nodded, duly impressed. He listened intently as Vinny went on: "I have a theory about the mazes, Frank. Don't stomp on my neck if I'm wrong here, but I don't think the mazes are random. I'm reading the files last night, and my first thought is to arrange them chronologically. I took the hotel stationery and put the state abbreviation on the outside of each folder.

"It's like he's working his way up the east coast. Like we shouldn't be here, we should already be in Virginia, waiting for him there. I think the mazes are road signs, not clues. That's what I think."

"And what if he turns left, Vinny?" asked Frank. "What if we find a girl with a maze sticking out of her nose in Mississippi? Or New Mexico? What if one of the mazes is a map? What if he's following his own twisted maze?"

"I thought of that," Vinny nodded, pushing away his coffee. He was too high on the adrenaline of the mental chase to partake of the brewed variety. "But none of the mazes matched up. None were linear enough. They all zigged when he zagged. Went north when he went south. Even upside down, flipped over, turned sideways, or folded in half there was no correlation to any kind of map."

Frank nodded. "So what we're left with is that old Catch-22: We don't want him to kill again, but we actually *need* him to kill again before we can catch him."

Vinny nodded back. "I don't think we have long to wait, Frank."

Frank sighed, signaling the waitress for the check as Vinny reached for his wallet. "Me either, Vinny. Me either."

30

Bernie Segal was watching three of the five TVs that dominated the bookshelves across from his desk. It was lunchtime, and his dutiful assistant, Guy (pronounced "Gee") Junger had just delivered a plastic to-go box full of bright and vibrant raw fish straight from Bernie's—and the rest of Hollywood's—favorite sushi bar.

It had taken Guy an hour to pick up the food, even though he'd faxed Bernie's order in, as usual, by 9 a.m. that morning. He didn't mind, though. Standing in a winding queue between Brad's personal assistant and Spielberg's PA, he was in pretty good company.

After twenty minutes of gossip about their respective bosses, Guy was more than willing to dish the dirt on Bernie's star client and notorious killer catcher, Frank Logan.

"I don't know how Bernie does it," Guy had bragged. "It's like he and Frank share this crazy Clarice Starling and Hannibal Lecter type connection. The minute a body shows up, I try to get to work early to man the phones, knowing the press is going to be all over Frank and asking for interviews, but Bernie's already there, funking up my headset with his cheap cologne as he tries to answer the phones. That's when he's even in town."

Guy had left his fellow PA's impressed as they all went their separate ways, clutching signature boxes containing rows and rows of expensive raw fish pricey enough to take a hefty chunk out of their weekly paychecks, had they been paying for it themselves.

In LA, office space was at a premium and everyone on the street was either a PA or a secretary returning to the office, carrying varying assortments of three-hundred-dollar lunches. Making his own way back, Guy munched on a breath mint snatched from the crystal bowl on the hostess stand.

Now here he was, watching LA's top literary agent tear into a portable buffet of delicacies as his stomach growled and he wondered if there would be any left when it came time to toss it into the trash.

The expensive watch on Bernie's arm ticked away the moments until the noon flood of all-day news coverage heated up, and in anticipation, Bernie flicked his open chopsticks at the bank of TVs that sat among his client's bestsellers, doing his best aging Harry Potter imitation. Like magic, the first one, then another, then the next, flicked to life with the same tragic scenes: a string of family snapshots detailing the nearly half-dozen victims now attributed to what the media had dubbed "The Maze Murderer." CNN, MSNBC, the Forensics Channel—they all led the lunch hour with the case. Frank's case.

"Guy," he spat around a mouthful of imported raw tuna, his deep, penetrating voice slicing through the open door to his assistant's desk just on the other side. "I can't believe how well this is all playing into our hands. Little did I know when I set Frank's latest book up for release this Halloween that this kind of shit would hit the proverbial fan. I must be a fucking mind-reader. We've got to capitalize on all this free publicity.

"For now, get me the producers at Scarborough Country, the Abrams Report, that new Norville show, and the guy who does the countdown. What's his name? Uberman? Overalls? For the life of me I can never remember his name."

"Sure, Bernie," Guy said, a surprisingly non-effeminate personal assistant dressed impeccably in the latest metro-sexual fashions. His spiked hair was outdone only by his cobalt blue glasses and dyed blond goatee. "Who's first?"

"First?" Bernie asked, flexing his chopsticks in the direction of the flickering bank of sleek TVs at the precise moment in which Frank Logan stepped forward from a mass of uniformed officers and rumpled detectives to answer a reporter's question. "You see this coverage? Fuck first, get 'em all on the line at the same time. They should be calling *me* at this point, shit."

Guy hesitated, and then pressed a button on the cord attached to the sleek silver headphone perpetually glued into his ear. "Yes," he spoke sternly as someone answered on the other end, "Bernie Segal for Debra Norville, please."

More clicks, more requests:

"Bernie Segal for Joe Scarborough, please."

"Bernie Segal for Keith Olbermann, please."

"Bernie Segal for Catherine Crier, please."

Bernie sat, smug and satisfied amidst his favorite aromas: desperation, achievement, raw tuna, aromatic ginger, and pungent wasabi. Frank Logan, the only working FBI Special Director with balls enough to write bestsellers about his cases while he was *still* working them, had long since left the airwaves, but the impression remained: The Maze Murderer, or "Maze" as most TV anchors now simply referred to him, was the country's mass murderer du jour.

Wait, that's the wrong terminology, Bernie thought as he downed the last of his fresh conch, chopsticks flicking like nunchucks in his deft hands. *What is Frank always telling me the new buzzword is? Ah, that's right: Special circumstances killer.*

Whatever it was, Maze was it. And Frank was the man who would catch him.

Bernie's eyes fell to the left of the TVs, to the shelf that held his hottest-selling titles. Among the Pulitzer Prize winners, actresses, hookers, and prosecutors whose books had topped the bestseller lists for weeks, sat copies of Frank's books. Each profiled a case in which Frank had used his decades of experience, quick thinking, worn shoe leather, and plenty of good luck to bring a savage killer to justice. The spines held both the killer's nicknames and the titles of Frank's latest bestsellers: The Funhouse Killer, a deranged psycho who stalked the country's carnivals looking for marks to, quite literally, scare to death.

The Pillowcase Strangler, a vicious and cunning killer whose pillowcases left little evidence needed to track him back to his job at a Manhattan Bed, Bath and Beyond. And Bernie's favorite, The Mile-High Murderer, a ballsy assassin who took the famed Mile-High Club to a new level by first raping, then killing his victims just before landing.

And his client, Frank Logan, had caught them all. Single-handedly, most of the time. His new partner, what was his name? Vinny something or other? A good-looking kid who would add a little much-needed sex appeal to the Maze Murderer book jacket when it was finally released next year. Too bad there was no time to get the good-looking Vinny on Frank's upcoming Halloween hardcover release, but maybe there'd be time to squeeze him onto the paperback next summer.

"Well," Bernie sighed as he pushed his empty lunch box aside for Guy to dispose of later. "Vinny might do some fancy footwork along the way, but I've no doubt that it will be Frank calling the shots when they slap on the cuffs."

"Corrine from the Norville Show is on 2, Bernie," Guy said, simultaneously interrupting Bernie's post-lunch reverie and clicking the cord to his headset twice to receive another call.

Bernie smiled and picked up the phone, preferring to be hands-on, "old school," as opposed to plugging some damn headset into his ear. "Corrine, Bernie Segal here. How do you feel about doing a remote with Frank Logan on this Maze Murder thing? Exclusive? Of course you'll be exclusive, dear. This is Bernie Segal you're talking to here."

31

For the second time in a week, Vinny Smalldeano was back in a bookstore. He couldn't remember how long it had been before that. One year? Two? No, three. Three years, and that was only because he'd had to get his wife that dream journal she'd been squawking about for Christmas three years earlier.

One bookstore. Three years. And now he'd been in two bookstores in a single *week*. He stiffened as the line of customers slowly dwindled. Now there were only three people left in front of him. Plenty of time for someone to shout out, "Hey, Vinny? Didn't you wait until first grade to learn how to read? Don't they teach that in, like, preschool or something?"

It didn't help that Frank had sent him to the biggest Barnes and Noble in all of South Carolina. The thing was three full floors of nothing but books. Rows and rows of them. Hardcover. History. Biography. Textbooks. Workbooks. You name it, this place had it.

He smirked, imagining Frank addressing yet another conference room full of "yokel locals" as he called them, filling them in on just enough details to help him solve the case, and leaving out just enough to keep them focused only on their victim, not the teenager down in Daytona or the mother of two in Durham.

"What about me?" Vinny had asked like a petulant schoolboy after two days spent joined at the hip with Frank at the crime scene. "What am I supposed to do while you interrogate the local boys about clues? Make nice with the coroner?"

"Try the bookstore," Frank had said, writing the address down on a page from his little black notebook and ripping it off for Vinny's sake. "I need to start getting a feel for these mazes. Where do they come from? Who publishes them? Are they local? National? International? You need to get the skinny on that and, until we're back at home base, if ever, a bookstore's as good a place to start as any."

And so here Vinny was, standing next in line to talk to another fresh-faced, perky bookstore clerk in another bookstore. *Where will all this end?* he thought wryly as the old geezer in front of him harangued the young lady because he couldn't find Andy Rooney's latest volume of wrinkled wit. "This case has already taken me into two bookstores. Will I have to attend the ceremony for this year's Pulitzer Prize before it's all over?"

"Try Popular Culture, sir," the co-ed cashier said in response to the crusty senior citizen. "You'll find that over in aisle eight."

"Who the hell put it there, missy?" the old codger asked. "He used to be in the History section. And before that, he was in Biography."

"Quite right, sir," she replied diplomatically. "But since he's so entrenched with *60 Minutes* now, he's considered entertainment and, unfortunately, entertainment goes in Pop Culture so, for now, that's where you'll find him."

"Where will he be next?" grumbled the old man to no one in particular as he trudged off toward aisle eight. "Do-it-yourself? That's all I seem to do around here. Do everything for myself!"

"Try the obituaries," Vinny muttered under his breath, or so he thought.

"That's terrible, sir." The cashier giggled, motioning him forward with long, elegant hands that hadn't seen the sun for weeks, if not months. He was struck by how closely their milky-white paleness resembled the pages of Frank's latest book, still resting only half-read on his hotel room nightstand.

Coincidence? he thought as he stepped forward to lean on her spotless counter.

"My grandmother's the same way," she went on. "Thinks Andy Rooney's the only writer worth reading these days. Well, he and Tom Brokaw, that is."

"What about Dan Rather?" Vinny asked.

"Tom's more handsome," she whispered conspiratorially. "At least, according to my mom, anyway."

Vinny nodded knowingly. "I figured you for a Matt Lauer type," he said with a wink, noticing that her nametag said, "Audrey."

Audrey, he thought. *Perfect. What a pale, perfect name….*

She laughed. Prettily. Playfully. A laugh so full of promise it was almost bulging. Making him twist his wedding ring nervously as the old temptations of life on the road came back to haunt him. She didn't seem to notice the thick gold band on his thick hairless finger, instead gazing into his eyes as she awaited his question.

Attention to customer service? he wondered in response to her expectant smile. *Or just me?*

In a dozen years of marriage, he'd never been unfaithful to his beautiful wife, Tina, and yet how many nameless, faceless stewardesses, concierges, clerks, cashiers, or co-eds had caught his eye as he traveled from case to case, town to town, city to city in all that time?

He wiped the thought from his mind, reveled in the fact that there was no one in line behind him, and posed his question to the helpful, attentive clerk with the pale hands, deep green eyes, and quick, young smile. "Maze books?" he asked, leaning forward on an arm still sore from his morning workout. Even he couldn't help but smell the waft of semi-expensive cologne as he shifted position, his firm chest pressing against his ever-present cotton Oxford and striped prep school tie. "What can you tell me about them?"

She smiled seductively, leaning forward. "Why do you want to know?" she asked, startling him. He wasn't quite ready to flash her his badge just yet. "I'm not trying to be rude," she laughed, easing back to a standing position as he thought he caught a faint blush cross her high cheekbones. "It's just that, ever since this Maze Murder thing, we've had a real resurgence in maze books, so much so that the shelves are empty and, well, until shipments arrive in the next day or so, I've only got half a dozen or so behind the counters; safe under lock and key, if you know what I mean.

"So, if it's maze books you're looking for," she concluded with a snappy smile and a flick of her wrist, "you're going to have to start being a whole lot nicer to me. After all, I'm something of the resident expert around here."

At that precise moment, as if on cue, Vinny's flat stomach rumbled.

They laughed nervously. "Is that an invitation to lunch?" she flirted mercilessly. "If so, I accept. I'm due for a break anyway and, if you buy me a cup of chai tea at the café over there, I'd be glad to tell you everything I know about mazes. And anything else you'd like to know."

"About mazes?" he asked, as if he'd lost all control of his tongue.

"Or anything else, for that matter," she said, taking off her nametag to clip it on the strap of her young, pink, funky purse. "So, is it a date, *officer*?"

He guffawed, accompanying the tall, waiflike bookstore clerk to another counter where he ordered her a chai tea, and after studying a frou-frou coffee menu that was as foreign to him as a thick copy of Homer's *Iliad*, bought himself a bottle of Diet Coke. He grabbed a bag of biscotti on impulse and joined her at a cozy table for two as she stirred honey into her tea from a wheel of condiments that was so extensive it could have served for lunch, if they'd been so inclined.

"How did you know?" he asked after a sip of much-needed caffeine. It had been another late night and early morning.

"What, that you are a cop?" she asked. "Well, for one, it's 10:30 in the morning and no one but businessmen wear ties these days, and what businessman can get off before lunch, right? Plus, we've got a TV in the break room and it's been tuned to CNN ever since they found that woman's body last week and, well, when the camera's not panning in on that old dude, I've seen you standing in the background once or twice."

Vinny grinned. "That 'old dude' is the FBI's most respected special circumstances killer agent," he scolded her. "And, if I'm not mistaken, he has about four or five books sitting in this very bookstore."

She rolled her eyes. "Well, like I said, I specialize in maze books, not true crime."

"That surprises me," he said honestly. "You're quite the detective, otherwise."

She blushed at the backhanded compliment, then pressed forward. "It doesn't take a special circumstances killer catcher to spot a cute detective on TV," she blurted despite herself.

"I'm with the FBI," he blurted back, then backpedaled. "That is, if you were talking about me, I mean, on the TV. Oh God, I'm too old for this."

"Yes, I was," she said sweetly, reaching out to touch his dark hand with her pale one. "Talking about *you*, that is. And no, you're not. Too *old*, that is."

They sat in comfortable silence for a moment. Eyeing each other. He felt free here, and more comfortable now. No one knew him here. Frank was at the local PD, grilling them about this clue or that. And his hotel room was one block away. He was anonymous. She was friendly.

What they could do on her lunch break, amidst the laptop and crime scene photos and file folders, whirred through his head, making him feel light and foamy like the whipped topping she was currently sucking off her stir stick.

But then he smiled. He knew it wouldn't happen; knew he'd never see past those fair, pale hands to the fair, pale arms and the fair, pale shoulders and the fair, pale breasts he so longed to caress. He was married. Happily. A father. Proudly. And he wouldn't have the faintest idea what to do with a beautiful bookworm in the first place.

He felt that she knew this. And, perhaps, like himself, that was the only reason she was still flirting with him. Harmlessly, he continued. "So?" he prodded. "You were telling me about mazes? Or, more specifically, what you knew about them?"

She nodded. Smiled. This was her cue to wax eloquent, and she dutifully launched in: "There used to be a lot of them sitting around here gathering dust. Mazes, you know? Like crossword puzzles or word finds, mazes aren't exactly bestselling fiction, you know what I mean? Then this killer started popping up on the news every day and, suddenly, we couldn't keep 'em on the shelves anymore."

"How many would you say you'd generally keep in stock?" he asked, trying to assess the killer's access to maze books, in general, and mazes, specifically. "Before all this happened, I mean. Ballpark figure."

"Forty to fifty books," she guessed, her tongue licking wickedly at the corner of her pale, puffy lips as she unconsciously calculated the number in her mind. "Ballpark figure."

"And how many bookstores are there in town here?"

"Six or seven, ranging in size from our Megastore here to the two or three mom and pop bookstores downtown. But you can get maze books anywhere these days. Drug stores. Supermarkets. Airports. Bus stations. Train stations. Dollar stores. Newsstands. Even online. I hear Amazon.com can't even keep 'em in stock these days."

He wondered if she could see his face blanch as she continued her litany of possible places the killer could have found his mazes. "What about the publishers of these books?" he asked. "What can you tell me about them?"

She licked the same corner of her mouth again, frowning. "Any fool with a computer program and a printer can put out a maze book. The paper is cheaper than a 'real book,' typically recycled crap that, if it gets wet, turns to mush pretty quickly. I see a lot of different names on the spines, you know. Game Press. Playful Publishers. Puzzle Press. Maze Merchants. Stuff like that. I get the idea there's a fairly small profit margin involved.

"None of the big boys will touch them, you know, like Random House or HarperCollins? The prices are pretty low. You can get them for ninety-nine cents here, two for a dollar at other places. They're more like magazines than books, so only a few real players come to mind as far as publishers go."

He listened attentively as she reeled off half a dozen names, quickly recording them in his notebook. She watched him writing, then had a brainstorm. He could tell by the licking of her lips.

"If you give me your email address," she suggested, "I can pull together all the purchase orders we do each month of the maze publishers. That way, I can merge them into one document and zip it off to you. It'll have the publisher's name, sales rep's name, address, phone, email, fax number, book titles, release dates, ISBN numbers, the works."

He nodded, impressed. "That will be very helpful, Audrey. Thanks."

She blushed at the mention of her name. Quickly recovering, she asked, "Or, if you'd like, I could, like, print it out and you could come back and get it later."

He stood up abruptly. She watched him from her chair as he fumbled for his business card. "Email will be fine," he said calmly. "That way I can split the file with my partner, that 'old guy' you're always seeing on the news."

She remained seated, the flare of disappointment already clouding her face. Still, she pressed on. "Or I could bring it by your hotel room later? I'm off at six?"

He shook his head calmly. "My email address is there at the bottom, Audrey," he noted. "It will be a great help to us, to the case, to the victims, if you could send me that sometime today."

She brightened somewhat. "I'll do it right after lunch." She spotted the untouched bag of biscotti. "Thanks, by the way," she added.

He nodded, not realizing how much he was trembling until he reached across the table to hand her his card. She took it with long fingers, which brushed his as the card left his hand. A jolt sizzled his insides, and he quickly backed away.

"T-t-thanks again," he sputtered like a blushing schoolboy, rushing out the door and banging his head as he pushed when he should have pulled. He heard her laughing in his wake but, as he turned around for one last peek through the café door, he saw it was a sweet laugh and for that, at least, he was glad.

He wanted to remember her just like that.

32 Maze stood in line at yet another Rent-A-Car booth at yet another airport in yet another town. Neither the name of the town nor the state was important. He'd be leaving there soon, the state line approximately 42 minutes away from the exact point where he was standing.

A wad of cash burned a hole in his plain khaki pocket, all part of his "anonymous American guy in the Rent-A-Car line" outfit. The plain khaki pants, bought for cash at a mall on the way to another airport in another town, matched the gaily patterned golf shirt, too-thick tan socks, and still new, squeaky topsiders that were half-a-size too big should, by some miracle of science, they track down his shoe size and try to match it to his foot.

The inevitable ball cap and non-prescription glasses topped off the picture of yet another modern traveler in yet another airport in yet another town on yet another trip. In the rental car office alone, he counted half a dozen men who looked just like him. Multiply that by the people in the airport itself, the planes both coming and going, and the protective pall of anonymity fell over him like a cloud.

He felt a slight surge of adrenaline as he noticed the newspapers and magazines clutched in the other travelers' hands. Frank Logan peered out from the cover of every other one.

He smiled smugly, but not too smugly, should the surveillance cameras hidden between the ceiling panels catch his happy visage. He remained calm, serene, and, as always, in complete and utter control. After all, the hooker back in Tennessee had bought him some time. Her death was so quick, so easy, so anonymous, so well-planned, it would be months before Frank Logan and his brilliant mind found her.

He'd studied the crime to a T. Everybody knew hookers went unnoticed. Look at the Green River Killer. He'd killed almost fifty working girls before anybody began to care. And he'd killed hookers before. Plenty. They were so easy. So quick.

Once they were in the car, a quick jab of the forearm to the throat and they were mercifully quiet, racking back sobs in their ruined voice box and painfully compliant as they slowly choked on their own tears. It was a skill that took practice but, after all, wasn't that what hookers were for?

But more than that, he'd been an ardent fan of the Weather Channel for weeks before the murder, patiently awaiting the first early cold snap of the year as October quietly inched along in its first few, drizzly weeks.

When he'd learned that Tennessee was this year's victim, when he'd studied the intricacies of cold fronts and cloud cover and convergence, he'd timed the death perfectly. Four days after the kill, the first cold snap of the year would blanket the lower half of northern Tennessee. Some experts were even expecting snow.

What better way to wipe away whatever invisible trace evidence he'd managed to leave behind? What better way to cleanse the body of blood, vomit, and snot? What better way to mask the time of death?

The line moved. He fingered the wad of cash in his pocket and thought about what he was missing back home. The phone calls. The messages. The urgency. The haste. He smiled some more. There was killing to do, and he was leaving the South, at long last. No more signs for boiled peanuts and fresh peaches. No more toothless gas station attendants admiring his fat wallet and slick watch. No more soulless women with their too-thick accents serving him fast food and bad food and fried food and worse food as he passed from town to town and state to state.

Now he was breaking the pattern, now he was moving on, now he was kicking it up a notch. The hooker would be the first sign, but at the same time, not the first. Maybe it wouldn't be months before she was found. Maybe it would only be weeks. Either way, it didn't quite matter to him.

All that mattered now was the lag. He would be doing plenty to keep the famed Frank Logan and his miniscule new partner Vinny Something busy in the meantime. There would be a string of bodies in the future. The near future, that is. And a suspect, too. We couldn't forget him, now could we? And in the midst of it all, with snows and melts and snows and melts, they would eventually find the last southern victim and wonder, "Was she the first? The last? The next to last?"

It was a small touch, a minor detail. But as he'd always been taught, it was all in the details. Money. Time. Work. It didn't matter. Only details mattered.

Death, it seemed, was *all* about the details.

33 Gracie Allan took a rare night off. She wasn't sick. She wasn't on vacation. She didn't need to stock up on lettuce or eggs for Basil's Diner. She was on a mission. She passed on her grease-stained pink uniform and ketchup-splattered tip apron for a pair of comfortable jeans, her favorite fisherman's sweater, and the hiking boots her grandson had given her for Christmas last year that she swore she'd never need. She needed them now.

As October slowly gained momentum and Tennessee braced itself for another roller-coaster winter, Gracie grabbed her car keys from the teapot-shaped hook by the front door in her one-bedroom, rent-controlled apartment and strode down the creaky front stoop to her twelve-year-old Datsun.

It started after two cranks and out into the night she puffed, her hands blue and cold on the cracked steering wheel as the heater slowly sputtered to life and filled the small car with lukewarm air.

She didn't live far from the diner, and though she eased the tiny car into the half-empty parking lot of Basil's, she walked straight past the cowbell-clanging front door and onto the sidewalk in front of the diner's grease-smeared widow, splashed with this week's specials: "Early Bird Meatloaf, $5.99." "Ham and Eggs Special: Only $1.99 after midnight."

She didn't even glance inside. It had been three days since Gina had come into the diner for her midnight meal and Gracie was nervous. The first night, she hadn't thought twice about it, though it hurt her personally to think that the tall, strapping prostitute would take her midnight snack business across the street to the local I-Hop or, worse, the Waffle House around the corner.

She'd shrugged, mentally calculating how much money she'd

make without Gina's nightly tip, and quickly forgot about her favorite hooker with a heart of gold as an endless stream of hungry streetwalkers demanded her time, coffee pot, and attention.

The next night, though, Gracie began to get a strange feeling in her gut. For six nights a week, going on three years now, Gina had been coming into Basil's for a cup of coffee and a plate of ham and eggs. She'd missed a night or two along the way, sure. There had been that bad beating about a year in, and the run-in with her pimp that left her too scared to leave the house until the cops had finally locked him up. But other than that, she'd been in, without fail, during that entire time.

Gracie had been talking to the other girls as they wandered in, doing her best Angela Lansbury imitation as she poured coffee and tried not to trip over her admittedly rusty Forensics Channel speak. "Have you seen Gina lately? Anything going down out there I should know about? Did the cops nab her? Any violent Johns out there?"

The girls, normally grim-faced and mute, seemed just as concerned. And so when Gina hadn't come in for a third night, Gracie knew something had happened. Sure, she knew the streetwalker had rented an apartment in Nashville, where she'd be safer, more anonymous, and free to start her life anew without looking over her shoulder for a former John to make eye contact and gear up her sleaze meter. But that was still a week away. As long as Gracie had known Gina, both women had held fast to their routines. There was no outside socializing between the two women, of course. Gracie needed her rest during the day, and Gina needed even more, but there *was* a motherly-daughterly connection between the two that had kept Gracie coming in on those nights when her arthritis, asthma, or shingles would have otherwise kept her homebound.

And now Gina was gone.

Missing? She didn't know. But she planned to find out. She started on the streets, asking the other girls anything, everything they knew. "When did you last see her?" "Anything strange about the last John she was with?" "Anything remarkable about his car? His profile? His license plate?"

As far as she could tell, the last time anyone had seen Gina she was coming out of Basil's Diner three nights earlier. A hooker named

Star had seen Gina fix her lips, adjust her skirt, and then sidle up to a nondescript rental car just before 1 a.m. the last night Gracie had talked to her, the night Gina had shared with Gracie her plan of escape.

Maybe someone had wanted her to stick around a little longer? Or, perhaps, never get away in the first place?

Now, Gracie looked up at a towering black woman with orange hair and green lips whose street name was Lola. "Can you remember anything about the car, dear?"

"I keep telling ya, Gracie," said the hulking hooker as patiently as possible, her eyes nonetheless wandering over Gracie's coiffed blue hair for potential tricks in the background, "wasn't nothing specific about the car. It was silver, it was gray, it was shiny, it was new. I seen two dozen cars just like it tonight."

Gracie was at a loss, but didn't let it stop her as she pestered the girl. "Did Gina look disturbed that night, Lola? Scared? Nervous?"

Lola shook her head and picked at a yellowed tooth with one of her too-long, wickedly curled, purple fingernails. "No, honey. She looked like, well, Gina. She smiled, did her stroll, flashed some tit, and got into the car."

"Where might she go?" Gracie pondered, looking past Lola to the dirty alleyway between Basil's Diner and the boarded up jewelry store next door. "Did she have a regular place she took guys? When she got in their cars, I mean?"

"Oh sure," Lola said. "We all do. Mine is this hotel around the corner. But Gina, she was saving her money and didn't want to spring the five bucks for the hourly rate. So she took guys just up the road to the town dump, you know, out past the water plant? There are picnic tables out there, you know, for the sanitation workers on their smoke breaks? She said they weren't too bad for doing business and, well, she saved herself a pretty penny each night not renting out a room for every trick."

Gracie nodded, then shook her head, then nodded again. She was getting quite an education. "How about the guy?" she asked, now liberally borrowing lines from her favorite cop shows. "Anything about him? Did you get a good look?"

Lola shook her head, spotted approaching headlights, and apologized once more. "I'm sorry, Gracie, you know. I wish I could tell you more. I just wasn't paying attention that night. I didn't know it would be anything special. But she could be anywhere. Maybe she took off early. Maybe she split without telling you. Sweet or not, the girl was still a hooker. We don't answer to no one, no how."

And then Lola was off, clomping away on towering pink heels to lean her ample frame into yet another passenger side window on yet another anonymous car belonging to yet another man willing to part with a few crisp twenties for the pleasure of her company.

Gracie shook her head and ambled off to her own car. She knew the area Lola was talking about, though the thought of Gina pulling her skirt up and her panties down for some man in the shadow of the town dump made her sadder than ever.

Still, she crumpled herself into the driver's side of the Datsun and puttered out of Basil's parking lot. It took her only three minutes to get to the dump, made less odorous now with the recent cold snap but no less ominous as huge piles of refuse and scrap towered high enough to almost blot out the moon. Their shadows mixed with the inky darkness as Gracie's old eyes struggled to stay with the crooked dirt road that she'd been following ever since the pavement ended half-a-mile back.

A chain-link fence cordoned off the town dump proper, but out of the corner of her eye, Gracie spotted a row of three sad-looking picnic tables that caused her heart to flutter. It made perfect sense: No one would be out here after hours, not with the gate keeping them out, but with the picnic tables on the open side, she'd be free to conduct her business and get right back to the strip.

Gracie felt a grudging tug of respect for the long-legged hooker, mixed with a twinge of sadness, as she put the car in reverse, turned counter-clockwise, and then inched forward toward the tables, illuminating them in the weak glow of her dim headlights. Even with the cold, the smell seeped into the wheezing Datsun.

"What a vile, rank place to do your business," she thought out loud.

The smell was even worse when she stepped out of the car, the headlights illuminating the forged plastic shapes of the trio of tables as they stood silent just outside of the heavily-secured gate that separated the town from all of its trash. She thought briefly of the Dempsey dumpster outside of Basil's, and how it had smelled two weeks into the sanitation strike of 1994. This was three times worse.

Still, she grabbed a hankie from the pocket of her jeans and kept it close to her nose, the lavender smell of her dollar-store body spray suddenly heavenly in her assaulted nostrils. She crept closer to the tables, the tread of her new hiking boots making crunching noise on the crisp frost of the after-midnight blades of grass.

She had no idea of what she was looking for, and realized pitifully that she did, indeed, watch far too much TV. "Heavens, Gracie," she exclaimed as the moment suddenly struck her as supremely surreal "If Sippowitz could only see you now."

She touched the tables, the bench-like chairs affixed with nuts and bolts. Was this where Gina did her naughty business? She smirked at her prudish thought, realizing that she knew only one side of Gina. The only side she chose to know, anyway. The side that strolled into the diner each night, steady on her long, shapely legs, garish in her short skirts and tight tops, but kind of word and soft of voice and easy of smile.

Gracie realized now that she had never formally asked what she did to earn her money, nor did she consciously think of how Gina earned those crisp, folded fives Gracie found under her coffee cup each night.

But this place? Well, this was ground zero in Gina's sad, lonely life. A cluster of cold, hard, plastic picnic tables just outside the town dump. Cloistered by a clump of trees that hid them from the road, and graced with ample parking should she have a busier than usual night.

Gracie watched the glow of the headlights as they illuminated every blade of grass, nut and bolt, and piece of trash that made up Gina's place of business. Directly behind the bank of picnic tables lay a row of brush, thick and clumpy and dark despite the car's headlights.

She shook her head, knowing that if she was indeed out here looking for clues, this was where they would be. She crept closer, feet trampling more frozen grass, and kept her hands clenched tight within the folds of her rich, thick fisherman's sweater. Every step found her stomach more fraught with distress, her tired fists clenched tighter against the sweater's rough fabric.

Behind the bushes, the twigs poking through the denim of her jeans, Gracie could scarcely make out a pile of beer cans, condom wrappers, and cigarette butts. Light somehow managed to sneak through, creating a cascading, strobe effect as her body trembled there in the brush and leaves temporarily scattered to let in light, only to snap back into place and blot it out a second later. She tried to focus her eyes past the intermittent clusters of trash, not knowing what she was looking for, but feeling in the pit of her stomach that this was where she should be. She crept closer, finally breaking through the thick brush and finding herself plunged into darkness as the bushes snapped closed behind her with a frightening finality.

She clung tightly to the slim penlight on her keychain and flashed it in front of her, creating a tight slice of light as it illuminated this used condom or that discarded French fry. A bolt went through her as she realized she was spying on Gina's world. Were those *her* fries? Was that *her* lipstick on an errant cigarette?

She crept farther and farther from the protective row of brush, now several dozen steps behind her. As it grew darker her penlight grew thicker, brighter, and she found herself relegated to its dim, cruel world.

Then she stepped on something outside of the pen's view. Something hard. And flat. And sharp. She bent down, hands quivering, to find her penlight's beam focusing on the heel of a shoe. Broken. Bent. Twisted. It was Gina's.

She cried out. A simple, "Oh." Nothing more. And then she moved forward, bound and determined to find the rest of the shoe and, God forbid, whatever other clues she might find. She pressed ahead on wobbly knees and too-stiff shoes. There were many clues in her path. Gina's skirt was next. Crumpled and discarded, no bigger than the handkerchief still clutched tightly in Gracie's other hand. Then her tube top, scarcely any bigger. A pair of those tiny panties, what did the skinny, brash girls on MTV call them these days? Thongs? That's it. A pair of purple thong panties were next. She looked behind her, running her penlight's beam up the path she'd just walked, and realized that the clothes were strewn almost like a swath of crumbs. Like a trail.

Was it she who was meant to follow them?

It mattered little. She didn't touch them. She knew enough from the Forensics Channel to let them lie, though her heart longed to pick them up, collect them, gather them, in preparation for Gina's return. Though the rest of her knew the broken hooker was never coming home.

Five steps from her purse, found just after her purple unmentionables, Gracie found Gina's body. It was pale and bright in the darkness, even without the small, thin flashlight beam that danced across her naked, mottled flesh.

Gracie didn't realize she was crying until the teardrops spattered across the girl's thin, dusty back. She'd thought the humming, croaking, gagging sounds coming from her mouth had been the Datsun's tired motor straining against the night.

She said a silent prayer over Gina's body, and quietly, quickly walked away from the corpse—that's what it was now, just a corpse—past the underwear, the top, the skirt, the broken shoe, and straight to her car.

It was only five minutes to the police station. She made it in two.

34 Maze cursed, watching the chartered Lear jet in the background, as Frank Logan and his sniveling, tag-a-long new partner, Vinny Something, disembarked into a clamoring crowd of scrap-snapping newshounds on the small color TV.

The hotel room around him, cheap and orange, blurred in and out of focus as he seethed with the news that his secret weapon, his time capsule at the town dump, had been discovered weeks too early.

What a fool he'd been to trust the Weather Channel. How naive. After all this time, too. Without another word he dressed, dumping his take-out dinner, his half-empty beer, his unused toiletries, all of it, every piece of himself, into the laundry bag hanging in the closet and dragging it with him as he turned his back on Tennessee for good.

He'd been hiding out, laying low, hoping for a little R and R, but now the Feds were entirely too close and it was time to cut bait and run. He hated the running. It implied failure, and failure was loss, and Maze was a man who could no longer afford to lose. Not now. Not anymore. The stakes were too high this time.

He stepped into the deep, dark night and threw the trash bag into the trunk of his spotless rented car; he would discard it miles up the highway at the first available rest stop. He couldn't help but feel the quiet tug of pride that occasionally merged with his reeling, maddening brain.

Frank Logan had not been up to the task this time. For once, the famed Lone Wolf had been forced to take on a partner. Not another grizzled old veteran like himself, either, but a young one, full of piss and vinegar, Maze imagined, zigging when Frank zagged, zagging when he zigged.

Ah, the caper was taking on a Laurel and Hardy feel now, but even as the thought slipped into his frenzied mind, it quickly retreated. It was too early to discount the old master, nor write-off the new pupil. Either man alone could have caught Maze quickly, if only they held the key.

Two men together? They might be able to catch him without it.

Of course, he'd already seen to that. Soon they'd be handed the key on a silver platter, *if* only they could find it. Then, and only then, would the real hunt begin. Was he up for it?

He dashed into the night, careful not to burn rubber and awaken any of the cheap motel's restless guests, nor exceed the speed limit and attract any night-owl cops as he raced from Tennessee due west, to parts better left to chance.

It didn't matter where he went next. The key gave him three options, and any one of them would be ideal for his purposes. Wherever he went, whatever he did, *whoever* he did, it had to be big. Bad. Bold. And, best of all, unmistakable. It had to read Maze Murderer all over it. And it had to be soon.

35

Cassie Spencer kissed her boyfriend Marc, got out of the passenger seat, and stood up straight and tall. He peeled off in his Camaro, a car he could neither really handle nor afford. Still, it was part of what she liked about him. Like herself, Marc was aimless, floundering, and loved the night. She knew he'd go straight to his favorite bar to catch a quick beer or two before he hit the stage with his hapless grunge band at whatever dive bar they'd be playing at later.

He might or might not pick her up nine hours later as the sun rose over Tyler, Missouri. And that was okay, too. After all, you never knew who you'd meet hitching home at sunrise. Could be a drifter on the way out of town; could be another loser on the run into town. Could be a guy looking to hide out, or some fella just looking. She liked Marc, sure, but they weren't exclusive. At least she wasn't.

She listened to the familiar clang of the cowbells above the door at the Stop 'N Pop, a fading orange and yellow convenience store on the wrong side of town with the wrong, outdated theme. No fancy coffee accoutrements, ATM, or imported beer here, just plenty of pickled eggs, beef jerky, cheap motor oil and cheaper potato chips. Bertha, the night manager, smiled at her and grabbed straight for her purse and keys, not even remembering to clock out as she gave her favorite part-time employee a quick high-five on the way out the door.

"Tag," she said, smiling broadly. "You're it. And just in time, too. I got a hot date. Wish me luck, girl. I'll see you back here tomorrow night. Same bat time, same bat channel."

"Good luck." Cassie smiled as she clocked her boss out and clocked herself in. Then she went straight to the cooler and grabbed herself a tall can of Budweiser, knowing the opening to the giant fridge was just out range of the security monitors. Pouring the can into a Super Swallow Slurpee cup on the way out of the cold storage, she greeted the night the only way she knew how: With a slight beer buzz paid for by those greedy pigs at Stop 'N Pop Corporate.

Smiling, she took up her position behind the cash register and wished she could smoke. It was the only thing missing from her own private nightcap. "Oh well," she sighed as an old Wham song cued up on the overhead Muzak, outdated by only a couple of decades, just a few years away from being cool again.

Cassie sipped slowly at her beer, knowing she'd have to pace herself for the long, dull night ahead. But that was okay, too. She had a system. One tallboy, one coffee. Another tallboy, a soda. And on and on. The sodas and coffee were free, of course, but the beer was most definitely not. Still, those damn delivery boys were always dropping a six pack or two, leaving a stray behind in the corner and, when they didn't, she'd ask them to, just for shits and grins. They all did it. And why not? They were all out to get the man, be he—or she—the CEO of Stop 'N Pop or Amber Ale. And so, her night began, a sip of cold beer, a flip through a tabloid magazine, the odd trucker or hooker stopping in for beef jerky or condoms, Mountain Dew or Boone's Farm.

She smiled at them all, game for conversation, bored out of her skull, but in a few minutes they were always gone, out into the night, pulling away from the convenience store in a rush of diesel and gravel as they drove somewhere far, far away.

She turned her attention to the rack of newspapers flanking the front door, realizing it had been some time since she and Marc had checked in with CNN. She stared at the local rag, the *Tyler Gazette*, then the greater Missouri paper, then the *USA Today* just below, and thought she was seeing double.

No, make that triple.

Each one had an eerily similar headline that blared the words "Maze Murderer Strikes Again." She read them from afar, sipping at her Styrofoam cup full of beer and trying to digest the headlines as best she could from behind the counter. As soon as she was out of beer, she stepped out from behind her protective barrier, grabbed her first soda of the night, and one of each paper.

In half an hour, she was sufficiently creeped out. The way the papers put it, the murder in Tennessee was the first surprise in the Maze Murderer's northward trek up the East Coast.

Florida, Georgia, South Carolina, North Carolina. Then, out of nowhere, a detour west into...Tennessee?

Cassie gulped at her soda, eager for the caffeine to revive her tepid mind. Tennessee. Tennessee. How many times a night did she see a license plate from the bordering state? A dozen? Two? Three dozen?

Thirty-six cars coming or going from the nearby state. Where would he strike next? North? South? East? West? Nobody knew. That was the thing. Nobody, not the president, not the FBI, not even Peter Jennings, knew where this crazed killer would strike next.

Suddenly she burped, too much fizz in too little time, she guessed, blushing at the security camera pointed right at her face, and then suddenly grateful for its presence. To date, Maze had avoided convenience stores, according to the papers, which theorized the deranged killer was smart enough to avoid being recorded.

She thought about the row of cheap security VCRs recording away in the manager's broom closet-slash-office and, for once, thanked goodness for those corporate clowns at the Stop 'N Pop home office. At least they'd keep her safe from this Maze character. Whoever he was.

Cassie smiled and burped again, excusing herself graciously to the camera before finishing her soda and disappearing once more into the labyrinthine beer cooler to find one more stray tall boy for round two. She was busy deciding between Budweiser, for taste, and Bud Light, for the calories, when the lights went out.

"Shit!" she said, stumbling into a stack of beer cases and dinging her skinny knee. "Double shit!"

She reached into her cheesy orange and yellow work bib for a flashlight, realizing she'd taken it out in favor of her Slushee cup, into which she could pour her beer. "Triple shit!" she laughed, sure that some drunk had slammed into a power line somewhere up the road and that it would only be a matter of minutes before the geeks at the power plant would reroute enough juice to keep this glitzy strip of convenience stores, fast food dives, and girly bars going at full tilt.

She willed herself to calm down, tapping cases of beer with her toe until finally spotting the orange glare of an emergency light through the frosty window of the cooler door. She made her way in that direction, slowly, coldly, the beer nipping at her hands as she opened the door and stepped into the lukewarm air of the store proper.

The emergency light flickered in the corner above the door, all but unnecessary as moonlight spilled in through the wide glass walls that made up most of the front of the store. Aside from the odd shadow cast from this beer sign or that, she had clear sailing as she stepped behind the counter, safe again.

She knew she was supposed to lock the doors during a power outage, standard operating procedure and all, but she wasn't moving squat until she'd had her second beer and by then, she reckoned, the power would be back on.

She sipped greedily, hungrily, nervously tearing at the Styrofoam cup as her nerves jangled her chattering teeth together and the cold, soft beer met the back of her tight, clenched throat. Outside the road was deserted. Not a truck, not a taxi, not a motorcycle, not a bike, not even a skateboard.

It was like a ghost town out there, and she couldn't help but feel all alone. She reached for the cordless yellow phone beneath the counter to call Marc, but couldn't even get a dial tone.

"Shit, shit, shit," she seethed under her breath, those Maze Murderer headlines blaring out to her in the moonlight spilling through the front door.

"What was *that?*" she gasped as a shadow cut through the night just outside in the moon-drenched parking lot. Her heart stopped, her hands clenched, nearly breaking her flimsy cup in half as she raced to put it down. There was a baseball bat under the counter. She reached for it now, feeling around her purse and a pair of salt and pepper shakers until she grabbed hold of the rough wooden handle.

She blinked twice, staring straight at the doors, where only a moment earlier she'd seen, or thought she'd seen—there it was! It did it again. A flash of a shadow, a blur of a shape, a figure darting from left to right in front of the doors. Blinding fast, cold and dark as the night that swallowed it up.

She was too scared to curse, too shocked to think. This couldn't be happening. It was all those newspaper stories, she told herself, freaking her out. Too much beer, too fast, with too little to eat. It had to be something else, a UFO, a plane, a raccoon, something, anything, other than what she now knew resembled a man's form.

A big man's form. Tall and lank. Wide or massive. Black or white. She couldn't tell. She knew the security cameras couldn't, either. Weak-ass on a good day, in broad daylight, they were worse than worthless in the dark.

There it was again! Only, this time, it stopped. Just out of sight. The shadow zipped, then stopped, and just beyond her line of vision, she couldn't tell if she saw a shoulder or the top of the ice machine, padlocked tight just to the left of the door.

She clutched the bat, realizing that if she'd just move beyond the cash register, she could bolt the doors tight, and then it wouldn't matter how big, or tall, or fast the shadow was. Then she could grab the cell phone in her purse and call the cops.

It might be nothing, or it might be something, but either way she'd have some company and that, most of all, was what she needed at this very minute. She took one step, then another, her toes still smarting from banging into all those cans of beer in the cooler. Still, she picked up the pace as she crossed the floor.

Stumbling, sprinting, almost there now, keys in hand, fumbling for the right one, the top bolt a deadlock but the bottom one requiring a key and she definitely wanted both locks tonight.

She reached the doors, her heart pounding, standing there, stock still, fumbling with the keys, until suddenly something caught her eyes, short-circuited her common sense, and made her stand there, dumbstruck, as a strange man loomed large, right in front of her.

Time slowed down—nearly stopped—as the man kicked open the door and split her lip, the rough edge of the glass shattering her top tooth in the process. Blood clouded her eye as she realized the broken glass must have cut her forehead, too.

There was no time to think, no time to react, no time to record his face or his hair or his ears for posterity. He had her, bound tight, under his arm, out in the parking lot, away from the store, away from the security cameras, the cell phone, the bat rolling across the dry pavement futilely until it came to rest against an unleaded gas pump, as useless to her now as a crisp paper credit card receipt.

She thought she heard sirens in the distance, and began to cry, realizing she might be safe after all. The sirens were getting closer, and closer, and closer, and then she stopped smiling, stopped crying, realizing they weren't sirens at all.

They were her own tortured screams, bleeding into the night.

36

Frank Logan was on hold, a feeling he was familiar with, to be sure, but always found unpleasant, no doubt. His cell phone burned against his cheek, slick with sweat despite the October chill of a desperate Tennessee night.

While he waited for the FBI communications rep to relay the latest "urgent" development in the Maze Murderer case, he watched as Vinny Smalldeano took over dealing with the locals.

It was a delicate balance, one minute strong-arming to get respect, the next soft-pedaling to get information, and either Vinny was a quick study from the South Carolina crime scene or the kid really had the right stuff after all.

Vinny talked with confident ease to a rumpled detective, calming him down as he elicited the wheat from the chaff of his scattershot testimony. Frank watched the rookie pursue critical facts with the scent of a pro, ignoring the hokey Muzak twinkling from the holding pattern in his ear to concentrate on his partner.

"We understand that, Detective Phelps," Vinny purred, as he eased the large detective away from the uniformed patrol officers at the site of the murder. "Can I call you Clarence? We understand that, Clarence, but regardless of what the old lady touched, we'll need to know the last time sanitation workers actually did a sweep of the picnic area. The temperature, the state of the body…it's going to be easier to determine date of death if we know the last time the dump was cleaned up."

Frank watched Vinny wait patiently as the detective grumbled something about "sanitation schedules" not being "part of my job." His hand clenched against the sweaty phone, ready to throttle the lumpy dick, but Vinny simply blinked and responded by saying, "No one's blaming you *or* your department, Clarence. We're all on the same team here. You, me, Frank Logan over there, hell, the whole FBI. We just want to catch this guy and, with your help, we'll do just that. Now…."

"Special Director Logan?" came a voice on the other end of the line, interrupting Frank's eavesdropping, not to mention his favorite Beatles song, or at least an instrumental flute version thereof. "Are you there?"

"I'm here, I'm here," Frank grumbled, the bright lights and noxious fumes from the scene at the city dump making it hard to concentrate as all the stimuli assaulted his senses. "What's so important you take me away from a crucial interview at three in the morning?"

"I'm sorry, sir," said the sincerely apologetic, sincerely *young*, male voice on the other end of the line. "I'm on direct orders from Senior Director Sharpe himself, sir. He's got a new crime scene for you, sir, and…."

"Repeat transmission!" Frank barked, unable, or perhaps unwilling, to trust his ears amid the sirens and blinking lights surrounding him. "It sounded like you said 'another crime scene.' Please confirm."

At the words "another crime scene" Vinny's ears perked up. Frank watched the rookie's alert young eyes move imperceptibly in his direction, even as he continued scribbling down notes from the now-placated local detective.

"Yes, sir, confirm that," said the now-nervous cadet in the communications center, where only the newest of the new toiled, relaying messages to senior agents out in the field. Frank himself had spent a solid year in communications before his first "live" case. It wasn't a job he relished, particularly in moments like this one.

"There must be some mistake," Frank said, trying to lower his tone and take it easy on the new recruit. "I'm already *at* the new crime scene. I'm standing here, right now, not four hours off the plane. Are you sure you're looking at the latest transmission, son? Check out the time stamp. You've got to…."

"Uh, there is no time stamp," the communications rep blurted. "Senior Director Sharpe is standing right here, right now, telling me what to say to you."

"That chicken shit!" Frank spat, only half joking as he pictured the hawk-like supervisor riding roughshod over the nervous young kid as he made him relay the unpleasant message to Frank in the field. "Put that old bastard on the line."

Frank heard the kid murmur diplomatically on the other end of the line in Washington: "Director Logan would appreciate a word."

"*A* word? A *word*!" bellowed the agency's most senior director, a vain and bellicose man who had, nonetheless, had Frank's back on many an unpopular occasion. "I've got three words for you, Frank: NEW CRIME SCENE. I've got another gal here relaying the coordinates to your pilot, and you're to be on that helicopter in no less than thirty minutes. It's en route now, should be there in twenty."

"How?" Frank muttered, speechless for the first time in months. "When?"

"How? When?" Sharpe bellowed. "A maze was found curled in our latest victim's hand, shoved into an empty tallboy beer can. Bud Light, to be exact. When? About forty fucking minutes ago! Where? Since you forgot to ask: Some shit burg named Tyler, Missouri. Looks like our boy is continuing on a westerly course, Frank. Get on that chopper, get out there, and catch that son of a bitch before he gets all the way to Hollywood and kills someone important, like your literary agent. Are you reading me here, Frank? This is starting to get embarrassing."

"What am I supposed to do about *this* crime scene, Sharpe?" Frank asked calmly, trying in vain to reconcile this new information with the hectic crime scene surrounding him. "We just got here."

"*We* is the operative word in that particular sentence, Frank," Sharpe spat. "You've got a partner now, old boy, use him. He's a good man. Wouldn't be standing there, otherwise. I suspect you know that by now. You've got about nineteen minutes to brief him on sucking the life out of an FBI crime scene, and one minute to board the helo. Understood, Frank?"

Frank paused, already listening for the familiar sound of rotating helicopter blades. "Understood, sir. Logan, out."

Frank slid his phone shut, realizing his hands had suddenly gone from clammy to ice cold in a span of sixty seconds. Vinny listened to the detective, nodding, until he couldn't take the suspense any longer. Excusing himself, he walked over to Frank in less than six long strides that wore Frank out just watching them.

"What's up?" Vinny asked, his finger in the middle of his little black notebook, noting where he'd left off the interview so he could return to it immediately after the impromptu conference with Frank was over. "Did I hear you say something about a new crime scene?"

"You did," Frank confessed, pulling Vinny gently to the side as they found refuge in one of the rare spots not blinded by the towering klieg lights hauled in from the local parks and recreation department. "And there is."

"When? Where?" Vinny asked, the blood rushing to his face. "Is it our guy? Confirmed?" Already the adrenaline was throbbing through his veins, making it hard to concentrate.

"Let's put it this way," Frank sighed, none too eager to get into a recitation of all he'd just learned, "I just got off the phone with Senior Director Sharpe...."

"Sharpe?" Vinny gasped. "I thought he was just a painting on the wall."

Frank had to smile, despite himself. He was faintly sure he could hear the helicopter rotors in the distance already. "Yeah, well, he's that and then some. Anyway, he confirmed it himself, and you don't get a guy like Sharpe out of bed at 3 a.m. unless you're damn sure it's the real deal. They found a maze, stuffed in a beer can, like a message in a bottle. Missouri, Vinny. He's moving west. Leaving us behind with our thumbs up our asses while we try to second guess him."

Vinny nodded. "So," he began, saving Frank the trouble as the two men scanned the skies for the helicopter they could both now faintly detect in the near distance. "We're splitting up. You'll go west, I'll stay here, and we'll meet up, where? In the middle? Back at headquarters in DC?"

"Not likely," Frank warned, shaking his head as if for emphasis, already scanning the crime scene for his briefcase and finding it on the top of a rental car nearby. "This guy's heating up, not cooling down. DC is for after the case, when we write up our reports, put the interviews in chronological order, wrap this baby up. Between you and me, we won't be back in DC for weeks, if not months."

Frank watched a flurry of conflicting emotions pass across

Vinny's expressive young face before the young agent asked, almost in a whisper, "What the hell am I supposed to do here, Frank?"

Frank smiled encouragingly as he inched Vinny over to the rental car where his briefcase lay. "You do what I'd do. Forget the bullshit, screw the hype, ignore the reporters, hone in on the facts. You know what we're looking for. Time. Opportunity. Motive. Clues. You gather them, and wait for me. When it's time, I'll call you out to the new scene and we'll compare notes. Two days, three, tops. You're up for it, or they wouldn't have sent you to the SCCU, right? I don't have time for pep talks or pats on the ass. Let me put it this way: If you weren't up for it, I wouldn't be getting on that helicopter, all right?"

Vinny nodded, watching as Frank picked up his briefcase and pre-programmed his cell phone for the battery of calls he'd have to make in order to coordinate the new task force that would be waiting for him the minute he landed in Missouri.

"Okay, Frank," Vinny said with a sigh, watching now as the menacing helicopter took rest upon the gritty, deserted highway just east of the trash dump. "I won't waste time with doubt. There's no time for that. I'll learn everything I can, and hopefully we can stop this asshole before he gives us a reason to split up again."

"That's the spirit, Vinny," Frank said, but both men knew his heart was no longer in the impromptu pep talk. He had a helicopter to catch, phone calls to make, and a killer to capture.

37

Bernie Segal sat at yet another Internet café, printing off the front pages of the top news magazine's websites, most of them, if not all, featuring his star client's grimacing face, trademark sunglasses, and FBI badge.

Next to the laptop bolted to the table, his cell phone danced across the Formica like a Mexican jumping bean, its vibration setting getting a good workout. From time to time, he'd look up from his reading, smiling smugly to see the caller IDs of half a dozen news channels, networks, or cable start-ups appearing there in the ambient aquamarine glow.

Although it pained him to do so, every day he forced himself to shut his cell off at least every other hour. Though it was typically attached to his hip, he knew it gave him the impression of aloofness to be unavailable, even if he was sitting right there.

In many cases he was waiting for the call, desperate for it to be this network exec or that talking head. And yet discipline, and half a dozen bestsellers on negotiation, had taught him that the image of aloofness was often more valuable than that of accessibility.

He no longer needed Frank to spoon feed him sensitive information; now he could get it all from the Internet—just like the producers who were calling him. "Be careful what you wish for, Bernie boy," he muttered to himself, spooking the college freshman downloading porn in the cubicle next to him.

It wasn't just the Forensics Channel and its whiz-kid Peter Heifitz on the other end of the phone, but the majors as well. HBO. Fox. Discovery. TLC. A & E. Hell, even the Sci-Fi Network was pitching a new fact-based crime series and wanted to use Frank as a consultant.

There'd be no out of pocket expenses for that season pilot, after all, and now that the locations were almost all scouted, he would soon be returning to LA, eager to let some overworked Assistant Director and a location scout team take over the grunt work he'd been forced to do himself while the Maze Murders heated up.

It was no longer a matter of if the Maze show would get picked up, but when and, more importantly, by whom. Nice problem to have, he knew, and whether Frank knew it or not, the two of them had just gone from under the radar to smack dab in the center of the media frenzy bull's-eye. Right where he'd wanted to be all along.

The last of his full-color pages was printing and his allotted half-hour was almost up when the alarm on his watch beeped, telling him it was time to turn his cell phone ringer back up. *Who would the lucky winner be?* he wondered as he punched two buttons, switching the vibration mode to a ring tone. Heifitz? Sci-fi? CNN? MSBNC? Katie? Matt? Tarantino? Hell, it could be anybody.

So when the *Daytona Daily* appeared, he was only slightly annoyed. His annoyance, in fact, quickly turned to amusement. It had been a long time since he'd pulled a power play on anyone; who better than some free rag out of the Florida boonies?

He let it ring twice more, swallowing his lukewarm cappuccino in the interim, and then flipped the phone open, doing his best Hollywood hot shot routine as he spat, "Segal here, speak."

"M-m-Mr. Segal?" stammered a hesitant voice, sporting an accent just shy of Britney Spears and just north of Jodie Foster. "I…I…I'm sorry to sound so surprised, but I was expecting to get an assistant or, I dunno, an assistant to your assistant. This is truly an honor, sir. I have to say I'm a big fan. I've read all your books, well, Frank Logan's books, that is, but I always look for your name first in the acknowledgements section and it's truly a thrill to…."

"Thanks for the pucker up moment, doll," Bernie oozed, logging off from the laptop and stowing the printouts in his distressed-when-he-purchased-it retro messenger bag, "but your moment of opportunity is ticking by. Get to the point or leave a message, got it? I've got Norville holding on Line 2 and Rather on Line 6. Convince me I shouldn't dump you to voicemail in favor of either one."

"Oh, yes, of course, sir," she recovered, her voicing growing stronger with purpose as she continued. "It's just that, with the Maze Murders blowing up so far so fast, I thought it appropriate that the *Daytona Daily* do a follow-up piece on Frank Logan, sir."

"A follow-up piece on Frank Logan," Bernie mimicked, enjoying himself and none too eager to squeeze back into his compact rental and make the half-hour trek to the airport. "How original? Not for nothing, toots, but I'm sure you could find all the source material you need on the Internet. That's where the other reporters get it. So why clog the airwaves and bother me?"

"Well, sir, it's just that I'll need a formal interview in order for Special Director Logan to…."

"An interview? Get in line, babe. You think I'm giving some Florida rag an exclusive with the blood and guts go-to guy? That's rich. Who's next on your list? The President? Or lemme guess: his mistress, right? Indulge me, won't you, and explain why Frank Logan should stop chasing the country's most elusive serial killer and spend half an hour talking to some 25K a year reporter from, where is it, Daytona? Please, doll, enlighten me."

"Well," came the slightly southern, slightly northern voice, no longer hesitant, "I assume he'll want to defend himself in the face of new allegations that he had an affair with the first victim. Mr. Segal, sir? Bernie? Are you there?"

He was there, all right. So busy dancing a celebratory jig he could hardly be expected to speak right away. This was it; what he'd been waiting for. The first salvo fired against Frank Logan's impeccable public persona. It was what the case had been lacking: a scandal.

Ever the opportunist, Bernie Segal couldn't give the Daytona reporter Frank's personal number fast enough.

38 Marcie Collins flipped her cell phone shut and smiled smugly. "One down," she thought ruefully, staring at a stack of Frank Logan clippings at her cluttered cubicle desk. "One to go."

She stared out at the storefront of her little newspaper office, empty now, with the copy editor, managing editor, and secretary all at lunch across the street at the local Bennigan's. She heard the shouts of the instructor through the plywood wall separating the *Daytona Daily* office from the karate dojo next door; fortunately, the laundromat on the other side of her was slow this time of day.

She was thankful for the silence, and had timed her phone call to Bernie Segal well. Now, as she dialed the secret digits she'd just conned out of his literary agent, she hoped her call to Frank Logan would be as equally well-timed.

There was no affair, of course. No allegations, no evidence, no nothing. Why, the Maze had been so prolific in his crime scenes—the case heating up so quickly—that Frank Logan hadn't even had time to visit the Daytona crime scene yet. Or had he?

She was about to find out.

"Logan here," came the legendary voice she'd heard so often on one late night newscast or another, at last causing the unflappable cub reporter to flap. "Speak now or forever hold your piece. I don't know how you got this number but…."

"Mr. Logan," she interrupted curtly, realizing Bernie hadn't had the time or the inclination to warn the FBI legend of her call, "this is Marcie Collins with the *Daytona Daily*. It was your agent, Bernie Segal, who gave me your number. He's coordinated this interview in order for me to fact check some items that came up in copy edit."

A hard sigh on the other end of the line told her Logan was

weighing his options. "Fine," he relented, "if Bernie gave you the number, he must think it's important. Though, forgive me if I sound like a prima donna, I didn't think he even got out of bed for anything less than the *Post* or the *Times*."

"I understand, sir, but I'm with the AP, so this will be hitting the wires later today, and he thought it best if I...."

"Fine," Frank sighed heavily, "but I'm on my way somewhere, so let's make it quick, huh?"

"On the way to a new crime scene?" she asked hopefully, showing her hand. She didn't mind lying about being with the AP or scamming Bernie for the guy's number if it meant getting the inside scoop, though she had to admit, she was slightly disappointed that one of the FBI's top guys was so easily duped.

"No comment," he spat, and for once she could tell he meant it. "Moving on?"

"Yes, indeed, moving on." She took a deep breath, gazed once more at the highlighted cities on a quick spreadsheet she'd printed up that morning after plugging in over seven dozen news stories from across the Web, and plunged forward. It was do or die time, and she had a feeling Frank Logan was anxious. "I'm looking at your flight itinerary for the past two months and...."

"No you're not," Frank corrected her, calling her bluff. "It's an absolute impossibility; moving onward."

"Fine," Marcie said, smiling. At last, a worthy response from a most worthy adversary. Still, she would not be deterred. "So I'm not looking at the actual itinerary, but the dates, the times, the durations, the cities, the states, are all right in front of me, I assure you."

"They may very well be, Ms. Collins, I'm sure with enough digging anybody can tell where I've been. My point is, don't lie to me again, or Bernie or no Bernie, we're through. Got it? Now, my itinerary. What's your point?"

"My point, sir, is this: In following the Maze Murders, I've noticed a direct correlation between yourself and the murders."

"Congratulations, Marcie. I may call you Marcie, right? You've managed to sleuth out the fact that I'm working the Maze Murderer case. Who did you say you worked for, again? The Daytona Dumbshit? They must be quite proud. Anything else?"

Marcie managed a weak laugh, as menacing as it was intimidating. "Not after the murders, sir, before. I'm showing a trip to South Carolina in September, one to Orlando at the beginning of October, a layover in North Carolina the week before that. Are you getting my drift?"

A cold silence met her question. At last, the realization of what she was doing—of who she was accusing—hit her like a furnace blast. The sound of Frank's silence was chilling. "Oh I get yours, cubby. Get mine: If a word of your accusation—and that's exactly what it is—if a word of your accusation hits the papers, I will send down a legion of Feds to arrest your, no doubt, pert, blond, cute little ass for obstruction of justice." Frank paused, letting the steel grit of his agitated voice sink in before continuing. "After that, we'll track down every email, snail mail, Christmas card, and gift basket you've ever sent. I will personally make your life a living hell if you do anything further to hamper this investigation. Get me? Print what you want after I catch this sick, twisted fuck, but if a word of your so-called conspiracy theory leaks out before a conviction, I promise you you'll wish you'd never made this call. Are we clear, dear?"

"Crystal," she said, hanging up with a trembling hand. She breathed slowly for the next three minutes before she was able to hit the playback button on her micro-cassette recorder. Only when Frank's voice, as clear as a bell, cut through the deafening silence of the *Daytona Daily* front office did she at last breathe a sigh of relief.

Of course, she had no desire to go to jail or have Frank Logan for an enemy. What she did have, however, was Bernie Segal's unlisted cell number and the outline of a true crime book of her own: How Frank Logan was, for a time, considered the main suspect in his own Maze Murderer case.

Nice, huh? Whether it was true or not remained to be seen, but she'd obviously touched a nerve, and Frank's "quote" to her would be the first line of her query letter to perspective literary agents, starting with none other than his own: Bernie Segal.

Marcie stared through the plate glass window that fronted one of Daytona's laziest streets. She looked at her watch, noticed there was still time to catch her colleagues for lunch, and stood on suddenly sure legs to stride across the street to their favorite table at Bennigan's.

Whoever the Maze turned out to be, Marcie's days of covering Bike Week and the annual Gidget look-a-like contest were finally over. She was headed straight for the big time. Frank Logan had just seen to that.

39

Vinny watched from over the coffee-stained lip of his Styrofoam cup as half a dozen stiffly suited agents ran from phone to phone, booking leads, making appointments with witnesses, tracking down the various publishers of the maze books they'd put out feelers to. He sighed, drained the last of his coffee, looked at the few remaining grounds left at the bottom, and tossed the cup into a nearby trash can, already well past overflowing, as an admittedly conscientious housekeeping staff failed to keep up with the rapid caffeine consumption of six alpha males on high alert.

It was 4 a.m. and the brightly lit conference room of the Holiday Inn Express was still a beehive of activity. Five more agents were sleeping in shifts in two rooms upstairs, while Vinny himself was going on hour 28 without sleep. It barely registered. Beneath his hands lay five distinct mazes, five separate blood types, and a stack of maze books he still had to compare before he could even think about shutting his tired, straining eyes.

Already on the floor were nearly fifty publications he'd already discounted. Too big. Too small. Too dark. Too light. Wrong texture of paper. Wrong color of type. There was always some reason to toss the book aside, only to have one or more of the agents on duty scavenge the "evidence" for his crossword-loving wife, girlfriend, or mistress.

"Free mazes for everyone!" Vinny felt like shouting, a few of the six thousand coffee grounds he'd ingested over the last 28 hours sparking a synapse or two in his tired brain and short-circuiting his mood from gloomy to giddy. It wouldn't last long. That much he knew from experience after taking one trip too many on the caffeine express.

His gaze fell once again on the five original mazes, pristine and pure beneath the polyurethane baggies with their tell-tale red crime evidence tags. He blinked his eyes, once, twice, and again. He'd been staring at them for hours, and wondered if this was, indeed, the priority he should be spending his time on.

He watched the other agents for a second, glad to be looking away from the blood-tracked pages of print that, after all, represented the deaths of five innocent, harmless women. They talked, they listened, the phones clipped directly into their ears as they wandered the room checking files, maps, weather charts, the works. They were capable men, men to trust.

Frank had said to delegate. Well, now Vinny was delegating. Something told him, deep in his gut, that the mazes *were* the thing. With no other clues, in fact, they were the only thing. "Let Frank profile this guy seven ways to Sunday," Vinny half-muttered, half-whispered to himself, looking up to see if anybody was watching. "These mazes will speak to me eventually."

In a way, they already had. The mazes had told him their texture, their feel, their look, their sheen. Or lack thereof. He knew their cheap paper, knew their carefully sliced perforations, knew their rounded borders as well as he knew the nape of his wife's long, elegant neck or the scar on his son's pinky toe—an early tricycle accident.

They were like faces in an interrogation room, each one individual, each one eerily identical. Like a code only he could read. A civilian, a crucial witness in one of his first serial murder cases, had looked at the half-dozen thugs in a six-pack Vinny had carefully prepared and rolled her eyes. "These guys all look the same to me," she had complained, visibly frustrated as her eyes flitted from creep to creep and thug to thug. "I wouldn't know how to begin telling them apart."

It was a common refrain, heard in countless cities in countless squad rooms from countless witnesses, but one, for the life of him, Vinny could not understand. He had looked at the six faces in that long-ago six-pack and thought, "How can't you tell them apart?"

By the time he'd finished trimming the edges on the mug shots and slipping them between the magnetic frame with its six telltale slots, he'd memorized every scar, blackhead, tattoo, piercing, dreadlock, and earlobe.

So it was with the mazes. By now he could pick up a book of

puzzles and not only know from which publisher they'd come, but what year they'd been printed and, in some cases, even what printer had done the job.

He'd spoken to twenty different sales reps from the twenty leading maze book publishers and, by now, understood page counts, distribution, readership, copyright, and cover art as well as any publishing intern or senior editor.

He knew that, the minute he saw the book from which the mazes had come, he'd know it. Trouble was, it could take days, weeks, months before that happened. It certainly wasn't from lack of trying. Day after day, FedEx, Airborne, and UPS trucks dropped off stacks of representative samples from the gaming lines of the industry's top puzzle publishers.

The stacks grew and diminished and grew and diminished by the hour. They ebbed and flowed like the tides, replenished by each day's delivery, depleted by Vinny's tireless inspection. Each new stack got Vinny's personal treatment, and still they came. And somehow, stack after stack, Vinny knew that wasn't the way he'd solve this case.

Oh, he knew it had to be done. And he knew he was the one to do it. By now he was the unofficial "maze man" among the younger agents.

"Where do you want these?" was the common refrain as delivery man after delivery man wheeled box after box into the hotel's cramped conference room.

"Give 'em to the maze man," an agent would invariably say, pointing distractedly to Vinny's converted picnic table where, at the mention of his nickname, Vinny would poke his head out from behind his latest stack of maze books and grin good-naturedly. Some of the delivery men had dropped off so many cases that they knew right where to go. "Morning, Maze Man," they'd say as Vinny grunted, as unhappy about the mindless moniker as he was about the six new cases of maze volumes awaiting his personal, blurry-eyed attention.

He sighed, rubbing sad eyes, and slipped quietly out of "maze mode" and desperately into "map mode." Vinny had been keeping a map since day one, something that came about by chance: A rental car agent had passed him a complimentary map of the United States. Idly, as he waited for his car to be washed, detailed, and assigned, he'd begun circling the points on the map where each murder had occurred.

At that time, the map had three circles. Now there were nearly twice that many and the map was tattered and torn, the silent, innocent victim of a dozen different ways of folding, crimping, cramping, in jacket pockets and laptop bags and hotel room dresser drawers and glove boxes.

The map never left his side. It rested there now, next to the six mazes. As Vinny pondered whether or not it was time for another cup of coffee, a junior agent crossed the room holding a fax.

Vinny tensed until the kid smiled. *Jesus*, Vinny thought, catching the gleam in the kids' eye, the cut of his jib, the pace of his step, the lack of wrinkles around his young, green, alert eyes. *This kid's just a...kid! Literally! When the hell did I get so old?*

"No worries, sir," the kid said. Vinny fought vaguely with the hour to recall "the kid's" name. Hopkins? Tompkins? Hop-Tompkins? Shit. "It's just a note from accounting. They need a senior agent to sign off on Logan's expenses thus far. If you could just initial the hotel charges in each state, I can fax it tonight and we can both get back to doing something more important."

"Good thinking, uh..." Vinny said, purposely leaving the sentence unfinished in case the junior agent cared to fill in the blank with his last name.

The kid smirked, getting the hint. "Franklin, sir. Agent Tony Franklin. From the Tennessee field office."

"Franklin, right." He nodded noncommittally as Franklin stood there expectantly. Vinny's eyes blurred as he stared at the dates, the time zones, and the states on Logan's expense report.

As his retinas scanned the plain sheet of white paper, blurred, and then refocused, he found himself staring at the rental car map just out of focus. Despite his deference to the senior agent, Franklin impatiently shifted his weight from foot to foot as Vinny went from map to fax, fax to map.

Florida.

Georgia.

North Carolina.

South Carolina.

Tennessee.

It was like one of those match-up games you did in *Highlights* magazine as you were waiting for the doctor to come back out into the waiting room and tell you it would cost $200 for the antibiotics to treat your kid's sinus infection. Dog to bowl. Cat to litter box. Bird to cage. The states were matching up, no doubt, but wasn't that to be expected?

"Sir," Franklin interrupted, eager to get back to work. "Your initials?"

"Right, right." Vinny nodded, wondering how long he'd been transfixed by the mental match-up. He quickly scribbled his initials next to each state and handed it back to Franklin. "Listen, kid," he said, scrambling to sound casual, "make me a copy of that fax, will ya? Logan will want it for his records, and if I don't have it by the time we hook up next, there'll be hell to pay, know what I mean?"

Franklin nodded seriously. Vinny paused, mouth open but unmoving, unsure about whether or not to press his luck. *In for a penny*, he thought, before continuing. "Also, do me a favor. Frank made mention in passing the other day about some big Halloween book signing he was going to be doing next week. Can you track down the details for that, if it's possible? I just want to surprise him when I show up and buy a copy. Long as we're dealing with the travel department, might as well line up all my ducks in a row, right?"

The kid made a mock salute. "Be right back, sir." He smiled, turning on the balls of his spit-polished shoes to zip over to the copy machine.

Vinny looked at his map, anxiously awaiting his copy of the fax.

Was this another maze?

Or just a bleary-eyed red herring?

40 Frank Logan stood outside the roped off convenience store and opened a fresh pack of Marlboro Ultra Lights. He hadn't smoked in, what was it now, three cases? Or four? Other ex-smokers kept track by years; Logan kept track by the gory case files of special circumstance murders he'd solved.

It didn't matter. He knew the warning signs: More than five murders, he knew he'd be smoking. Now, with a bittersweet Missouri winter shaping up as the morning kissed the sky, he flicked a brand new Bic lighter for the first time in months, the salty-sweet infusion of smoke reaching his grateful lungs as he sucked in the desperately familiar tang of nicotine and ash.

The reporter's phone call might have had something to do with it. He'd yet to speak with Bernie, but there'd be hell to pay when he finally did. Frank knew there was no credence to the story, but for years Bernie had been urging him to "let out some of the skeletons hidden in his closet."

"You're too clean," Bernie had complained, as if that were a bad thing. "You're never gonna top 100 million in sales if we don't dig up some dirt on you."

Was this his thinly veiled attempt? Hauling in some smart-ass reporter with a conspiracy theory and a chip on her shoulder?

"Shit," he spat as he finished the first cigarette in six long, taut bursts. "Shit, shit, shit."

"Hell of a case, huh, sir?" asked an older agent, serving in the Missouri branch.

"Yeah," Frank grunted, eyeing the man severely. "But that wasn't what I was shitting about. It's these damn coffin nails. I promised myself I wouldn't smoke again."

The agent smiled knowingly as they both lit up fresh cigarettes. "Hate to say it," the old man confessed, "but I'm grateful that you did. When my wife heard I was working this case with you, she made me promise I wouldn't smoke unless you did. I was afraid I couldn't hold out much longer."

Frank laughed despite himself, the universality of human frailty bringing him momentary comfort in the wake of so much loss, pain, and tragedy. Somewhere in the world, a world he no longer inhabited, housewives still cared that their husbands impressed their bosses. "That's why you're out here, Agent…."

Frank knew he'd been introduced to the man before, maybe twice by now, but for the life of him couldn't remember his name. Or anyone else's on scene, for that matter.

"Sherman," the man said as a trail of smoke rushed from his open mouth to punctuate his reply. "Stewart Sherman and, yes, I was just about to sneak around back and 'inspect something' until you hopped yourself right back on the smoke wagon and saved me the trip."

Frank nodded, squinting against the acrid smoke blown back into his eyes from a sudden breeze that swept off the vacant lot across the road from the Stop 'N Pop parking lot. "Glad I could oblige, Stewart," he said.

The two men smoked in silence for several minutes. Inhaling. Exhaling. Inhaling. Exhaling. The pattern at once familiar and comforting and yet slightly surreal in the face of an austere, painfully fresh crime scene. Suddenly, Frank looked up and broke their silence. "What time is it, Stewart?"

Both men realized that Frank had his own watch, and a pricey one at that, but Stewart knew it was just the senior agent's way of making conversation. He smiled to himself, trying to preserve the moment for posterity. All the better to tell his wife over supper that night. "6:45 a.m., sir," he replied in the dim, gray light before stamping out his second cigarette to Frank's third.

"Do troopers still have the road cordoned off, Stewart?" Frank asked. It was a game he played with himself: When he wanted to remember someone's name, he'd say it three times in conversation. Once to familiarize himself with it, another to remind himself of it, the third time to cement it in his short-term memory.

"Not since 4 a.m., sir," Stewart nodded.

"So, Stewart," Logan sighed, mentally ticking off the number three in his head. "Is it normally so quiet at this time of day? I've been to a lot of crime scenes this month, and this is pretty much prime time for traffic to get humming, isn't it? I haven't seen nary a trucker since I walked out here. That strike you as odd?"

He resisted the temptation to make his fourth and fifth usage of the agent's name in the same sentence, trying to sound less like a formal letter and more like a friend. Or at least a colleague.

"Not really, sir," Stewart admitted after struggling with the answer. It was a toss-off comment for a man like Logan. For Stewart, it was an audition. "I'd hate to think how sparse traffic was when he snatched that girl."

Frank looked up, admiring the elder man. There would be no need to use his name anymore. At least not his last name. "My thoughts exactly, Stewart. I'm thinking our boy had all the time in the world. So why was he so sloppy?"

Stewart pondered whether or not the question was rhetorical. He hoped so, as at the moment he had no answer for the man whose latest bestseller was currently resting on his wife's nightstand, a bookmark bearing the poem "Footprints" marking her place. He'd seen many killers in his thirty-four years with the FBI, but nothing like this. Most of them had been drifters passing through, bikers, ex-cons, that kind of thing. Not exactly masterminds.

And those had been the hard ones. The rest of his cases were less bloody, more technical. A bank robbery here, a case of mail fraud there. Now he was standing with a guy he'd been seeing on the news for the last six weeks straight, not to mention for years on the Forensics Channel and MSNBC, and he's asking *him* if something was strange or not?

Luckily, Frank was just thinking aloud, and followed his statement quickly by answering his own question: "I mean, he's got no traffic, half a dozen cameras, twice as many blind spots, and nothing in the beer cooler where he actually snatched her. Quick strangle, no funny business. There was no, style. No...panache. You know? This may have been our guy, Stewart, but he certainly wasn't himself last night."

Stewart nodded, knowing well enough not to speak unless spoken to. He knew, despite Logan's use of his name, that he wasn't really talking to him anymore.

"It's almost like he felt rushed. In a hurry. Like he had some mental deadline he was racing to meet. But what? This is his masterpiece, this whole crazy thing. Piece by piece, girl by girl, maze by maze, he's been so careful to build up this house of cards. And now *this*? These guys work out this shit for years. It's all they do. Every day. All day.

"They may work, and be good at it, pros, the top of the their game. They may have wives and kids, but it's in their heads even while they're making conversation, making house payments, making dinner, making love. That loop just never ends, and they're good enough to fake being human to see that their plans are fulfilled. That's why it's so hard to catch 'em. No way can we ramp up to speed that fast. Playing catch-up is all we can do, at best, and they're often years ahead of us, literally, when it comes to the planning.

"So this slop job just doesn't make sense. There has to be a reason for it. I've counted three cars, two of them long-haul truckers speeding by with hardly a glance in our direction, and we're surrounded by crime scene tape and blinking squad cars.

"Last night must have seemed like the surface of the moon. And all alone, he doesn't enjoy it. Doesn't work his magic. So what was the reason? What was the purpose? Unless…unless he's trying to divide and conquer. He knows I've got a new partner, knows I've got to adjust to our new dynamic, make compromises all of a sudden. He knows the rules have changed. So maybe he saw us getting too chummy on the news, maybe he caught us finishing each other's sentences, hunched over a few too many files, getting just a little too comfortable for our own good.

"Maybe he didn't feel comfortable getting teamed up on, you know? Maybe this one wasn't planned. Maybe this one wasn't in his grand scheme. Maybe this is just his attempt to pit my new partner and me against each other.

"I just don't know, Vinny."

"Stewart, sir," the older, though still junior, agent corrected him quietly.

"What's that, Stewart?" Frank frowned.

"You called me Vinny, sir." Stewart blushed at having to correct the senior agent.

"No shit." Frank nodded vaguely, whipping the quickly thinning pack of cigarettes from his trademark charcoal gray jacket. "I don't know what came over me. Sorry, Stewart. That was exceedingly rude of me."

Stewart opened his mouth to reply, but stopped just short, choosing to light up instead. He could tell from the faraway look in Logan's eyes that he wouldn't have heard him anyway.

41 Franklin was once again standing expectantly at Vinny's makeshift desk, a four-legged picnic table with a padded plastic cover that sagged in the middle where his laptop glowed, its vibrant screen filled with enough charts and graphs to make an Algebra teacher giddy. After clearing his throat several times, Vinny finally looked up. "Apparently another housekeeping issue has popped up, sir," said the eager young agent. "Literally. Seems Director Logan didn't have time to check out when the command center demanded he go right to Missouri the other night."

Vinny waited for the punch line. When it wasn't forthcoming, he looked at his watch. 7 a.m. Where had the last three hours gone? "And?" he spat, reaching instinctively for a cup of coffee he'd thrown away two hours ago.

Franklin looked hurt. "Oh, well, sorry, sir, but, now they need someone to go up and clear out his stuff. There's a convention of pediatricians checking in, and I guess they need the room. I was going to take care of it, but I wasn't sure what type of classified information Director Logan might have lying around in there, so...."

"You did the right thing." Vinny smiled, making pains to be overly condescending after snapping at the eager beaver. "You got a key? I need to take a shower, anyway. Maybe they gave him an extra bar of soap. My room's plumb out."

The kid laughed. Friends again. Vinny was glad. Franklin handed him a generic looking passkey and whispered, "Room 217," as if perhaps the walls had ears and Maze himself might be listening.

Vinny smiled, earnestly, a knee-jerk reaction to the kid's obvious sincerity. "Got it, uh, Franklin," he said, standing up on weak legs.

"Kitchen opens in a few minutes. Can I grab you something on my way back?"

Franklin stammered, "Oh, no, no, thanks, sir. I just had a Power Bar and that'll keep me running until at least nine. But, thanks, I really appreciate that."

Both men stood there expectantly, eyeing each other, until a fleeting memory of the previous 180 minutes forced Vinny to ask, "Hey, listen, did the home office have any idea where Logan was going to release his latest bestseller next week? I'm not trying to be a snoop, I just think I could score some major brownie points with the old man if I popped up and bought a few copies, you know?"

"Oh right, right," Franklin stammered, fishing through his pockets until he found a scrap sheet of hotel stationery. "I remember you asked me to get you that information. Far as I can tell, Frank's got a book signing in none other than Batesville, Arkansas on Halloween Eve."

"Arkansas?" Vinny spat, surprised. "Who the hell launches a national book tour in Arkansas? I was thinking New York, Chicago, or LA, right?"

Franklin grinned. "Well," he explained, grateful to be in on the scoop, "word around the home office is that his agent set it up because Batesville will put people in mind of Norman Bates and, since the new book is about serial killers, what better place to kick it off than a town named for one of Hollywood's first serial killers?"

Vinny nodded, the logic suddenly clear, though the timing far from convenient. *Who the hell interrupts a national special circumstances investigation to sign copies of his latest book?* he thought as Franklin gave him a quick mock salute.

Vinny returned the gesture, careful to wait until Franklin had turned once more on his heels and headed back to his own sagging picnic table before grabbing up his map and Frank's expense report.

His palm was sweaty on the pass key as he took the fire stairs up to the second floor, grateful for the first rush of blood below his neck in the last dozen or so hours. He passed a room service cart and two housekeepers fighting over the vacuum before finally standing, knock-kneed, in front of the door to the room his partner had spent less than thirty minutes in two days prior.

He felt the blood rising to his face, as if he were being monitored, but he knew the set-up at the Holiday Inn didn't allow for it. This wasn't Vegas, after all. There were no "eyes in the sky" watching his every move. He was alone. And he knew it. Worse yet, he knew what was on his mind, and he knew it wouldn't go away until he satisfied his own morbid curiosity.

He slid the key into the lock slot, watched the light turn green, turned the knob and quietly crept inside. The room was untouched, pristine, and felt hollow. The only thing Frank had had time to do before heading to the crime scene was wash his hands, as evidenced by the single soap wrapper in the trash can and a nearly fresh bar of flat, generic, white hotel room soap lying in the clam-shaped divot next to the dripping faucet.

A clothes hanger, unzipped, remained in the closet. A matching carry-on was just to the left of the in-room safe, the door of which stood open, revealing empty shelves. Had Frank had the bellboy drop off his bags?

Vinny purposefully avoided the mirrored closet door as he bent down on tired knees and carefully unzipped Frank's duffel. It was predictably full of clean black socks, carefully rolled, prescription reading glasses, most likely a back-up pair, as Vinny had seen Frank reach for his main pair in the pocket of his jacket on countless occasions, and five unopened two-packs of XL boxer shorts, striped, not plaid, and a bound review galley of his latest book, *The Killing Kind: Theories and Practice from a Master Mind Hunter.*

"Subtle, Frank," Vinny mused as he put the book back. "Real subtle."

The hanging bag was more of the same. Stiff suits, white shirts, a row of muted ties, breath mints, golf tees, of all things, and a dopp kit full of over-the-counter aftershave and prescription painkillers. He felt embarrassed again, prying through his partner's personal effects, but he couldn't shake the gut instinct that kept him moving forward, from pocket to pocket, zipper to zipper, until he'd physically examined every single one of Frank's left-behind possessions.

He justified his actions by theorizing that Frank would do the same thing in his shoes, only probably a lot quicker, and grabbed the bags to leave the room. As he finally allowed himself a quick look in the mirror, he noticed for the first time the shaft of light seeping into the room from a tiny part between one side of the curtain and the other. More specifically, he saw that, as the light fell onto the chaotically patterned comforter, it revealed a slight depression mid-mattress.

Just where someone would sit if he were sticking something in the nightstand. Vinny crossed the room, watching the colony of dust mites he kicked up dance merrily in the single shaft of light. He lost the impression the closer he got to the bed and wondered idly about fate: What if he'd still been too embarrassed to look into the mirror? What if he hadn't looked at precisely the right time? What if it had been cloudy out?

He shook his head. "Keep thinking like that," he muttered, sitting on the spot on the bed where someone's—Frank's?—rump had recently sat, "and you'll be taking another trip to the nearest bookstore. Only this time you'll be wandering aimlessly around the self-help section with all the other relapsed beatniks."

He hesitated, for just a moment, then reached quickly for the drawer. "In for a penny," he whispered reverently as he pulled at the brass knob on the pressed board dresser. Inside rested a Bible. Nothing else. No suicide note. No clue. No "gotcha" in the form of a stink bomb or other embarrassing trap. Just a giveaway Bible, with nothing wedged between its gold-leaf pages or slipped underneath.

He sighed, then smiled, then laughed, then stood up, then walked away, then turned back, as if on instinct, his legs, arms, eyes, and gut taking over where his training left off. Quickly he flipped up the mattress and immediately spotted the bound book with the purple cover. Thinner than a book, actually, but kind of thick for a magazine. In garish yellow print the spine read, "Mazes for Masters."

It wasn't just a book of mazes. He knew even before opening the cover, even before flipping to the first missing maze, that it was *the* book of mazes.

So what the hell was it doing in Frank Logan's room?

42

Guy was making excuses. Again. "I'm *not* putting you off, Mr. Brilstein," he sighed for the third time into the mouthpiece clipped to his $90 silk shirt. "Mr. Segal really *is* out of town."

Brilstein barked something unintelligible into his speaker phone, forcing Guy to take his well-manicured finger and press it gently against the metallic earpiece to better hear the famed Hollywood producer's request.

"Yes, I know it seems like he's been on the road a lot these days," Guy protested, trying in vain to do a little damage control as the espresso machine coughed temptingly across the room. "But with this Maze Murderer thing heating up, he's had to go hands-on with the pre-publicity for the new Frank Logan book. In fact, if I'm not mistaken, I believe he's headed south this time around, something about setting up a book-signing for his favorite client. As you well know, Mr. Brilstein, if it wasn't for Senior Director Logan, Bernie would be glued to his desk chair awaiting your phone call."

Brilstein muttered several vague obscenities, which Guy promptly ignored, before hanging up. Guy smirked. He saw no reason to tell Brilstein that Bernie traveled for *all* his clients. Day. Night. Week. Weekend. Coach. First class. Chartered. Lear. Didn't matter.

He was a glorified ambulance chaser, after all. It was nothing for him to see some girl get pulled out of a well during the evening news and be on a plane to Armpit, Ohio or Ass Crack, West Virginia the very next day to sign her up as a client.

"Of course, ma'am," Guy could hear him say, both ass cheeks firmly planted on a plastic slip cover as the child's mother offered him a plate of stale Fig Newtons and slick Vienna Sausages, "fifty percent of your daughter's profits is more than fair. Industry standard, after all, is *sixty* percent! Why, yes, I'd love another glass of sweetened ice tea, thank you kindly. Can you tell me, is it powdered or from a can?"

Guy returned to his laptop and scrolled down to the schedule button, revealing his boss' itinerary for the rest of the week. Scrolling down, humming, he soon began singing. His hands fumbled nervously for the button on his headset as he fumbled to hit "redial."

"Hampton," he said, leaving a message for his boyfriend, a model-slash-actor-slash-waiter-slash-screenwriter-slash-caterer-slash-producer currently between all of the aforementioned jobs. "Bernie's away until this time tomorrow. If you hurry, we can make it on his bearskin rug before the FedEx guy gets here. Or, hell, if you're up for it, we can wait until he gets here and see if he's interested. Catch you in ten."

What the hell, Guy thought to himself as he propped open the front door in anticipation of a little afternoon delight.

43

Frank Logan sat in the darkened movie theater and waited for the previews to begin. It was midday, he was missing no less than three meetings with the locals, and here he was, sitting in a strange Missouri theater. But it was the one place no one would look for him and the only place he could get away with muting his eternally ringing cell phone—at least for one hundred and twenty sweet, solitary minutes.

There was a bag of popcorn to his left, a diet soda to his right, both of which would remain untouched throughout the two-hour-long hiatus Frank had just begun. The cell phone was buried deep in his pocket, the case files back in his car, the case itself fresh and clear behind his tired, aching eyes.

He dug into his shirt pocket and retrieved two Excedrin, popping them into his mouth and chewing them dry, and old habit, even though he knew it was the remotest of possibilities that they'd even touch, let alone cure, his three-day-long migraine.

Finally, the screen flickered to life in the antique theater. First one preview then another blared out at him from the screen as the theater's vain attempt at anything as modern as "surround sound" faltered back and forth: One speaker would shut out in the back, then another spring to life in the front, and vice versa. It was like watching a movie and listening to a tennis match at the same time.

It mattered little. Frank was there for the peace and quiet, discovering on a long ago case in a long ago town that he could think best when lifted from the crime scene and plopped into a darkened movie theater.

Now, on every high profile case he'd ever solved, a movie theater had played a vital role. He could clearly remember his epiphany years earlier while watching the second, or was it the third, *Nightmare on Elm Street*, when he put two and two together and discovered his latest killer was a woman and not a man.

Thus, the Cross-Dressing Killer was solved thanks to Freddy Krueger and a glove tipped with scalpel-sharp knives. Other movies, immediately forgettable, had helped solve now-legendary crimes and yet few—in fact, only Margie back in DC—knew his "dirty little secret."

He knew right now the locals were screaming into their cell phones, barking at the brass, who would soon be screaming even louder into *their* cell phones. That didn't matter, either. What mattered was that this was the only place in Missouri where he could get some peace and quiet, even if it *was* between blaring previews and the screams and hollers of some B-rated horror flick.

He dug deeper in his seat as the house lights went down, somehow able to block out the gore of the opening scene and managing instead to zoom in on the real horrors that marked his own life, both personally and professionally.

Soon the theater was gone, the movie was gone, the sounds were gone, and all he could see was the killer as he brutalized his victims. Calm and detached were both men, as Frank knew this was less about the blood, sex, and gore and more about the thrill of the chase.

Killers were smarter today, this much he knew. They learned police procedure from the Forensics Channel, read about what not to do in true crime books, and devoured court transcripts like others did the daily crossword puzzles. They cleaned up better, hid smarter, and destroyed evidence more thoroughly than any other generation of killers before them.

But the one thing they *couldn't* do was enjoy the perspective of any veteran cop. Most big city cops saw more murder scenes in one year than even the most prolific serial killer could imagine in an entire lifetime.

They saw what guns could do, and what knives did. They knew who'd been raped and who'd just been posed to look like they'd been raped, even before the first med tech took the first swab out of the first rape kit. They knew which killers were organized, which were targets of opportunity, which were gay, which were straight, which were high on crack, hell, they could even get it down to the caliber of gun if they'd been doing it long enough.

Long enough? Days like this made Frank feel as if he had been doing it longer than anybody on the planet. He knew just what this guy was about. He sensed that Vinny felt it, too, even with his limited experience. Though that, too, was quickly about to change. This wasn't a lust killer, a spree killer, or even a serial killer. This was a guy who had it out for authority, in general, and Frank Logan, in particular.

Frank felt it was personal. Hell, Frank *knew* it was personal. Perhaps it was his vanity, but he didn't think so. The mazes were just too...too...theatrical. Too forced. Real killers kept trophies. Stupid shit no one else knew about. An earring from the very back of the jewelry box. A Christmas gift from under the tree. Hell, he'd once studied the cold case of a killer who was arrested two decades after the murders when a toy Batmobile had been found in his possession and the victims' son remembered it had gone missing the night his parents were murdered some twenty years earlier.

Only mind fucks left such obvious signature clues. Only vain, egotistical, star suckers left mazes shoved up cigar tubes or lurking in ice cream coolers or hidden in empty beer cans.

This was a guy who hadn't had a normal erection in years, maybe even decades. This was a guy who'd never fit in, who was most likely successful, if only because he tried so very, very hard. This was also a guy who never, ever, not for even one single solitary day, felt comfortable in his very own skin.

It all came down to the mazes, this much Frank knew. But how? He wished Vinny would call him, wished Vinny would figure it out. He'd given him one task: figure out the mazes.

He knew it was an impossible task, something it might take a team of forensic specialists with decades of experience more than six months to accomplish, but for some reason, Frank had a feeling about Vinny.

A gut instinct that said, "If anyone could do it, Vinny could."

But now he wasn't so sure. The kid was still playing by the rules. Finessing the locals, adding up clues, working with the team, faxing in updates to the home office four times a day, going straight by the book.

How could Frank tell him that the book, like the clues, was for pussies? That the book was written by bureaucrats who hadn't gotten off their asses in years and who hadn't actually been in the field for decades?

Frank needed a gut player. He could tell Vinny was his man, but he needed a few more years of blood and guts experience—literally, in this case—to bring him up to speed. Years they didn't have right now. Still, young was the only way to go.

There were a dozen agents more experienced than Vinny that he could have gone with, and yet where Vinny would have to be brought up to speed, those men and women would have to be something even worse: retrained. Vinny was fresh clay, waiting, ready, and willing to be molded. The vets were old dogs who were unable, or unwilling, to learn new tricks at this late stage of the game. Frank was all alone. Partner or no, he was flying solo.

He took a rare look up at the screen, watching as some half-baked killer in cheap gloves and cheaper shoes dispatched a pretty teen victim whose firm, naked breasts fairly glistened, awash in cheap red movie blood, placed just so to enhance maximum mammary potential. A wet T-shirt contest, without the shirt.

He thought of Maze's victims. Candace. Lisa. Rhonda. Gina. Cassie. He thought of their families and the years of grief, tears, and therapy that awaited them. He thought of the locals, scratching their heads as Maze, Frank, and even Vinny left them in their dust.

It made no sense. The women were worse than unconnected, they were entirely *unrelated*. There was nothing tying them together, except for the killer. He knew they were random. He knew it. So why involve the locals? The locals were secondary, as were the crime scenes, the hour, the temperature, and the order of victims.

Yes, even that was irrelevant. As far as Frank was concerned, they too were interchangeable. Florida might as well have been Georgia might as well have been Tennessee. What did it matter? Unless the mazes weren't only mazes. Unless the mazes were something more. Unless the mazes were...*maps*.

Frank looked up at the screen to find two rumpled cops straight out of central casting sitting in a squad car discussing the fake movie killer. He didn't hear their words; he was already digging into his pocket for his cell phone.

44

Vinny Smalldeano's cell phone was ringing, but he dared not answer it. Not yet, anyway. He saw the name of the caller clearly without even opening the phone: "Logan, Frank." But it was too soon to talk to the man whom he now suspected of killing six women in as many states.

Vinny stood awkwardly in a phone booth six blocks from the hotel, sitting next to a stack of 60 minute phone cards and talking to the only person he could trust in the world: his wife, Tina.

Tina had never taken a class in forensic criminology, never lectured extensively on criminal profiling. Hell, she'd never even fired a gun. Unless their annual 4th of July Super Soaker swimming pool fight counted.

And yet on every big case he'd ever worked, there came a point where her objectivity, her clear head, her street smarts, her common sense, were not only valuable to Vinny, but vital. She could see things he'd long since forgotten, misplaced, or misread. He just hoped she answered.

"Hello," she gasped on the sixth ring, clearly out of breath. Vinny could imagine her juggling three sacks of groceries as their two boys fought over a bag of candy bars in the driveway.

"Tina," he said, relief coloring his words.

"Vinny?" she gasped. Then, recognizing the fear in his voice, she added, "You're stumped, aren't you? Talk to me, baby."

Those were the words he'd longed to hear.

So Vinny did. He told her all of it, right there on that unsecured land line a mere six blocks from where some of the finest agents in the FBI were probably looking for him at that very moment. He spilled it all: the clues, the crimes, the mazes, Frank's room, the light, the dust, the drawer, the book, the works. It took her exactly ten seconds to whisper, "Jesus, Vinny. Frank Logan. Really?"

"I hope not," he sighed, a sleepless night translating into panicky vocal chords the next day. "You've got to play my devil's advocate on this one, Tina. You've got to shoot holes in my theory. One by one."

"Got it," she said, unemotional, detached, instinctively knowing that every second counted and that this very conversation could color the rest of the investigation—not to mention Vinny's entire career—for better or worse. "Shoot."

"Florida," he said. "Scene of the first crime. Teenage girl, Candace Myers, butchered in the ice cream parlor where she worked. First maze found."

"And Frank?" she asked. "Where was he at the time?"

"Dunno," Vinny mumbled. "I was busy wrapping up that local homicide in Massachusetts and didn't even know about the Maze Murderer. Nobody did. She was his first."

"So, Frank could have been there, or he could have not. You're gonna have to get his travel records, somehow. Not the ones after the first crime, but before. You've got to go back a week and figure out if he could have been there."

"How?" Vinny gasped.

"His secretary?" Tina offered before quickly discounting that theory and answering herself. "No, she can't be trusted. What about...."

"Forget it," Vinny muttered, suddenly realizing their predicament. "I've got a fax listing his movements *after* each murder, and it's bare bones. Hotel room charges, room service, rental cars, outsourced photocopying. He'd be too smart to log his pre-murder miles. This guy's the king of dark tricks. Why would something as simple as logging in with an airport trip or putting in an expense report for a trip to Disney World trip him up?"

"Okay," Tina soothed, her voice receptive and calm even in the face of this obvious setback. "So until you came onboard, he could have been anywhere, done anything. He wouldn't have recorded those miles, his secretary wouldn't give them to you anyway, and that's a dead ball, right?"

"Right. And I met up with him in South Carolina. Since then, we've been stuck together like glue, so how could he have murdered the hooker in Tennessee and the latest, this convenience store clerk in Missouri?"

"I thought *I* was the one supposed to be playing devil's advocate?" Tina asked.

"You're right, you're right," Vinny admitted humorlessly. "It's just that I don't want this to be true, this just can't be true. I've been troubleshooting myself all night. I just can't see clearly anymore."

"Okay, Vinny, relax," Tina said calmly. "We'll figure this out. Together. The first thing you've got to do is look at it logically. You're too caught up in this, too emotional. You've bought into the whole Frank Logan mystique, the myth, and you want it to be true. But you've told me a thousand times if you've told me once, 'The minute a cop starts trying to fit the clues to the suspect, they've already shot themselves in the foot.' So you've got to release yourself. Either Frank's the killer, or he isn't. It's that simple. What do the *clues* tell you?"

"The clues tell me there's no way he could do this. No way he could be gone long enough to slip over to Tennessee and kill that hooker and then get back to South Carolina the next day to have coffee with me. We've got meetings every day, all day. How could he?"

"You're exaggerating, right?" Tina asked, zeroing in on Vinny's soft spot. "Do you *literally* meet with Frank every day, all day? Think about it, Vinny. How could you? Weren't there opportunities for him to slip away for hours at a time?"

"Hours, sure," Vinny admitted somewhat reluctantly. "But it's a trek from South Carolina to Tennessee and back. And the guy's gotta sleep sometime."

"That's right, Vinny," Tina said quietly. "So, do you two sleep together? Do you know where he is from, say, midnight to six a.m.? Or eleven at night until seven the next morning? Even an extra fifteen minutes at night and twenty in the morning gives him close to 40 stolen minutes. It adds up. That's a lot of hours to account for."

"But *six* hours, Tina? He'd have to be a speed racer to zip from South Carolina to Tennessee in that amount of time. Right?"

"That's not entirely true, Vinny. You say South Carolina and Tennessee like they're different countries. But if you're talking going from the West end of South Carolina to the East end of Tennessee, well, that's not very far at all. Plus, didn't you say he has the luxury of a Lear jet or helicopter at his disposal?"

"He wouldn't involve a pilot." Vinny dismissed the notion out of turn. "There's just no way he'd leave a witness behind. He knows I'd get to him eventually."

There was silence on both ends of the phone for perhaps thirty seconds, and then Vinny piped up. "The weather," he said finally. "There was a cold snap in South Carolina, and we never even identified that particular victim. Nor could we tell if she was killed before or after the victim in North Carolina. We assumed she came first because that made sense, geographically speaking, but chronologically we could never be sure. Same with Tennessee and now Missouri," he concluded, already picturing the crime scene photos in his head.

"So, theoretically at least," Tina posed, "he could have killed them out of the order they were found. Georgia before Florida, South Carolina before Florida…."

"No," Vinny argued. "The girl in Florida was seen only hours before she was killed, same as the girl in Georgia. Those dates and times of death are more firm. The unidentified victim in South Carolina is a variable we can't determine, and the hooker in Tennessee hadn't been seen in days by the time a concerned citizen found her, so those two aren't firm dates by any means."

"So he could have killed both of them while he was on the case in Georgia, or North Carolina, right? Before you were brought on?"

"I suppose," Vinny said with a pained expression. "But no way Missouri. I was with him night and day when we found out about her. He couldn't have slipped away. Not a chance."

"Unless…," Tina began.

"He's got a partner," Vinny finished.

"Shit," husband and wife said simultaneously.

"I gotta go, babe," Vinny said, already collecting his unused phone cards and vibrating cell phone.

"I know, baby," Tina murmured. "Go get 'em, and call me when you can."

"Could be days, baby, could be days," Vinny warned.

"Whatever it takes, Vinny," she said even as he hung up the phone.

45

Frank tried Vinny's cell phone, then his hotel room phone, then the front desk, then the converted war room in the hotel. Then he tried them all over again. Twice. Three times. Four. All in vain. No one had seen him. No one had even heard from him.

Frank quit calling. He'd left enough messages by now to go hoarse. He knew the kid would call him, he just didn't know where he was. It tripped him up. Contact was vital; the flow of information, key. Vinny knew that; it was lesson number one in FBI Procedures 101. So where the hell *was* he?

Frank thought about his extravagant two hours in the darkened movie theater and felt momentarily chagrined, worried that somehow he'd been the proverbial pot-calling-the-kettle-black. Another reason to feel guilty loomed on the horizon: He'd soon have to go "off reservation" and enter the civilian world for his much-anticipated Halloween Eve book-signing in Arkansas, of all places. A contract was a contract, and Bernie was nothing if not a stickler about their various legal agreements.

Alternately, Frank flushed for another reason: anger.

By God, he'd earned those 120 frickin' minutes of radio silence. And, truth be told, a few stolen hours at the launch of what could turn out to be a *very* lucrative book tour. Vinny was still wet behind the ears. He should have been glued to the phone. Night. Day. Day. Night. And every other minute in between. What the hell was *wrong* with him?

Frank felt alone once again. He sat in the car outside the movie theater and pondered his next move. The scene in Missouri already felt dead. He knew the killer had moved on, that he was maybe 48 to 72 hours ahead of him, and in this day and age, that meant he could be virtually anywhere by now. A quick flight to Tahiti. A slow shuttle to Seattle. A bus ride to Pittsburgh. Or a rest stop four miles down the road.

To date, they hadn't obtained a single shred of physical evidence, save for the mazes. Not a hair, not a fiber, not a description, not a car, not a…wait, that wasn't quite right, either.

Frank picked up his latest report and noted the address of the hooker stroll in Tennessee where their prostitute named "Gina" had disappeared. The old woman who'd found the body had given them voluminous details about the victim, but only one lead about the killer: Lola, the last person to see Gina alive.

She'd described a man in a car. A "silvery" car, to be precise. The transcript of the first interview was too vague; Lola was too hopped up on this drug or that to see clearly in her mind's eye. They would need another interview. Soon. Before she went on another bender or smoked a few more hits of rock and killed those particular brain cells they needed to tap.

Where the *hell* was Vinny?

46

Maze was making tracks, but even as he crossed the state line he could feel the buzz following him. Even as the news stories heated up, he knew there was a story *behind* the story, the one the reporters weren't getting, the one even the FBI agents couldn't fathom. He could sense that they were on to him. Not "him," per se. That would be impossible at this early stage of the game; he'd been much too careful and was flying much too low to even show up as a blip on their radar screens. But they were on to the *essence* of him.

The reasoning, the drama, the game, the folly, the mazes. He knew the more he killed, the more of himself he gave away. Not physically, maybe. He'd been too careful there. But psychologically speaking.

Every murder revealed more and more about himself. No matter how clever he got with the knife or a syringe, no matter how clean—or dirty—he left the victim, no matter how he posed them or where he shoved that maze or from where he snatched the girl, there were clues he just couldn't hide.

His eagerness, perhaps. His impotence. His mock cunning. His insecurity. His distaste for violence. Or thirst for the same.

He could only outthink them for so long before they would finally put one and two and three and four together and solve his game. He was what they called "escalating." That much he knew. That much he recognized in himself. Getting wilder and wilder, too protected by the safety of his ruse, too cocky and swagger-sure of his abilities to get away with it.

But even that was part of the fun. The control, and then lack thereof, thrilled him. To go back and forth twelve times a day: They're on to me, no, they can't be, yes, they are, no, they can't.

Even that, in and of itself, was something of a turn-on.

He was almost glad the end was near. He was tired of the killing. Tired of the hunting. It was hard work. Sitting long hours watching some tramp walk her beat or white trash co-ed sip her Sex on the Beach when all he wanted to do was get it over with and move on to the next one and, a few months down the line, collect his prize.

It was droll and self-indulgent and boring. Only the chase thrilled him anymore. Only the rival whom none had ever beaten before. Only the man, the legend himself, could drive him forward, keep him renting these cars and hiding these mazes and killing these poor, boring, dull, already lifeless and far too innocent girls.

He didn't care how many he killed, as long as the game was fun. He knew the stakes were getting higher, knew his time was running out. They could only last so long, the Feds, before the headlines would turn sour and "Frank the legend" would become "Frank the loser."

The press was exceedingly fickle, the FBI brass doubly so. Frank was still the star, still the sole, last hope against a merciless killer too cunning for anyone else to capture. It would be no fun to vanquish Frank the loser. Nor, in fact, would there be any profit in it for him if he did so.

He still wanted, still *needed*, to master Frank in his prime. But how long could *that* last?

He put Tony Robbins back into the rental car's CD player and tooled along, feeling bittersweet and loathsome about the kill ahead. He would have to wait a little longer for this one. Sit tight on her, watch her, stalk her, and wait until the Feds were just a tad closer before he could finally kill her right in their own backyard.

This prey was special. This victim unique. And no Fed could resist coming to her aid. Least of all the great and mighty avenger Frank Logan.

It was Maze's job to make sure he was just a tad too late.

47

Vinny watched the last of his staff leave the war room for their own hotel rooms. The minute the door slammed shut in the junior agent's wake, he pulled out a crisp bag from Kinko's and cleared the fold-up picnic table before him to give the effect of a tabula rasa—a clean slate.

Directly after leaving the phone booth following his conversation with Tina, Vinny had raced to the busy copy shop near the college and had the mazes run off in every conceivable manner: on regular copy paper, on hard-to-find and doubly expensive onion skin, on clear transparencies, on different colors, paper stocks, weights, thicknesses, whatever, however he could.

Now he spread the vast array of mazes out on the table and tried to visualize how they went together. It was hard working alone. Even in the short time he'd known him, he yearned for Frank's expertise, for his vision. For his uncanny ability to follow the lead wherever it went, be it to the killer's doorstep or his own best friend's.

The objectivity Frank, and Tina, to a smaller degree, possessed was the one piece of the puzzle that Vinny lacked. He could see the forest. He could see the trees, too. He just couldn't see them both at the same time.

It had always been that way. Growing up, he'd wanted nothing more than to be the reigning champ of all things video game. Galaga. Space Invaders. Pac Man. Centipede. Frogger. It didn't matter which game, or how many quarters he invested in mastering it. His legend, his dream, never made it past the first few stages. He could only get so far and then, just as the high score was in reach, it eluded him.

He'd practice for hours on end, toiling away in a tiny game room on the wrong side of town just so no one from his neighborhood would know what he was up to. He went without lunch money, pissed away every cent of his already meager allowance, even traded in some of his best baseball cards, all in search of that elusive next quarter.

He was good, no doubt about it. But the real legends of the game, the real masters, were kids who could see not just the missile aimed at their ray gun, but the three ships they needed to shoot *before* they dodged the missile.

Vinny always felt like he was playing catch-up, and in turn, the game's high score always eluded him. He imagined himself standing there, cool and aloof, the bells and buzzers and blinking lights falling on deaf ears as he coolly calculated the effects of this shot versus that one.

Zigging when he should zig, zagging when his instincts said zag, firing, exploding this neuron bomb at just the right time for the greatest effect, watching as the high score disappeared in the distance and feeling the crush of onlookers as, finally, the crowd closed in to see the new kid take over.

And yet, the reality was quite different. He was but a passable player in a short-lived fad that nonetheless haunted him to this very day. Now the murder game was no different than the video games. He could see the blood of this crime scene or the gore of that one, but putting the two together was a skill he lacked. How could he ever be a Frank Logan if he couldn't even *catch* Frank Logan?

The question bothered him, and as he sat there at his desk, rearranging maze after maze, color after color, onion skin to transparency, he wracked his brain for an answer. How could Frank possibly be the Maze Murderer?

It was impossible. It had to be. And yet, how could the maze book have wound up under his bed? He knew he should have told Frank about the book by now, but as it turned out, he hadn't returned a single one of Frank's messages. He knew he wouldn't be able to control his voice, not when a killer was on the other end of the line.

It had been hard enough to bask in the legend of Frank Logan, FBI hero. How would he ever handle Frank Logan, mass murderer?

Still, he knew to catch a killer meant you had to think like a killer. And, in this case, that meant thinking like Frank Logan. And if there was one thing Vinny knew about Frank, it was that he was a merciless interrogator.

Rarely loud, vaguely threatening, quietly menacing, he took his time with a suspect. Drawing him out, screwing him over, tricking him, befriending him, flipping him, twisting him, until the poor schmuck eventually thought the only way out was to confess.

He was equally ruthless with clues. In the short time they'd partnered together, Vinny had watched Frank noodle over a single crime scene photo for days on end. He'd spend an hour in one quadrant of the photo, zeroing in on a shoe or earring, only to spend another two hours staring at a folded overcoat or an open purse three inches to the left.

Now Vinny would have to do the same. Forest. Trees. Forest and trees at the same time. This much he knew: professional courtesy was no longer a concern of his. If Vinny knew Frank at all, he knew that if Frank considered him the killer, he would pursue him until the end of time. Friendship, professional courtesy, or otherwise. The job came first. And he did his job exceedingly well.

Vinny blinked his eyes, downed his twelfth cup of coffee of the day, and took another look at the mazes. He quickly decided there were too many. Reproducing them had been a good idea; staring at them all at once was not.

He put away all but the transparencies, admiring them over and over again. Stacking them on top of each other produced a momentary thrill, until the lines printed on the maze blurred with the path to the solution left by the killer.

He separated them next, laying them end to end, then side by side. The hour was growing late, and the lines were beginning to blur together once again. He could all but hear the pings and pongs of those long-distant alien invasions as he dumped his last quarter into the final game of Galaga for the night.

Forest. Trees. Forest and trees.

"Fuck the fucking trees," Vinny spat, sliding the clear mazes off the folding picnic table and onto the floor in a rare display of pent-up emotion. "I *hate* fucking trees."

Vinny closed his eyes. Vinny blinked his eyes. Vinny rubbed his eyes. Vinny reached for his empty Styrofoam cup, then cursed the similarly empty coffeepot halfway across the room.

Looking from the coffee-stained pot to the maze-scattered floor, Vinny suddenly saw the forest, the trees, *and* the forest-and-the-trees. But first and foremost he saw the floor-length map some of the junior agents had had blown up and taped on the floor in the corner of the cavernous room.

There, they'd plotted the killer's past moves in hopes of seeing his next. Now the transparent mazes lay scattered across the map, nowhere near each other, not touching each other, not arranged perfectly, but nonetheless something clicked.

Vinny rose calmly out of his chair, bent down on one knee, and arranged each maze along the map. Carefully. Quietly. Patiently. He started with Florida, realizing that the solution to the maze brought him all the way up from Miami to Daytona Beach alongside the state's main artery, I-95. He moved the map of Florida, forward, backward, and there it remained. A well-trafficked interstate was, in fact, the solution to the first maze.

Next came Georgia. The corresponding maze found near the butchered mother of two traveled exactly along rural interstate I-75. In South Carolina, the maze followed I-20 from border to border. Same with Tennessee and Missouri.

Two more states. Two more popular interstates.

His breathing slowed, his pulse leveled off, and the serenity and calm he'd always lacked as a fumbling video game champ reigned supreme in the SCCU junior agent. He reached calmly for his briefcase, removing the stack of mimeographed sheets of the remaining pages of the maze book he'd found in Frank's room.

He'd made a copy of each unsolved maze in what he now referred to as "Frank's book," solved each with deep, dark ink, and had them all transferred to different colors of copy paper at another Kinko's halfway across town. He took out the eighteen transparencies now and spread them out from the latest crime scene, Missouri, across the entire country.

He matched the first maze to I-70 in Illinois, but, though it was closer to the latest crime scene than he would have liked, to date the murders had occurred in contiguous, matching states.

Next it was I-40 in Oklahoma. Again, too far.

Maze after maze, state after state, interstate after interstate, he placed the mazes across the blown-up map. His pulse never faltered or spiked. His palms remained cool and free from moisture. His breathing stilled to an almost Zen-like state. And that's when he found it: I-30 in Arkansas. The maze matched perfectly.

He could see the progression. He could see the mazes line up from state to state, victim to victim, crime scene to crime scene. Now he knew. Vinny knew where the killer would strike next. And maybe he should have known a day earlier when he'd first had the balls to ask junior agent Franklin the location of Frank's upcoming book signing in a few days. What had the kid said? Batesville?

Batesville...*Arkansas*?

The crime scene was incomplete, his staff was clueless, but his work here was done. The maze had shown him the answer, the coincidences too many. His path was clear, and there was only one way to beat the killer.

That was to get to the next killing ground before he did. But first, he had to do the unthinkable: He had to call Frank. To put it off any longer would make it obvious that something was up, especially if it was, in fact, Frank who was committing these murders. To catch a killer, he would have to beat the killer. But first he would have to call him.

48 Frank hung up the phone and immediately contacted the three support people he needed in order to get to Arkansas in the next six hours. He had already been planning on visiting the Razor-back state to launch his book tour, but that had been a solo trip—a civilian jaunt, quick in, quick out, and then right back to work. Now he would have to do double duty and bring along the troops he'd need. Looking around his room, he packed quickly and efficiently, even as his gut fluttered and he found himself in a taxi on the way to the nearest airstrip.

As Missouri farm country passed outside his window minutes later, Frank considered Vinny's call and found it odd. While he'd certainly been impressed with the brilliance of the junior agent's discovery, there was no accounting for the four hours Vinny had been, for all intents and purposes, incommunicado.

Sure, he'd explained it conveniently enough, "Sorry, boss, the battery on my cell phone died," but it was an excuse he himself had used once too often with the superiors back in DC, and he didn't feel entirely comfortable with it.

His voice was off, too. A little too high for Frank's taste, like someone making excuses to a distant aunt who's in town and wants to spend the weekend together.

What was going on with Vinny? At first, he'd scoffed at himself, claiming a combination of paranoia, stress, and not enough sleep. "You're seeing spooks where there are no spooks, Frank," he'd said aloud in the elevator on the way out of the hotel. But now he wasn't so sure. Never before had Frank been unable to trust his partner. True, he'd gone solo long enough that the word "partner" itself seemed like ancient history, but there had been enough in their day to prove to him that the men and women of the FBI were, for the most part, extremely trustworthy and if not, they weren't around for long.

From their initial meeting, Vinny had all but radiated trust. But from the moment Vinny had been asked to retrieve his luggage from the hotel room, Frank suddenly realized, communication between the two partners had been almost null and void.

What had happened in the hours since Frank's departure from Tennessee? Frank had seen partners burn out in the past, but that was after weeks on a case, not days. True, this case was as big and bad and ugly and national and newsworthy and stressful as they got, but Vinny had been on big murder cases before, and Frank didn't think that was the problem at all.

Was it him? Had Frank somehow pissed the junior agent off? Assigned him one too many dull chores? Was Frank getting bossy in his old age? Go there? Do this? Find that? Copy this? He doubted it. And even if he was, who cared? That's what paying dues was all about. So what was up? Frank didn't care personally, of course. He'd long since given up on trying to not piss people off, but his concerns were a distraction from the case. This was exactly why he avoided having partners. It was easier to do things by himself.

Still, he'd thought Vinny was different. How could he have been so wrong?

Frank chose to ignore the personality clash and instead focus on Vinny's news: he had finally figured out the maze. Frank had congratulated him, both of them full of the false hope that comes from figuring out a long-elusive clue. Now all that remained, of course, was to catch the killer.

Frank had neglected to mention to the rookie that the killer might have actually "let" him figure out the maze. Or that the killer could be picking victims out of order. The map was interesting, the interstates vital; no doubt about either of those discoveries. But what if the victim in North Carolina really *had* been killed before the girl in South Carolina?

The thought had always troubled Frank, and now it came back to bite him in the ass at the absolute worst possible time. Vinny was onto something, but there were still a few too many threads hanging to tie a big fat bow around their perp.

Still, having a partner—and more importantly, *being* a partner—was all about trust. Hinky feeling or no, loose ends or split
ends, Frank had no one else but Vinny to trust. So trust him he
would.

49

Maze had found her. His latest victim. His last victim. The victim to end all victims. Of course, he chose to think of her in terms of his specialty. Therefore she was the crowning jewel of his internal movie plot. The elusive sequential arc. The climax before his resolution. The piece de resistance. Enid McManus was a retired schoolteacher who lived alone off Route I-30.

Of course, killing her in her home would be too easy. He knew that the Feds would have, by this point, triangulated every single crime scene to its nearest interstate, airport, bus station, etc. To whit, he'd been careful to always kill a victim as far away as possible from the nearest highway.

Killing Enid at home would have been out of character for Maze. Too easy; not enough of a challenge. Worse yet, it would have been untimely and conspicuous; a sloppy end to his carefully orchestrated charade. Though pressure was running high and his baser instincts made the offer tempting, he knew in his deeper core that the end to this long, frenetic ride could be no more sloppy than the beginning.

So far, so good. Not a single piece of his intelligence—and his source was as close to the case as you could get—had mentioned the interstate connection. Though each of the victims had a tie-in with their road of choice—the teenager's school was right off I-95 at the Daytona Beach exit, and the hooker's favorite diner was a quick left off I-65 in Tennessee—the Feds had apparently been too busy dusting for prints or breaking in new partners to run down the list of old standbys.

Even so, he couldn't let *his* guard down just because the FBI had done the same. The only way to beat them was to be better than them. Obviously, he was. Obviously, he always had been.

Now Maze tracked Enid as she left the house at the same time she'd left the day before—2:45 p.m.—to attend a water exercise class at the local senior center. Maze had even stuck around to watch the previous day's workout, if it could be called that: thirty minutes of flapping arms and neon-colored "noodles" being bent into various positions that constituted cardiovascular exercise.

He thought the choice was perfect: an old dawdling senior citizen to wrap up a murder spree that began with a sprightly, innocent teenager. The culmination was at hand; they made perfect bookends to the internal story he'd created for himself and, just like the rest of the country, had watched live on CNN. Maze smiled, passing the teacher's white picket fence on the way back to his hotel.

He didn't look forward to another night of take-out food and answering client calls on his cell phone, but savoring the next kill made it all the more worthwhile. He eyed the neon strip of take-out dives dotting the interstate exit and thought to himself, *What do I feel like tonight? Chinese? Fried Chicken? Pizza? Or would I like all three?* He decided on the latter. After all, the end was near.

It was time for a celebration.

50

Vinny waited in Frank's hotel room, feeling a vague sense of déjà vu as he sat on Frank's bed. In the next room, a crack team of agents sat poised with listening devices, stun guns, digital recorders, and anything else they thought they might need in the course of Vinny's "interrogation."

Directly across the hall was a similar team. All of the agents were backed up by a parking lot full of armed men from various contributing agencies. Between them all, there was no way Frank Logan was getting away from that hotel without an armed escort and a cuff on each limb. It was supposed to make him feel safe. Vinny felt anything but.

He had beaten Frank to Arkansas by less than three hours. Along the way, he'd presented his case to Frank's superior, making sure to record the entire conversation should Senior Director Sharpe heed his loyalty to Frank instead of his loyalty to the FBI. He shouldn't have worried. It turned out that Director Sharpe was no fan of Frank Logan, or his legendary ego, and the man listened eagerly as Vinny laid out his case against Frank.

Intrigued by the clues, shocked by the discovery of the book of mazes in Frank's room, and convinced that the next murder was to occur in Arkansas, Sharpe had promised to devote a team to compiling Frank's travel records and, in response, Vinny had gotten a call halfway to his destination that alerted him to the fact that not only was *he* booked at the biggest hotel midway between the origin of I-30 and its endpoint, but so too was a team of elite officers.

Ultimately, the travel records had been inconclusive. Was Frank there? Was he *not* there? The verdict seemed to be that Frank was everywhere; that proved his innocence as well as his guilt. But once the doubt was there, Sharpe had seen enough evidence to warrant apprehension, or at least an interrogation.

Already, Vinny dreaded the confrontation with his mentor, superior, and personal hero. How was he, a green rookie, supposed to interrogate the most famous interrogator of them all? This was the man who'd made Bundy weep, Dahmer tremble, and, rumor was, John Wayne Gacey piss his pants. Now Vinny was supposed to accuse him of being none other than the Maze Murderer?

His ears and attention perked as he heard Frank slide his magnetic key card into the slot. His stomach lurched as the clasp on the door clicked and light from the hall entered the darkened room. Frank Logan, a Fed 'til the end, saw just enough, as the beam of light washed over Vinny, to unholster his weapon and aim it squarely at the junior agent's head.

"Jesus, Frank, put that thing away," Vinny said nervously, the adrenaline making him stand up on the balls of his feet. "It's me, Vinny. Calm down, man. What the fuck?"

"You tell *me* what the fuck, Vinny?" Frank asked, doing nothing to holster his weapon or, for that matter, move any farther into the room. Vinny noticed that the veteran still had one foot in the doorway, leaving him not only a quick exit from the room should the need arise, but the shaft of light sitting squarely on Vinny's transfixed face. "As in," Frank continued, clicking on a light switch with his free hand, "what the fuck you're doing in my room, sitting in the dark, telling me to calm down?"

Vinny inched forward. Frank remained where he was.

"I was catching a few z's, Frank," Vinny lied. "I knew you'd want to meet the minute you got here. I had the maid let me in. I thought I'd save you the time of hunting me down and doing this in *my* room."

Frank nodded, finally letting his foot slip from the door. It swung shut with a metallic thud that surprised both men. When Frank looked back from the door to Vinny he, too, had his gun drawn.

"Put it down, Frank," said Vinny, literally willing his hand not to shake as he strode forward across the room. "Play it smart. It's not just my gun pointing at you here. It's the agents in the next room, and the room across the hall, and the half dozen men who followed you into the lobby, and the rest of the dozen who are sitting in unmarked cars surrounding the perimeter."

Frank nodded, then shook his head, then nodded again. He deposited his service revolver on top of the TV closest to the front door. Vinny took it quickly, shoving it inside his own holster and clipping it shut with one hand.

"I don't know what the fuck you think you're doing, Vinny," Frank said calmly as he stood where he was, "and I know this is being recorded so, for the record, you, Junior Agent Vinny Smalldeano, are one crazy motherfucker and, mark my words, I *will* have your badge for this."

"I hope you're right, Frank," Vinny said with all sincerity. "I really do. Because if Frank Logan can really be the Maze Murderer, then I'm not sure the FBI is worth fighting for. If we do find you dirty for this, then kiss my ass. You won't have to take my badge. I'll gladly give it to you."

Frank Logan smiled. Then he nodded. Then he shook his head. Then he set a hard line across his face that would stay there for the duration of their interview. "The Maze Murderer, huh? That's who you think you've caught, *Junior* Agent Vinny Smalldeano?"

Frank made the word *junior* sound like profanity. "Shit," he continued, chuckling dryly with irony rather than humor. "I can't win for losing this week. First some cub reporter from Florida, of all places, and now my own partner? And what kind of evidence do you have, Vinny? A hunch? Found my fingerprints at the crime scene? Boy, that'd be a stretch. What in the world would the senior-agent-in-charge's fingerprints be doing at the crime scene he's investigating? Well, gee, I wonder...."

"Try the book of mazes, Frank," Vinny said, revealing his trump card. "The same book of mazes from which each and every maze we've found to date has been pulled. The edges match, Frank. The edges from the book have been matched to the edges of the mazes we've found, all using the latest electron microscope."

"What book of mazes?" Frank asked, following immediately with the next vital question: "Where?"

"In your room, Frank. Remember when you wanted me to bring your bags with me to the next crime scene? That was very ballsy of you, by the way. What's that they say? 'Keep your friends close and your enemies closer?' Well, turns out I found the book when I was in your room, wedged between the mattress and the bed frame."

"Bullshit, Vinny. That is fucking 100% absolute, bona fide, unbelievable, Grade-A bullshit. With a capital 'B.' Bullshit!"

"Is it, Frank? I've since cataloged that piece of evidence and it's been in FBI custody since day one."

"You could have introduced it yourself, Vinny boy. To frame the old man. You weren't good enough to take the spot from me, so why not just frame me and get it by default?"

"That's ludicrous, Frank, and you know it."

"Do I, Vinny? It's about as ludicrous as me leaving a fucking book of mazes identifying *me* as the Maze Murderer right where you can see them and then asking you to go to my room and *get my bags for me*. How fucking ludicrous is *that*, Vinny?"

"Okay, so maybe ludicrous isn't the right word, Frank. Maybe *crazy* is more like it. Maybe we weren't getting close enough to you for your liking, so you decided to spice things up a bit by leading me straight to the biggest clue of all. Who knows what goes on in a killer's mind?"

"Well, boy, you sure don't, that's for sure. Okay. Fine. So that's all you've got? A book of mazes any maid, manager, or piss-ant lock pick could have planted in my room. If that's true, then I don't even know why we're having this discussion."

"Fine, Frank. You don't like that? Try travel records that place you in every kill zone *before* each murder. Don't like that one?" Vinny pounced, on a roll and swelling with a strange mixture of pride, regret, and overconfidence, "Then try *this* one: Don't you think it's a little odd that the next maze, the next interstate, points straight to Arkansas? And what are the odds that your book-signing just so happens to be in Arkansas, too?"

Frank paused, looking Vinny in the eye with a steely gaze. "Vinny," he began, more gently this time. "Vinny, I beg you, listen to yourself. Listen to what you're saying. This is a big case, I'll grant you that. We're all shooting in the dark right now. But it's no time to rush to judgment. I know your evidence seems good. Otherwise, Senior Director Sharpe wouldn't have approved a shitload of agents to take me in. I'm sure it seemed like the most logical thing at the time. But ask yourself, Vinny, *why* would I do it? Why would I lead the whole agency on this wild goose chase just to throw it all in the last quarter by tipping you off with the book of mazes? Why would I only kill in towns I could easily get to while at a previous crime scene? I don't mean to sound like a cheap cop show here, Vinny, but don't you think it's more likely that someone's trying to frame me?"

"Like who, Frank?" Vinny asked, his gun dropping ever so slightly. "Who the hell would want to frame you, Frank?"

Frank thought a minute, inching closer to Vinny as he did so. When he was close enough, he helped the frustrated junior agent lower his gun by placing his trembling finger on the muzzle.

"Let's start with those people who know my every move— where I'd be going, when I'd get there, when I'd be leaving—and narrow it down from there. There are only, what, half a dozen names on that list? A couple crack agents like you and I, shouldn't take us too long, now should it?"

Vinny nodded, then handed Frank his weapon back. "And just what am I supposed to do with the two teams of agents in the other rooms? Not to mention those in the lobby and/or parking lot right now?"

"Keep 'em around," Frank smiled. "This guy's obviously ready for a showdown and is drawing us a road map. Straight to Batesville, I presume. We're gonna need a few extra men to pin him down."

51

Maze scoured Room 9 of the Batesville Motor Lodge for clues, pouring the last of his three bargain bottles of bleach down any and all drains to obliterate all hair, fiber, and DNA evidence. He knew it was overload; by the time the Feds caught on, days from now, the room would have been cleaned each day after he left.

Still, you never knew about such things, and he hadn't come this far by being sloppy. He took up his single gym bag, disposable, full of similarly disposable clothes, and left the sleazy room behind. In the lobby, if you could call it that, he checked out quickly and anonymously, using his travel name—Tom Wadsworth—and credit card with the same nom de plume. It was as forgettable as white bread, thanks to his very unoriginal birth parents, and few desk clerks would look at it twice, let alone remember it under police interrogation months later.

From the lobby, he carefully skirted the pool, went to the lobby and returned to the pool. There, he found a Dempsey dumpster in which to stow his clothes, dopp kit, and empty bleach bottles. He'd save the murder weapon in his trunk for disposal in a nearby creek he'd scoped out days earlier.

At the car, he fumbled with his keys. It was only then that he noticed the cars in the parking lot. It wasn't the number, though there were twice as many now as there'd been when he'd gotten up that morning and looked out the window to see if his rental was still there. It was the make. And the model.

What were the odds of a dozen cars in the parking lot being exactly the same color, year, and make? That's when Maze knew they were onto him. He dropped his keys at his feet, backed up three quick steps, and turned quickly around. Only to find Frank Logan and his young partner, Vinny Smalldeano, standing in his path.

"Mr. Segal?" Vinny asked as he took a pair of thick cuffs from the small of his back.

"Bernie?" Frank asked as he did the same, his tone jovial, his smile fixed, his shoulders cocked and palms wide open, as if to say, "Fancy that. What are the odds of meeting you here?"

Bernie Segal had nowhere to go. He had only the final ruse in his dwindling bag of tricks to try. "Frank! Man oh man, are you one tough son of a bitch to track down. I've been trying to reach you for days. I just wanted to get to the bookstore early and make sure everything was ready for the signing and…."

Frank let the hammer fall. "Is that right, Bernie? Or should I say…Tom Wadsworth? Remind me to thank your personal assistant. What's his name? Guy? Not only is he very thorough, but he's extremely friendly to big, burly FBI agents who barge into your office unannounced, especially those his boss represents and who, from time to time, might need his real name to get in touch with him when he's on the road, especially when there's an exclusive opportunity to be on a little show we like to call *Oprah*."

"After that," Vinny bragged, "all it took was a few dozen phone calls to every hotel, motel, and campground along I-30—and bordering the Batesville Barnes & Noble—before we found where you were staying."

But Bernie Segal had been in show business a little too long not to have an acting chop or two hidden up his sleeve. "Tom Wadsworth?" he sneered. "Never heard of the man. Obviously there has been a mistake, gentlemen."

Vinny smiled and got to say the line he'd been wanting to recite for years now, ever since he and his father had watched all those cheesy 80s cop dramas on that tiny black and white TV in the break room of his grocery store. "Tell it to the judge, fella, tell it to the judge."

52

"There's not a single clue to tie me to any one of those women," Bernie Segal said as he endured the ultimate negotiation, that which would save—or end—his very life. "Not a fucking finger-print," he blathered on, eager to straighten his tie if only they'd unchain his hands from around his size-32 waist, "not a hair, not so much as a broken flower pot."

"You seem to be very familiar with the case, Mr. Segal." Vinny smiled knowingly, sliding a pack of cigarettes across the table, knowing good and well Bernie Segal couldn't smoke them, even if he'd wanted to.

"Yeah, well, me and 99.9% of the fucking country, junior," spat the accused supremely as he eyed the generic smokes with relish. "So sue me for being an avid reader. Not to mention my star client happens to be personally involved in the matter. You forget *that* little piece of evidence, *Junior* Agent Smalldeano?"

"Actually," Frank interrupted as he squared off against his for-mer literary agent, "he's just been promoted to *Senior* Agent Small-deano. Hey, here's a thought. Maybe you'll want to represent him, Bernie. Knowing you, you could probably finagle a cell phone on death row. Make all your big Hollywood calls to your big Hollywood friends. Get a movie deal out of it. Maybe it'll even get made before they strap you down for that lethal injection you've got coming."

Segal smirked, ignoring the obvious jab to raise his hackles. "Smalldeano?" he spat instead, taking aim at Vinny's last name. "Sorry, pal, the *Sopranos* fad is over and out. You'd be lucky to get mention in your hometown paper after I get through with you."

Frank couldn't help but smile. It was the kind of threat he'd expect from a man like Bernie Segal. "Why do you think we're here today, Bernie? Or should I call you Tom? I think we'll stick with Bernie for now, for old time's sake. So, what do you think it is clue-ing us in on you, Bernie? Could it be you're the only civilian privy to my travel schedule? Could it be you'd be the only one with a vested interest in me, your top client, being the killer?"

Bernie couldn't resist taking the bait on that one. "Top client?" he scoffed. "You think *you're* my top client? I can barely pay my cell phone bill with the chump change I make off your measly royalties, Frank."

"All the more reason to frame me as the killer, Bernie," Frank said, closing in.

"Yeah, Bernie," Vinny chimed in, piling it on. "That'd sure drum up some book sales, huh? I can see the headlines now: 'Read the con-fessions of a killer!' And who's to say you don't write your *own* book when Frank's locked up and they've thrown away the key, huh, Bern? Here's your title: 'My Client was the Maze Murderer.' Sounds like a bestseller to me. How about you, Frank?"

"Number one with a bullet, Vinny," Frank agreed.

The two men eyed each other over the interrogation table as Frank suddenly remembered Bernie's recent sales pitch. "Here's a thought, Bernie: What if your big "scouting locations for a new Frank Logan TV show" ruse just happened to cut a swath through the South, using the very same interstates and highways Vinny here used to solve the maze of all mazes? Now that's something a jury could buy into, don't you think?"

While Bernie remained tightlipped, too smart—or perhaps just too afraid—to engage in anymore emotional outbursts, Vinny and Frank smiled at each other. "You'll be interested to know, Bernie," Frank began, using his familiarity with his agent to play the good cop, "that we're working on a witness."

"That's *eyewitness* to you, Segal," Vinny spat, doing his best imi-tation of a bad cop.

"Yeah, right," Bernie said. "Eyewitness to what? Me sitting at my desk making calls to Larry King on your behalf, Frank?"

"Actually…." Vinny began.

"Far from it," Frank interrupted. "Try picking up a hooker in Hicksville, Tennessee."

"Look at me," Bernie said in all seriousness, leaning away from the desk so the men in the room get a better gander at his expensive tie, tailored suit, and trim figure. "I need a hooker like I need another deranged Fed for a client. I haven't had to pay for it since your mother sucked me off in college."

"Whose mother?" Vinny asked with a straining smile. "My mother never went to college."

"Mine either," Frank said. "Now my dad's another story."

The three men let the bad jokes die. There was no room for them anymore, and they all knew it. "Actually," Frank said, tiring of the claustrophobic nature of the room and eager to land his clincher, "the hooker in question just happened to be one of the Maze Murder's victims."

"Physical evidence?" Vinny chimed in. "Not so much. Unless you count the similarities in pages from the maze book you stashed under Frank's mattress, the type of pen used on each maze, and the hidden watermark the publisher printed in the corner of all five mazes."

"Well," Frank said, as if interjecting an insignificant point, "that and the partial print we found on the underside of my bedspread, the one you moved in order to place the maze book under my mattress and which has been in FBI custody since the day Vinny found it."

For the first time, Bernie Segal was silent.

The men enjoyed watching him squirm, until finally Vinny could take it no longer. "We figure you used the gloves the whole time, staying careful, keeping clean. But the positioning of the maze book was crucial to me finding it. So we figure you hid the book, sat on the bed just so I'd be sure to see that big ass impression the next day, all the while taking your gloves off in anticipation of leaving the room."

"And then," Frank took over, "just as you'd slipped those delicate little agent hands out of those gloves, your paranoia got the better of you and you just *had* to check to see if the maze book was sitting just so. So, very carefully, holding the gloves instead of wearing them, you lifted the comforter just as one of your manicured little fingers slipped past the glove, thereby transferring a partial print we've already identified as yours."

"So the eyewitness?" Vinny asked. "She's really just insurance."

"Yeah." Frank nodded, savoring the moment. "Insurance."

"Insurance my ass," Bernie growled, apparently approving of the best way to wriggle himself free of the implications. "So you guys have never heard of a little guerrilla marketing?"

His tone was embarrassingly inquisitive.

"Guerrilla?" Vinny asked.

"Marketing?" Frank muttered.

"Yeah, you know." Bernie nodded, getting more caught up as he went along. "So I knew your travel itinerary. So I set up a book-signing square in the path of some deranged killer. So I slipped into your room and hid the maze book. So I tipped that little reporter off to your private cell number. So I scouted a few locations for a TV pilot. So what?

"Think of the implications it would have for your book on this case if people thought, even for a day or two, that *you* were the killer? I was gonna fess up to it, and keep the publicity rolling all the more. I was days away from signing a six-year contract with the Forensics Channel, Frank. We still could, you and I. Vinny, shit, you too. Every Batman needs his Robin, right? You should be thanking me, Frank, not cuffing me."

"Nice, Bernie," Frank said admiringly.

"Very nice," Vinny agreed.

Both men looked at each other and smiled.

"Guess we'll just have to fall back on that insurance after all, huh, Vinny?"

"Guess so, Frank," Vinny nodded. "Better to be safe than sorry, right, Bernie?"

"Fuck you two," Bernie snarled. "You have any idea the kind of pull I have? The kind of connections I deal with? By the time I'm through with you, you'll be parking cars in Poughkeepsie."

Vinny nodded, smiled, grinned, then gloated, the reality of the moment finally settling in.

Frank smiled, too. "Fine with me, Bernie. I hear Poughkeepsie's awfully pretty this time of year."

53

Lolanda Walker Degrath Soshanna, aka "Lola," sat in the interrogation room in Arkansas, flirting with the local patrolmen. They'd already supplied her with a pack of generic cigarettes from some poor local's desk—wait'll he went reaching for a smoke the next morning—and no less than three Diet Dr. Peppers from the vending machine in the lobby. Now their patience was growing thin.

"Is there anyone to back up your story, Miss Soshanna?" asked the local agent in charge, a big man with a bigger attitude.

"Call me Lola, honey. And no, ain't no one to back up my story. Ceptin' for poor lil' Genie and she gone, as we all know. But I seen the car clear as day that night. Big gray thing. Run a few by me and I'll point it out for you. And the man driving? Him I recognize a week or so after Gina gone missing and old miss Gracie find her.

"See, I'm a big fan of E! TV," Lola rambled as the men rolled their eyes and began gathering up their badges, guns, and blank affidavit forms. "Now, just hold on a tic. So about a week or two, I can't remember which, after poor 'lil Gina passed on, I was watching this special on that big FBI man, the old guy, y'all should know him, looks like Clint Eastwood, shoot, I know you be working for him somehow."

"Frank Logan?" one of the Feds sighed.

"That's the one," Lola nodded enthusiastically, like a game show winner who's just answered the $64,000 question. "The one be writing all them books I can't afford. Anyhow, I'm watching a special on his life, you know, on account of the Maze Murders and them wanting to capitalize on all the publicity and whatnot, and all of a sudden the killer's face pops up on this program."

"Frank Logan is the Maze Murderer?" one agent asked in disbelief.

Lola merely shook her head. "If y'all would quit interrupting and let a sister talk you'd be hearing me better. *He* wasn't the killer, but the man what was with him was. They was at some big book signing in New York City. This about a year or so ago, according to the program on E! Somebody be talking about 'his longtime agent accompanied him' or something. Not *your* kind of agent, that's for sure. But his book and movie agent, I s'pose. Like a talent agent or something."

The men looked skeptically at the hooker, shaking their heads.

She let out a large, audible, dramatic sigh, worthy of talent agents everywhere.

"Oh, I sees where we're all at," said Lola, sucking lazily on another free cigarette in between sips of another free soda. "Nobody wanna believe some nasty little crack ho named Lola, huh?"

"If the HIV-test fits," cracked one of the Feds.

Lola spat into the corner. "That's funny," she said, deadpan. "Real funny. Just so happens Gracie wasn't the only one in Tennessee with a hurt in her heart over that little girl Gina, you know. I sees the car. I can identify your man. I'm telling ya straight up and plain simple."

The locals shook their heads. Lola sucked at her cigarette and free soda alternately. There was nothing here, they knew, already imagining trying to clean Lola up and sitting her in a courtroom, even as she sat there spitting in the aisles and asking the bailiff for a free carton of Salems for her trouble. No matter how they hosed her off and dressed her up, it's like they say: You can take the crack out of the crack whore, but at the end of the day the whore's still there.

Any lawyer making more than six bucks an hour would tear her credibility to shreds in just under three minutes. Looked like Segal was gonna walk after all.

"'Course," added Lola as she drained the last of her soda and crushed the can between her two man-hands, "for the price of another one of these sodas here, I might be inclined to tell you about the pawn shop next door to Basil's Diner...."

"Forget it, slut," one agent said, already reaching for the keys to her waist cuffs. "We're talking a serial killer, here, not some...."

"Damn," Lola muttered, "can't a girl finish? What I meant to say was how this pawn shop owner was one paranoid son of a bitch, not to mention impotent, darlings, but that's another story for another time. So this impotent paranoid SOB put these surveillance cameras up on his roof. One for each corner. Now, I've been inside his back room before—don't ask Lola why, but I'm sures y'all can figure it out for yourself—and he saves every tape from every day in a big glass gun cabinet. I seen 'em with my own eyes. July 1. July 2. July 3. And so on and so forth.

"I'm pretty sure if y'all hurry on down there, be sure you take a warrant with you so they don't toss your fine asses out of court, you can persuade that impotent, paranoid, pawnshop keeper SOB to let you look at the tape pointing down on my side of the street the very night Gina disappeared. See that sucker's big, white face clear as day when you—hey, where the hell y'all going? Come back here and unlock a sister, will ya? Damn. And bring me another one of these here sodas when you do."

54

Guy Junger was watching a *Sex & the City* rerun on one of Bernie's huge TV screens when the Feds burst in.

"Jesus," he spat over his half-empty jar of cold sake. "Can't a fella watch a few reruns on his own time without bringing in the Feds?"

A lead agent in a nondescript blue suit approached Guy sitting behind Bernie's huge desk and flashed him a search warrant. "My name is Agent Philip Anderson, sir, and this is a search warrant for your employer's travel records."

"Travel records?" Guy said with a sneer, as if he couldn't be bothered. "You want 'em, you got 'em. That Bernie's the cheapest man alive. You know what he gave me for my Christmas bonus last year?"

"Sir," one of the LA bureau's agents interrupted, "we really don't...."

"An Old Spice dopp kit," Guy finished, as if talking to himself. "Me, of all people. Old Spice? Please. Point being, *officer*, Bernie's very particular about his travel receipts. Sky Miles and all, don't you know? I have every airline ticket, rental car receipt, fast food coupon, and toll booth receipt for the last month. Look at this. Florida. Georgia. South Carolina. North Carolina. All under his birth name, Tom Wadsworth, of course, but legally he's entitled to the Sky Miles nonetheless. He'd kill me if I let that little cat out of the bag. I had to sign a confidentiality agreement to that effect, don't you know, but you're the cops, right? You can't tell Bernie what I'm saying and get me in trouble, right? What's so funny? Did Guy tell a joke? Why are you guys smiling?"

55

Frank and Vinny were going home. Precisely ten minutes after departure from Arkansas in the FBI chartered jet, Frank turned to Vinny and said, as quietly as a prayer, "By rights, I should throw your ass off this plane."

Vinny barely flinched. "By rights, I should shove your shriveled old carcass down the shitter."

Frank nodded. "Gimme your badge," he said in reply, his large, calloused hand extending from his seat to Vinny's.

Vinny looked nonplussed. "I...I thought you were kidding about that," he stammered.

"I told you I'd have your badge," Frank said with a grave face. "Now hand it over."

Vinny sighed. True to form, he turned over his badge. Frank smiled serenely, pocketing what amounted to Vinny's entire career in his coat pocket. Then he turned over a new badge, his index finger pointing squarely to the words "Senior Agent" emblazed above the badge number. His expert eyes caught the name to which the badge belonged: Frank Logan.

"This is *your* badge, Frank," sputtered Vinny.

"It's only temporary," explained Frank, shrugging playfully. "But no partner of mine is going to be seen with a junior agent badge when he's really a senior agent. Besides, I haven't had to flash my badge in years. One of the perks of being a famous media darling, don't you know."

"So," Vinny hedged, ignoring Frank's put-on airs and already guessing at the answer. "I'm forgiven then?"

"Oh fuck no," spat Frank, pouring two glasses of Scotch from the fully stocked bar aboard the speeding jet. "You've got about six years of shit duty ahead of you before I fully forgive you for thinking I could ever be the Maze Murderer. Just ask my last four partners. If you can get a hold of them in Siberia, that is."

"Frank," Vinny continued nervously, "you and I both know that, if you were in my shoes, you would have done the very same thing."

"Yes," Frank said after clinking Vinny's heavy rocks glass, "and that's the only reason your head's not zipping through Engine No. 2 right about now. Don't worry, Vinny, you'll have plenty of time to apologize. Not only is it a long flight back to DC, but we'll be sharing an office for the time being."

Vinny listened as Frank Logan, his boss, his mentor, his *partner*, discussed future cases, whose desk was bigger, and just exactly *how* he took his coffee. The junior—make that, senior—agent no longer minded.

He guessed he'd passed some kind of test and, in passing, it looked like he and Frank would be working together for a long time. He didn't know whether that thrilled him or scared him.

In the end, he thought, taking another sip of scotch as Frank rambled on about the "extra bump in pay translating into an extra bump in responsibility," it didn't really matter. Frank hadn't caught the Maze Murderer. Vinny hadn't caught the Maze Murderer.

They'd caught him together.

56

She began typing furiously, her fingers flying across the keyboard of the sleek new laptop she'd just purchased, maxing out her already overloaded credit card in celebration of the book deal she was shortly about to secure.

Dear Guy Junger,

My name is Marcie Collins, ace reporter for the *Daytona Daily*. I share with you now the words Special Director Frank Logan of the SCCU, spoken exclusively to me during the Maze Murderer investigation:

"If a word of your accusation, and that's exactly what it is, if a word of your accusation hits the papers, I will send down a legion of Feds to arrest your no doubt pert, blonde, cute little ass for obstruction of justice."

Fact? Or fiction? Trust me, they're word for word, and attached to this email you'll find a brief Wave file purporting my assertion. I suggest we talk about the fact that your boss, Bernie Segal, may be doing time for a crime he didn't commit.

Even if he did commit it, let's talk anyway. I think we could sell a few million copies of my new book, *Getting Away With Murder,* about why I still think Frank Logan is the real Maze Murderer.

"Am I serious?" you may be asking yourself right about now. My answer: dead serious. Do I really believe it? By way of an answer I'll ask you a question in return: Who really cares if he did it or not? By the time the dust clears

and Frank Logan proves his innocence, we'll both be a few
million dollars richer.

Marcie Collins admired the short, terse query letter with an
approving smile. She typed a few more lines of inconsequential ass-
kissing, double-checked Guy's email address for accuracy, keyed in
her own contact information, ran a quick spell check, and then pushed
the "send" button, watching impatiently as the short sound bite
uploaded and then soared through cyberspace. Mission accomplished.

She unplugged her laptop, threw it on top of the cardboard box
which held all of her earthly possessions, and walked out of the
Daytona Daily office without a word, ignoring the very people who'd
endured her various delusions of grandeur for nearly five long years.

Double-parked in front of the storefront office in which she'd
toiled ever since graduating with a Journalism degree from the U of F,
her Mazda 626 was gassed up and ready to roll. She ignored the $5
parking ticket she'd earned while typing her letter to Guy, watching it
flutter under her windshield wiper for a few quick miles before, just
as she got on the Interstate, it fluttered away, never to be seen again.

The cardboard box, the new laptop, and the freshly printed
directions to Guy's Beverly Hills office were all that remained of her
previous life. She left behind a boyfriend who wouldn't miss her, an
apartment she never liked, a job she liked even less, and a freezer full
of Lean Cuisines.

As the Interstate pavement yawned beneath her balding tires,
she flicked on the radio with the satisfaction of an inmate newly
released from the joint. That's what she felt: freedom. Freedom to
live the American dream, one scandal at a time.

She'd forgotten to change the channel from her favorite talk
show on the way into work that morning, and so had to endure yet
another cookie cutter story celebrating the great Frank Logan and his
hunky new partner, Vinny Smalldeano.

Boy, she thought as she eased into the fast lane, disregarding the
trio of cars she'd just cut off to do so, *he'd come out of nowhere, huh?*

She smiled to herself.

If he played his cards right, Vinny might just make it into the
sequel.

57

Guy Junger listened to Frank Logan's threatening voice for the sixth time that morning. Not on the TV, as usual, or even the phone, but on his computer, where he'd just opened Marcie's query letter and downloaded the verbal threat from Bernie's favorite client.

He liked it. He liked it a lot. He liked it even better when he googled her name and quickly found Marcie's perky picture next to her byline on the half-dozen generic stories she'd written about the Maze Murders for the *Daytona Daily*. None of them, of course, touting her theory that Frank had really been the mastermind behind the killings.

He admired her sense of timing most of all. She was just as he'd expected, just as Frank had predicted in the Wave file he listened to one more time: a "pert blonde" with what he just knew was a "cute little ass." Not that it mattered to him, of course. But it would sure enough matter to the press, who, in the wake of the Maze Murders, would be looking for the next big thing.

Now that Bernie was gone, it was his job to make sure she was it.

He worked furiously at Bernie's laptop, now his laptop, using the database he'd created, culled from every rejection letter Bernie had ever received, to quickly cut and paste Marcie's query letter into his own template, featuring Bernie's old signature line, with one quick modification: his name instead of Bernie's. He was sure the old man wouldn't mind. And even if he did, what was he going to do about?

In less than a minute, and with two clicks of his mouse, Guy sent the query to one of New York's biggest publishers, simultaneously cold-contacting the rest of New York's biggest publishers, not to mention the biggest publishers in Dallas, LA, Miami, Chicago, and all points in between. He then sighed, put his feet up on Bernie's desk, and waited for the phone to ring. Hearing his stomach growl, his smile grew even wider as he buzzed in his new assistant, a burly nineteen-year-old hustler fresh off the bus from Michigan.

"Yes, Mr. Junger," asked his new boy toy, already slicked up and duded out in LA's finest fashions, courtesy of Bernie's rapidly dwindling envelope of petty cash.

"Phillip, I want you to head down to that sushi restaurant where we did your interview. You know the one, around the corner on Rodeo? Right. I want you to ask the maitre'd for Bernie's regular. You remember, the little guy in the black suit? Don't worry, he'll know what it is. While you're at it, order two. I'm feeling generous today, my boy. And you sure do look hungry. Care for raw fish? Don't worry, it's an acquired taste. Kind of like me. I think our fortunes are on the rise, you and me."

Phillip looked out from under the garish ski cap Guy had insisted he wear—supposedly it was all the rage in Milan—with a mixture of envy, fear, and the faint stirrings of something he could barely recognize as desire. "Won't they have cut off Bernie's account by now, sir, seeing as he's in prison and all?"

Guy couldn't help but laugh. Boy, was this kid fresh off the bus or what? "Lesson number one, my boy: Hollywood has a short memory, and nobody cares where Bernie is as long as his money's still green. Besides, the old boy's paid up through the end of the month. You know what, come to think of it, grab four orders and stick two in the fridge in the break room. I have a feeling we're going to be working overtime tonight."

With that, the phone rang. Guy eyed it, using Bernie's rule of letting it ring four times before even thinking about picking it up. "You're not opposed to a little overtime, are you, Phil?" he asked on the second ring.

"No, sir," Phil said by the third, already heading out the door.

"Don't forget the extra wasabi," Guy yelled after him before picking up the phone.